KISSING MADISON

"You're staring at my mouth." Roark's voice came out low and gravelly.

"What?" She pinched her lips together, jerking her gaze to his eyes.

"My mouth. You keep staring at it."

"So?"

"So. I wanted to kiss you *before* the staring. You keep looking at me like that and I will."

Madison swallowed back a whimper, her heart hammering in her chest. She wanted him to kiss her. Then it could be his fault. She wasn't the one stepping out of line into the land of unprofessional liaisons. Roark was.

She looked away and counted to ten. Her door was right there. Turn the key, go inside. It would be so easy to be a good girl right now.

Madison licked her lips, slowly dragging her gaze to Roark's before intentionally staring at his mouth.

He said something on a harsh whisper, something like *thank god.* Then Roark grabbed her, and pressed his lips to hers . . .

A Moment of Bliss

Heather McGovern

LYRICAL SHINE
Kensington Publishing Corp.
www.kensingtonbooks.com

LYRICAL SHINE BOOKS are published by

Kensington Publishing Corp.
119 West 40th Street
New York, NY 10018

All Kensington titles, imprints, and distributed lines are available at special quantity discounts for bulk purchases for sales promotion, premiums, fund-raising, educational, or institutional use.

Special book excerpts or customized printings can also be created to fit specific needs. For details, write or phone the office of the Kensington Sales Manager: Kensington Publishing Corp., 119 West 40th Street, New York, NY 10018. Attn. Sales Department. Phone: 1-800-221-2647.

Lyrical Shine and Lyrical Shine logo Reg. U.S. Pat. & TM Off.

First Electronic Edition: August 2016
eISBN-13: 978-1-60183-836-0
eISBN-10: 1-60183-836-0

First Print Edition: August 2016
ISBN-13: 978-1-60183-837-7
ISBN-10: 1-60183-837-9

Printed in the United States of America

*To my Irishman. Thank you for your love,
laughter, and support.*

ACKNOWLEDGMENTS

With special thanks to:

My executive committee: Jeanette Grey, Elizabeth Michels, and Laura Trentham. None of this would be possible without your critique and consultation, and I certainly wouldn't be having this much fun.

The fabulous ladies at BadGirlzWrite.com, for the encouragement and friendship.

My agent, Nicole Resciniti; my editor, John Scognamiglio; and all of the wonderful people at Kensington for believing in me and helping me share my stories.

Chapter 1

Madison lifted her chin and sniffed the lobby again, thankful no one was around to see her bang-up bloodhound impression.

She was at the inn to work; to make the impossible happen with her skill and professionalism. But right now something smelled like fresh-baked heaven covered in sinful cinnamon frosting, and she had to find out what.

The reception area held no piles of cookies or cakes. No candles or bowls of potpourri; only a single flower arrangement centered on a mahogany table the size of her car. She leaned over and gave the flowers a good long whiff.

Someone behind her cleared his throat in a deep rumble.

Crap.

"May I help you?" A man—too good looking and looking too amused—stood beside the reception desk. Tall and broad enough to fill the doorway behind him, he struck a serious figure in his dress shirt and slacks, but he held a tiny, frilly edged, peach-colored towel in one hand.

"Your gladiolus smells like cookies," she told him.

One dark eyebrow crept up. "I'm sorry, my what?"

She pointed her finger, an accusatory arrow right at the lobby's floral arrangement. "This flower. It's a gladiolus, but it smells like cookies."

"It's not the flowers." He closed the space between them in three long strides, and Madison's pulse jumped at his approach.

"I'm Roark Bradley, owner of Honeywilde Mountain Inn and Resort. Is there something I can help you with?" His Southern drawl rolled the words off his tongue, like rough rocks that'd been tumbled smooth. He made the question sound so much more appealing than it really was.

She knew exactly who Roark Bradley was, from Honeywilde's website. She wasn't about to tell him that though, or that he was even better looking in person.

"Madison Kline." She stuck out her arm.

Her plan was to take charge of this meeting and keep the upper hand until she got her clients what they wanted. So far, she'd managed to get busted sniffing the flowers and eyeing the owner.

All she could do now was hope her palm wasn't sweaty.

Roark shook her hand, not tight and overpowering, but firm and polite. His skin was smooth enough that she could tell he took care of it, but not so smooth that he'd never known a day's work. Hands like his were a good sign for any business owner, and she always took note of the signs.

"You're the wedding planner."

"Event coordinator," she corrected him.

"Sorry. Event coordinator."

Polite, well dressed, well spoken—he was exactly what she'd come to expect from the hospitality industry. He was well built too. Not that it had anything to do with his business skills.

"So, you want to have a wedding here."

"No." She corrected him again. "I want to take a tour of the place to see *if* my clients might be interested in having their wedding here. That is all." All a big bluff, more like. Her clients wanted Honeywilde and nowhere else would do. Madison's job was to make it happen and pull it off in less than three weeks.

"I'm sure once you have a look around, it will be an easy decision."

The decision was already made. The trick was in the execution, but at no point could Roark Bradley realize the cards were dealt in his favor—like, royal flush in his favor. "We'll see. First, are you going to tell me why these flowers smell like dessert, or is it an inn secret?"

He shrugged and held up the little peach towel like it explained everything. Then he nodded toward his arm.

Madison followed his gaze to a huge wet splotch that covered the left sleeve of his dress shirt.

"It's me. I was in the kitchen right before you arrived, and our chef is baking for the afternoon tea. There's this vanilla and cinnamon and spices mixture he uses. He can be all elbows sometimes and..." Roark glanced up with a sheepish grin. "Anyway, there was a thing with some vanilla and now I smell like cookies. How about we get started on that tour?"

She forced her lips into a polite smile. The man smelled delicious. Of course he did. Because that's just how her day was going.

Roark held up the little towel. "Let me put this back in the office and I'll show you around." He strode toward the office with a lot of dignity for a man who was cookie-scented and carrying a little peach towel.

Madison gave Honeywilde's lobby another once-over. She could see why the bride-to-be insisted on getting married here. The inn held a unique charm. It was a well-kept secret that it had been off its game in the last several years, but what was bad news for Honeywilde might be good news for her.

This was her first big event since she'd struck out on her own, and if she succeeded, all the naysayers would have to eat their words.

Madison smoothed her hair back, making sure her chignon was secure. Her fingers trembled with nerves, so she clutched her portfolio tighter.

"We can avoid the kitchen for now, if you think the cookies are dangerous," she told Roark when he returned. Her comment came out unintentionally playful and she fought not to roll her eyes at herself.

With a lazy grin that proved he'd caught the tone, Roark clasped his hands behind his back. "Yes, we should probably save the danger for later. Play it safe. Since your main concern is most likely the location for your clients' wedding ceremony, may I suggest we start outside the inn, on the veranda? You'll find the view from there is second to none and it's the ideal setting for a ceremony."

Now was the perfect opportunity to take charge and lay down the groundwork for how this appointment would go. She couldn't let Roark charm her with his good looks and easy smile. No slick sales pitch, only to slap on an astronomical price tag when it came time to book the inn.

She might be desperate to hook Honeywilde, but he didn't have to know that.

"Actually, I'd like you to answer a few questions first, and I have an order I want to follow for the tour." She opened her black leather portfolio and whipped out her pen. "I have several main concerns, not just about the location of the ceremony, but the entire inn. You've recently taken over operation of Honeywilde, correct?"

"I worked as manager under my parents, but I became the owner a few years ago, yes."

"Word is, the resort fell off in the last few years, prior to your inheritance of the property."

His smile disappeared as he worked his jaw. "That is true, but now my siblings and I run things entirely. I've invested a lot of time and money into the resort and I assure you our place is in top shape."

She made notes, knowing it'd show diligence. With her former employer, Madison was known as "a hard-nosed broad." Yes, she'd really been called that, even in the twenty-first century. She was proud of the moniker, but what people left off was she *had* to be hard-nosed to crawl her way up from the bottom.

"Rumor has it you intend for Honeywilde to reclaim some of its former glory," she said as she wrote.

"Not some, all. It's more than just a rumor too. You'll see the improvements as we tour. Honeywilde will again be *the* inn to stay in."

"I like your enthusiasm, but the tag line needs work." Madison clicked her pen and pointed toward the front door. "Now, since I've seen the inn's entrance and lobby, rather than see the veranda, I prefer to continue on through the great room. Then I'd like to make my way to one of the guest quarters, then the restaurant and kitchen, and finally the exterior, including the veranda and the view."

Roark's eyebrows crept up. Surprisingly, she didn't detect the usual judgment she got for taking charge. He looked more impressed than offended.

"Starting in the great room works for me." He held one arm out, inviting her to join him.

They took the three steps down into the sunken great room and walked toward the center seating area. Roark was at least six foot two, built like the baseball player he was—according to a quick Internet search he'd played ball for all four years of college at Appalachian State, then went on to get his MBA there—and able to reach the center of the large room in about ten steps.

Lagging behind allowed her quite the view, but she knew better than to let him lead.

With her height and long strides, she easily caught up to him, and marked it down as a small victory.

Four people occupied the large common area, on the far side of the room, and she hadn't seen a single guest milling about since she arrived. Unless everyone was playing the most successful game of hide-and-seek ever, the rumors of slow business were true.

"Touring in the order I listed, I get to experience Honeywilde as if I were one of the wedding guests. I can see what they'll see and know if this is the right place."

"Of course."

"My clients are very . . ." She looked at the enormous stone fireplace at the end of the room, hoping the right word would pop down like Santa Claus. The bride and groom seemed like perfectly nice people, and for newly minted celebrity-status musicians, they were strangely down-to-earth. "Discerning. They know what they want and it's my job to make sure they have it."

Their business manager, on the other hand? Arrogant, intolerable, and insistent that Madison come in under his budget. But she couldn't say anything about a business manager or celebrities. Not right now anyway.

"I have to be one hundred percent sure of Honeywilde before I begin any arrangements," she told Roark.

Why did she keep justifying her actions to him? She was supposed to spin this as the resort being lucky to have her business. The goal was to exude confidence and command or a man like Roark Bradley would never respect her or her offer.

"I agree completely."

Trying to rebound, she gave him a curt smile. "You're just agreeing with me to be polite, but I don't need to be schmoozed."

Roark turned to her with a playful smile. "Actually, I legitimately agree, but I can disagree with you for the rest of the tour, if that's preferable."

She tilted her head, reconsidering the man in front of her.

This wasn't some Southern gentleman patronizing her, or a man offended that she'd come across bossy. This was Roark Bradley being a smart-ass.

She liked a smart-ass. A person who could give as good as he got, that was someone she could work with.

"Schmoozing isn't my thing either. I prefer to get down to business."

Madison unclicked her pen and clutched her portfolio in front of her. "Good. Then you won't be offended when I ask some pointed questions?"

"I welcome them."

She studied Roark for a sign he was bluffing to get on her good side. The line of his jaw didn't budge, his blue gaze steady, clearly confident in his claims.

"How many weddings have you hosted in the last three years?"

"Only two, but before we'd have at least two each season."

"How many other events in general?"

"A few in the spring and summer, but not as many as I'd like."

"When do you think you'll have the hearth around the fireplace redone?"

"Excuse me?" He finally blinked.

"The hearth." She pointed over with her pen and stepped closer to the floor-to-ceiling stone fireplace. "Some of the stones are missing on each end."

"Right." Roark cleared his throat, clenching his teeth enough that she could see the tension in his jaw. "That's on my list. It's the last item on the great room renovations, and we have a guy coming out next week."

She made a note in her portfolio, also noting she'd hit a nerve. "I hope you can appreciate why I ask. When I'm planning someone's wedding, I can't sugarcoat the questions."

His gaze met hers as soon as she looked up. "Ms. Kline, I can handle sugar-free. The hearth was supposed to be fixed last month. I'm not happy about it either."

She studied her notes again so she wouldn't stare at him. When he looked at her like that, a zing of pleasure rushed through her body. It seemed there'd be no BS with Roark Bradley, but working with him could still prove complicated. "That's good to hear. And you may call me Madison. Now, regarding the fireplace. Is it operational otherwise?"

"Fully operational and comfortable to use anytime, except maybe in the middle of summer. Even in September you can have perfect weather for a night fire. When the sun goes down up here, it can drop more than twenty degrees. Summer to early winter in one day."

"I remember."

"What's that?"

"I . . ." She'd gone and opened her mouth about it; now she had to spit it out. "I used to live near here."

"Oh yeah? Well, welcome back."

She glanced over, clicking the top of her pen. Roark's voice was pure warmth, full of sincerity like he was welcoming her home.

When Madison was fifteen, her mother's boyfriend of the moment got moved to western North Carolina for a job. They'd lived there for all of nine months. It was the longest she'd lived anywhere, until she turned eighteen and her mother told her to get the hell out and get her own place.

People like Madison didn't call anywhere home, even if they wanted to.

Her grip on the pen tightened. "What's beyond that door?"

"That is our game room, complete with a couple of billiard tables, darts, and foosball." He went past the fireplace to the door on the left and pushed it open. "We keep it separate so people can be enthusiastic about shooting pool without disrupting our quiet readers and lobby loungers."

She looked out over the lobby, with its scattered seating arrangements of couches, love seats, and chairs, all in the same comforting chocolate color, distressed leather with coordinating pillows. The furnishings appeared new and beckoned a person to sink down, relax, and never get up again unless forced.

"The furniture." She peeled her gaze away. "I'm assuming all of it can be moved? None of it is bolted down."

A short bark of a laugh escaped him as he turned toward her again. "Bolted down? Are you being serious?"

"Yes."

"Why? Do you think your clients will steal it?"

"Excuse me?" Madison gaped.

Roark's full laugh came out, as he put a hand up. "I'm sorry. I'm not laughing at you."

She fought not to smile. "I think you kind of are." He was joking with her. People never did that. She owned a sense of humor, just most were afraid to look for it.

"Maybe a little. But bolted down? Come on."

"You'd be surprised at the things I've seen while looking for wedding locations. Furniture that's bolted into place is the least of it."

"I thought they only bolted stuff down at the Super 8."

She shook her head. "I wish. This was at a well-known hotel that shall remain nameless."

"And you've seen worse?"

As a rule, she kept the dirty details she learned top secret, but sometimes she wanted to vent so badly. The crazy stuff she went through, most people wouldn't believe. Sharing one or two anecdotes with Roark couldn't hurt. Perhaps it'd even butter him up when she lowered the boom about the kind of deal she wanted. "Once, I toured an outdoor amphitheater with a shoddy sound system that would blast bluegrass music without warning. I convinced the couple not to use it because who wants the Soggy Bottom Boys in the middle of their vows?"

"You're joking."

She relaxed a fraction. "I wish I was. But the best was the barn wedding with the wayward cows. They got out of their barn—the non-wedding barn across the property—and migrated toward the ceremony. I've never moved so fast in heels in my life. Luckily, the owner of the place was a cow whisperer or something. He got the herd moving back in the other direction."

She was sharing too much and she knew better, but her job was the one thing she loved to talk about. Every event was a challenge and even when she planned everything down to the tiniest detail, something always came up at the last minute to keep things thrilling.

"You didn't want to try your hand at cow herding?" A teasing note played through Roark's question.

She was about to laugh but caught herself and cleared her throat. Too chummy, too early in the deal. "Um, no. So that's a no on the bolted-down furniture?"

"Definitely a no."

A handful of guests strolled by and Roark greeted them with a "good afternoon" while Madison made notes in her portfolio. "What about the rest of the common area?"

Roark showed her every inch of the great room, the groupings of furniture, the comfy yet elegant leather chairs and sofas, the enviable chessboard setup, and the reading nook, which was occupied by exactly one person.

"We also have modernized yurts if your clients have any adventurous wedding guests."

She stopped writing mid-word. "A what?"

He pulled out his phone. "Yurts. Souped-up tents. Circular. Ours come with amenities." Roark leaned in to show her the picture on his phone. The yurt was indeed a tall, round thing that was probably twenty feet in diameter.

But the tent with the funny name wasn't the issue. Roark still smelled like dessert and he stood so close. Close enough that his body heat warmed her side.

"No thank you on the yurts," Madison said, and refused to be disappointed as Roark stepped away.

"I didn't think so, but I love to offer."

They continued walking through the great room. The inn's restaurant, Bradley's, was in the back left corner. The back of the inn opened up with floor-to-ceiling windows and three sets of double French doors.

Before her was a view of the Blue Ridge Mountains like nothing she'd ever seen.

Everyone online said the inn's location was its crown jewel. Sitting on a westward-facing slope, the panorama and multicolored sunsets one could witness from Honeywilde were supposed to be its top draw. Her client bride had waxed poetic for a full five minutes.

Roark touched one of the French doors' S-shaped handles. "These of course lead to our veranda. In warm weather we set tables up out there and serve from the restaurant. It's a prime spot to see the mountains and where most people want to have their wedding ceremony."

Madison stepped forward. "So, you've shown me the view first anyway, only in a roundabout way."

Again he stood close, and when she looked over, she could make out the details of his pale gaze, the touch of blue in otherwise storm-gray eyes.

He glanced down, and quickly back up. The effect of his little eyelash flick might not have been intentional, but that didn't make it any less potent. Heat shot through her body like an electrical surge.

"This is more like second or third on the tour by now, right?"

Her face felt like granite as she fought not to fall into his gaze.

"Second. Still, you got your way."

"I wouldn't say that." He defended himself with a smile. "The veranda simply is where it is, and the view is undeniable."

Yes, the view was definitely undeniable.

"We can ignore it for now if you prefer. Just close your eyes. Look away and we'll pretend it's not there."

"Too late."

"Would you like to go outside?"

She tapped her pen against her portfolio and looked around, at anything but her tour guide. "I think I'd like to see the restaurant now."

"But you said . . . I mean, sure. Let's go check out the restaurant. We can just avoid the ki—"

"I'll need to see the kitchen too, of course." If he insisted on working the view in early, and doing that thing with his eyes, then she could insist on seeing the kitchen.

"A heads-up though," Roark said as he opened the restaurant door for her. "Our chef is still probably mid-cookie prep, and he's a messy yet amazing chef. Don't say you weren't warned."

The restaurant was quiet and mostly empty, which made sense for midafternoon. A small bar took up the wall to the left, just inside the door, and only a bartender milled about. At the table nearest the bar, a dark-haired man sat, fully focused on his laptop, paperwork spread out around him, cell phone clutched to his ear.

He glanced up and gave Roark a cursory nod, his gaze like a laser beam even from this distance. His dark hair was longer, but with the jawline and intense glare, he was definitely a Bradley.

Roark nodded back, but neither of them smiled or made any effort to approach the other.

Interesting.

"So this is Bradley's." Roark presented the restaurant without moving farther into it. "Steve is our bartender and he's a genius. The restaurant is full service, but we can do catering in or out of house, depending on what you need."

"Who is that?" Madison played clueless and nodded to the man still hard at work on whatever he was doing.

"That's my brother, Devlin. He's our hospitality manager. I can introduce you later." Roark held open one of the white swinging doors that had to lead to the kitchen.

Madison went first and the scent of rich sweetness hit her before she even made it in the door.

Her mouth fell open at the display before her, and she wasn't the type to ever let her mouth fall open. "That is *a lot* of cookies."

Several different types of cookies lay carefully arranged on three silver platters. The usual chocolate chip, oatmeal raisin, and peanut butter, but also a decadent, deep-orange colored cookie with a ribbon of creamy white, and the most elaborately decorated sugar cookies she'd ever seen. Thick frosting in chocolate, vanilla, and several other colors swirled over the tops. Some were even topped with a monogrammed H.

"Those look...." Madison swallowed back a little bit of drool. "Good." Would it be bad form if she face-planted into one of the serving trays?

"I tried to tell you, it's dangerous in here right now. Wright is messy, but he prides himself on his desserts, and what used to be a few simple tea treats has turned into this."

"Wright?"

"Our chef. He's probably outside with a produce vendor right now, but these are his pride and joy. He makes way too many. We always have leftovers, but every day he takes the remaining cookies to the children's hospital or an assisted living facility, sometimes the school. I can't complain about the extras without sounding like a—"

"A jerk?"

"Yeah." Roark puffed with a laugh, rocking back on his heels. "So I keep my mouth shut and let the chef do his thing."

Madison would've rolled her eyes at the halo polishing about giving cookies away to kids and the elderly, if he hadn't been so honest about having to keep his mouth shut.

"What are the orange ones?" she asked.

"Pumpkin Pleasure Rolls."

She cocked an eyebrow at him.

"Don't ask."

"Now I *have* to ask."

"Wright named them that. Says it's because they'll make your eyes roll back in pleasure. His words, not mine. And he calls the frosted ones Frosty Fixations."

She rubbed at her mouth to hide her grin over the ridiculous names.

"He's a fanatic, I'm telling you. But I can't eat just one. Would you like to try a Pumpkin Pleasure Roll?"

Would she like to try one?

She barely managed not to laugh like a hyena. Hell yes, she would like to try a whole plate of them and then roll around in the crumbs, but she was not going to fall victim to the inn's goodies yet. Not until she knew this deal wasn't going to blow up in her face.

"No, thank you."

"Seriously?"

She couldn't believe it either. The self-restraint she was practicing right now would impress a nun.

Roark stepped aside. "Suit yourself then. Feel free to have a look around the kitchen. You'll see the enormous vat of vanilla mixture over there. It's been known to attack. Give it a wide berth."

Madison turned away so he couldn't see her smile. She was here to work; to broker a deal that meant she was capable of succeeding on her own. That deal meant practically taking over his inn for a weekend and pulling off the impossible in about three weeks. She was not here to smile and laugh with the good-looking inn owner.

The kitchen was clean but recently used and cluttered. Wright might be a messy chef, but he tidied up afterwards. The revamps Roark had mentioned showed in the new commercial oven and appliances.

Luckily, she was capable of doing a thorough yet speedy overview of everything. The longer she spent in this kitchen, the more tempted she was to stuff a cookie in her mouth.

A scenario ran through her mind. What was the likelihood she could scarf down one, possibly three, cookies without anyone noticing?

She finished checking out the kitchen and wound back around to the front, right in time to find Roark polishing off a Pumpkin Pleasure Roll.

His cheeks full, he dipped his chin, color rushing to his face. When he got done chewing, the strong line of his jaw was back in place, but his cheeks were still pink. Roark's flush was a complete contradiction to his steady gaze and serious look. He wiped his fingers on a napkin and smoothed his shirt down, as though straightening a tie that wasn't there.

"Busted." He smiled, showing the tiniest hint of a dimple in his right cheek.

In that moment, Madison finally admitted the truth to herself. Between the cookies and the resort owner, Roark Bradley was the yummiest choice.

Chapter 2

"I need to see the outside now." Madison bolted past him like the kitchen had caught fire.

Roark followed, tossing the napkin aside. "I thought you said—"

"I know what I said. I changed my mind." She beat a quick retreat through the restaurant, to the French doors.

"The view from outside is pretty amazing," he called after her.

"Good." Madison stepped out onto the veranda and kept going.

The sudden urgency shouldn't surprise him. She'd done nothing but confuse him so far. Almost smiling, and then straight-lipped. Wowed by the cookies, then glaring at them *and* him.

Earlier she'd made it very clear she wanted to tour in a particular order, jabbing her pen around like a weapon, defending her choice of itinerary as though Roark wasn't going to let her have her way.

He didn't care how they toured, but she'd been so insistent, he couldn't help picking at her, just a little.

"You're sure you don't want to go to a room?"

Madison spun on him, her eyes so wide the green practically sparked. "What?"

Roark skidded to a halt so he didn't plow into her. "Whoa, what?"

"What did you just say?"

"You sure you don't want to tour a guest room? You said before, the order in which you wanted to tour: first the great room, a guest room, the restaurant and kitchen, and *then* the outdoors."

"Oh." She clutched her portfolio in front of her. "No. It's fine."

Surely she didn't think he'd meant . . . *Oh.*

"I didn't mean it like *go to a room.*"

Madison pinned him with a dead-eyed stare.

Damn. *Damn.* He'd guessed way off base. "Not that . . . I'm not saying that's what you thought. I'm saying, just in case it came out like that, I don't want you to misinterpret..." He was making it worse. A lot worse. Not quite as bad as being caught with a mouthful of two, count them, *two* cookies, but still pretty damn awkward. "Never mind. So, this is the veranda." He held an arm out toward the view.

He was a lot of things, but the smarmy guy who hit on a woman with some two-bit line? Hell no. She was undeniably attractive, but a woman involved in his business was strictly that.

"It's fine. I know what you meant." Madison took off walking again, her heels clicking on the stone flooring of the veranda.

A wave of relief blew over him like cool air and he hurried to join her. With her height, and a pair of long legs that he was working very hard *not* to notice, he had some catching up to do.

All right, that much was a lie. He'd noticed her legs. Wearing tailored gray pants and a matching jacket, cinched in to highlight her waist. The lady knew how to wear a business suit, but he was trying to be a gentleman and not fixate on . . . things.

Like the sharpness in Madison's green eyes, the smooth arch of her neck, the way she fought smiling, so that the corner of her lips curled up mischievously.

Dammit.

Devlin was right. He needed to get out more.

She finally stopped speed walking when she reached the wrought-iron banister. "This is lovely." Her shoulders rose and fell with a deep breath, her blond hair in a perfect twist at the nape of her neck.

"I told you." He finally caught up to her.

Roark threw a covert glance in her direction, under the guise of checking out a view he'd seen hundreds of times. All he could do was *try* to get a read on what she thought of the place.

She seemed to like Honeywilde, but she wasn't exactly telegraphing her reactions.

Everything about Madison was hard to read. She started to joke with him one moment, then completely shut down. She shared some information and went airtight on the rest. Roark was playing guessing games when it came to Madison Kline. He wasn't sure if he liked it or not, but it wasn't helping his confidence about this deal. Booking a wedding could be a boon for the inn, and they desperately needed a boon right now.

In the midst of their quietly taking in the view, Madison suddenly sparked to life. She stepped away from the banister and did a 360-degree turn, studying the veranda. "I think you could comfortably seat forty people out here. Wouldn't you say?" "Forty would be comfortable." He hopped topic trains to keep up with her. "You'd still have nice space for the ceremony official, wedding party, and musicians if you want them. Seating for fifty-five would be cozy but doable. The one time we had more seating than that, it was too much. Most people shoot for fifty."

"Thank you for the insight," she said without smiling.

"You're welcome." Part of owning an inn and resort was selling it, and he had to sell people on Honeywilde. He and his family relied on it, and he'd learned at the wise old age of seven, that if he didn't take care of his family, nobody else would.

"I bet the sunsets here *are* nice." She held her portfolio tight and looked out over the mountains again.

He joined her, taking in the sight of the Blue Ridge Mountains beyond and Lake Anikawi below. "Better than nice. They're amazing. That's not a line either, by the way, but my honest opinion. Legend has it the sunsets seen from here can soften even the hardest heart, and bring love and prosperity." That part was complete bullshit if you asked him, but so were most legends. Lots of visitors believed them, so who was he to point out the ridiculousness of it?

"I've heard that bit of folklore about the inn in general. Bringing love and luck and all that. Do you believe it?" Madison leaned her elbow on the banister and met his gaze.

She clearly wanted his opinion, but more importantly, a forthright answer.

As the inn's owner, he ought to weave in a little love and storytelling to improve a guest's experience. As a boy who grew up at Honeywilde, hearing about a legend that had done nothing to help his parents' troubled marriage, he had a hard time buying the myth. "No. The whole thing is mostly hype, but guests love the notion. Guess that's all the reason I need to play along." A long-nurtured bitterness crept into his voice, no matter how hard he tried to hide it.

Madison studied him long enough that heat spread over the back of his neck, then she gave him a quick nod. "I don't buy it either, but most people eat up that sort of thing."

"What are those over there?" She pointed to the spattering of cabins along the slope, next to the inn.

"Those are ours. We have a few private properties. Cabins, all heated with electricity, fully furnished. For guests who want more of a secluded feel."

"A compromise between an inn and a yurt."

She spoke the words with such contemplation, Roark had to chuckle.

Madison cut her eyes over at him.

"Sorry. You just sounded so serious saying the word 'yurt.' It's . . . sorry."

"The word 'yurt' is cracking you up?"

"It's not the word. It's how you say it."

"Yurt," she said, insistent in her volume, putting her palm out as though presenting some serious research.

Roark finally gave up and laughed. He wouldn't dare say that the way she said "yurt" was cute, but it was. "I'm—" He cleared his throat, pulling himself together. "I probably had too much sugar from those cookies."

She stared past him, over his shoulder, her lips slightly pursed, the inside of one cheek sucked in like she was chewing on it. At first he thought he'd pissed her off and potentially ruined the whole deal, but then she met his gaze, briefly. In it, he saw the sparkle of restrained laughter.

Madison wanted to laugh too, so badly she could hardly stand to look at him, but she flat out refused. And now he wanted to make her laugh. The goal felt like a mission, and he wasn't going to question why.

"Is there a finished lower level since the inn is built into the mountain?" She leaned over the banister to look down.

Roark didn't bother looking too. His view was better. "There is. It's about a quarter of the size of our main and upper floors. It's finished, with a common area, a long empty room that's yet to have a purpose, and eight suites. My youngest brother has one of the rooms down there, but I'd rather open it all up for guests so it could be something of use."

"Your brother doesn't need a place to live?"

Roark clenched his jaw on what he was tempted to say about his wayward baby brother, Trevor. He went with the politer option. "He hasn't been here in three months, so I guess not."

Madison quietly considered him for a moment.

"I'd like to come back out here at sunset," she said, gracefully changing subjects. "If the sunsets are all they're rumored to be, maybe we should time the ceremony accordingly."

Roark grabbed at the chance to talk sunsets instead siblings. "I think that'd be ideal for a wedding. And, if there's rain on the day of the wedding, we have the great room as an alternative."

"It won't rain. I don't allow rain on my weddings."

He bet the weather didn't have the balls to rain on any of her weddings.

They both studied the skyline again, Roark keenly aware of the woman next to him. She was a beautiful contradiction.

Stern and serious one moment, a teasing playfulness trying to break free the next.

He didn't want to think too much about her, or over analyze, like he was prone to do, but this time of day was always so quiet in the mountains. Like nature conspiring to make you sit and over think everything.

The air was thicker, heavy, muffled. A shower could pop up at any minute, lasting all of five minutes before disappearing.

Silence settled over the veranda as they both stood there, studying the cloud-dabbled sky. A combination of shadows and rays danced across the lake. The moment was oddly intimate, sharing serenity with a stranger.

Madison sniffed. "Is that the kitchen I smell or is it still you?"

Roark studied the dried stain on his sleeve closest to her. The sweet smell was definitely him, but he played along anyway. He sidestepped away about five or six paces. "Do you still smell it?"

She sniffed the air again. "It's gone. That's good though. You smell delicious, but I don't want other kitchen scents to travel all the way outside. No one wants eau de catfish while listening to Mendelssohn on harp."

Madison thought he smelled delicious. That was going to be his takeaway. "You won't smell any catfish. Nothing but fresh mountain air, maybe the scent of roses or whatever arrangements you use. It won't rain, the sun will be perfectly scheduled to set, on cue, and you will have the wedding of the year."

A quick laugh escaped. "I expect a lot. I know. What can you do about a cloudless sky, soft breeze, happy clients, and guests who are awed by the whole event?"

Roark saw the opportunity and jumped at it. He checked off an invisible list with his finger in the air. "Done. What about a flock of doves to fly by at precisely the right time? A migration of butterflies?"

"No, thank you. I've used doves before."

He tilted his head back. "Of course you have."

"Released upon the announcement of the new couple. All I could do was pray none of the birds . . . you know?"

"Lessened their load midflight?"

Madison laughed. Finally, with the quickest flash of white teeth before she covered her mouth, she let herself laugh. "Yes. Everything worked out, but I prefer to stay away from live animals at my events."

"I don't blame you. But I bet somebody, some day, will want to ride in on a horse. Or off on a horse. There will be something involving a horse in your future." He was teasing her, but she was laughing. He sure as hell wasn't going to squash it now.

Madison gave him a stern look that was nothing but playful. "Bite your tongue. I like a challenge, but you could curse me with some kind of cowboy-themed ceremony and horses all over the place."

He shook his head. "Potentially a lot worse than doves . . . if you know what I mean."

This time her burst of laughter echoed around the veranda. She clamped a hand over her mouth again. "Don't say that. Don't even put that out into the universe." She spoke from behind her fingers, but it sounded like she was smiling.

"I should take it back?" Roark grinned too.

She dropped her hand. "Yes, definitely."

"I take it back. No horse weddings. No doves. Butterflies will be the extent of any living props at your weddings."

"Butterflies I can handle. Thank you."

Madison was definitely smiling. No tight politeness from earlier, not a sly business smirk, but a full-on, light-in-her-eyes smile. Roark had finally managed to say something funny.

He wore a dopey grin right now, he just knew it. The pull in his face, the warm hum along his cheeks. Dammit, he probably looked ridiculous, but he couldn't help it. He'd gotten her to laugh.

Madison grabbed up her portfolio and straightened. "Um. I should probably . . . talk to your hospitality manager? And see more of the restaurant before the dinner crowd arrives?"

Roark dropped his smile. "Yeah? I mean, yes. He is in charge of hospitality, after all. Wright might be free as well. I need to finish up some things in the office."

A moment for Roark to refocus on business and not on whatever the hell he was doing might be a good idea, but he wasn't ready for Dev to take over the tour completely.

In fact, he downright didn't want to give her up. "How about, when you're done in the restaurant, you can stop by the office and we'll see the rest of the inn?"

Madison nodded, and her feet click-clacked, rapid fire, against the veranda's stone floor as she hurried back inside.

Roark followed, made the polite introductions, and got the hell out of the restaurant. He made it to his office, closed the door, and slumped in his too big, too old desk chair.

What in blazes was he doing?

He wouldn't deny he found Madison attractive. Insisting otherwise was pointless, and he didn't do things that were pointless—but damn. He needed to get himself together.

Madison was gorgeous, smart, and he was about two seconds from asking her out for drinks. The problem was, she wasn't some woman he'd met in town. She was a potentially *huge* client for Honeywilde, and clients and guests were off limits.

Not only that, but he knew better than to flirt with her. It was unprofessional. Madison probably got hit on by businessmen all the time, and he bet she loathed it. Roark wasn't going to be that guy. He *wasn't* that guy. That guy was an ass.

Now . . . if he'd met Madison at a pub or been introduced by friends, that'd be a different story. He'd ask her out for coffee or lunch, then a dinner date. But that wasn't the case here. She might be booking an event here, and that mattered above all else.

No. She *would* book an event here; he'd see to it. Honeywilde had to have this. Madison had done enough research to know the inn's business had been off the last decade or so, and they'd done enough research on her to know she coordinated the kind of events that could help the inn out of its financial hole.

His grandfather's pride and joy, the Bradley legacy, had gotten so close to foreclosure it still gave Roark heartburn, but his parents broke up the shares of Honeywilde and entrusted it to their children before they retired.

Roark inherited the majority, took out the loans to fix the place up, and he and his siblings would be the ones to turn it around. They had to survive this winter first though, the dead time for mountain hospitality, and the preceding fall season was looking pretty bleak.

"Where have you been?" Roark's sister burst into his office and circled his desk in a tornado of Post-it notes and riotous red hair. A huge mop of chocolate hair and four legs followed, tongue out like this was the best game ever.

"That apple vendor is trying to rob us blind," she complained, the dog, Beau, barking in agreement. "He's priced those apples like they don't grow *everywhere* up here. I told him no thanks, buddy."

She bumped around behind his chair, shuffling through the folders on the credenza until one fell off.

"May I help you find something?"

"I need the number for that produce guy. The one right outside of town, family farm. I bet he'd hook us up with some apples, and in the spring he sells strawberries. Wright wants to make his apple crumble thingie for Sunday brunch this weekend. Sunday brunch is the restaurant's busiest time."

She said it with such conviction, like Roark needed to be convinced. Right now, the restaurant was what kept them afloat.

"I know Sundays are busy."

"Then you know Wright *has* to make his apple crumble thingie and we kind of have to have apples for him to make it."

He scrolled through the contacts in his phone until he reached the number for Stewart Farms. He forwarded it to Sophie's phone and it rang in her pocket.

She wrinkled her nose again. "I do not have time to talk to anyone right now."

"It's me, Soph. I just sent you the number to the farm."

"Oh." She checked her phone, then almost dropped it when she clamped her hand down on his arm.

"Ow." For someone so tiny, she had a grip like the jaws of a pit bull.

"That event planner, the one who did the big wedding in Charleston—Madison. She's supposed to be here today."

"Yes. She is here."

"Oh my god. Where? When?"

"She got here about an hour or so ago and I showed her around."

Sophie threw her hands up. "Why didn't you say so? How did it go? What did she think? Is she going to book us? She used to work for Echols Events and they handle some big names. A big-name event is exactly what we need."

His little sister had done the recon on Madison as soon as she'd called to make an appointment. Sophie had said the name sounded familiar, and sure enough, Madison's name had shown up in a Charleston style magazine in an article about a big wedding, right before she left her employer to go into business on her own.

Roark stood, hoping to corral his sister's anxiety. Beau was right beside him. "This *might* be a big event, Sis. Let's don't get too far ahead of ourselves. She hasn't booked us yet, but I think it's going really well. She likes the place so far."

"We could use a successful wedding on our books."

He didn't have to be reminded of that fact. "Soph." Roark towered over her, so he put his hands on her shoulders and bent his knees so she wouldn't have to crane her neck. After all the years of reassuring Sophie that everything was going to be okay, he automatically took that position anytime she worried about anything. "I'm taking care of it. Everything is going to be okay."

"Where is Madison now?"

"She had some questions about the restaurant and a few details, so I left her with Devlin."

Sophie looked at him with bug eyes. "You left her with Dev? Since when is that a good idea?"

"Never, but I can't cut him out completely. He's already giving me the stink eye every chance he gets. If I interrupt him now, it'll be next year before he stops pouting."

"Don't be like that. See, this is why the two of you fight."

"We fight because he wants an on-staff sommelier, classes for yoga and cooking, even freaking ballroom dancing. He acts like we're the Sandals of the Smokies."

Sophie bumped his arm with her fist. "Dev is a good businessman, like you, but he's . . . creative. Imaginative, and that's a positive. Y'all balance each other out."

Roark barked out a laugh and had to dodge another one of her punches that looked like it held more force.

He put his hands out to block her tiny fists of fury. "The important thing is, the tour with Madison is going well and I'll finish when she's done talking to Dev."

"Oh, *you'll* finish it? You don't want your hospitality manager to take over?" She stepped back and somehow managed to look down her nose at him.

"No, I don't. Besides, Madison and I speak the same language. We have . . . rapport." He was not going to say chemistry, however tenuous it might be.

His sister gave him her patented flat stare that held about a thousand accusations and never failed to make him feel guilty, even when he'd done nothing wrong.

"What?"

"Rapport?"

"What?"

She rolled her eyes and turned for the door. "Nothing. Just get us this wedding. Then you can do whatever you want with your rapport."

Chapter 3

Madison squeezed her phone between her shoulder and ear, and made a beeline toward her Audi. The line rang and rang, until finally Whitney picked up.

"Hello," the future bride sang into the phone.

"It's Madison. You were right. Honeywilde is perfect."

Whitney squeaked into the phone. "I know, right? Did you get it booked?" The famous lead singer didn't have to tell Madison how eager she was to have her dream wedding at her dream location; it oozed from every word.

"Not yet. I just finished the tour with the general manager and I'm about to meet with him to make an offer. I have to play it cool versus gushing over how gorgeous it is up here." She walked around her car, enjoying the private moment to admit how freaking beautiful yet quaint this place was.

"You've seen it now, so you know why I have to have it. Growing up, we went there almost every summer. Pay them whatever they want to clear their schedule and book it."

Easier said than done. "You know I can't pay them whatever. Your manager already chewed me out about this event, then he went after you. I'd like to keep the price within reason and keep him off our backs."

Whitney groaned. "Phil is such a dick sometimes. I'm sorry. I know he's looking out for us, but still."

She wasn't wrong. The band's business manager was a nightmare. Regardless, Madison's job was to turn this whole thing into the couple's dream come true. Not just for them, but for her. If she pulled off this high-profile wedding, her one-woman business would be set. No more backstabbing coworkers, no more sexist boss, no more constant threats of losing her job because someone else didn't do theirs. "Try not to worry about Phil. You hired me so I can worry about all of the logistics and you don't have to. I'll make it work. You have music to tend to."

"When are you going to tell him we need the whole place for a week, in like, less than a month?"

"I won't be telling him 'we' need anything. He doesn't know who is getting married yet." Because that'd jack the price up enough to make manager Phil's nonexistent hair curl.

"So he could still say no and slam the door in your face? You can tell him it's us. Maybe it will help."

"He's not going to slam the door in my face." She bet it'd been months since Honeywilde was booked to full capacity. Madison wasn't just offering full booking, whether the rooms were used or not, but hefty events costs. The inn needed that kind of money, the same way she needed this wedding to be a success.

Besides, she wasn't letting the big-name cat out of the bag unless she had no choice. "I'll lay out an offer and we'll massage the deal until it's done."

"Oh, I hope so." The wistful longing in Whitney's voice betrayed her youth. The bride and groom were in their early twenties and, by all accounts, desperately in love.

Madison wouldn't say it to them—could *never* say it to any client—but she thought anyone getting married was out of their mind. She'd gotten close enough to dream about it once, when very young and stupid. Her dream had been built on lies, believed by a silly girl who should've known better than anyone else. Weddings were part of her job, not part of her life plan.

"There's no need to hope," she reassured her bride. "I'm going to make this happen."

Madison hung up and dropped her phone in her bag. This deal *would* be agreed upon and this wedding would turn out flawless. She didn't have anything else to fall back on, so she simply wouldn't fail.

As much fun as she was having dealing with Roark, this was the kind of high-profile gig that could make or break a career. She smoothed down her suit jacket and ran a hand over her hair. She wasn't primping for Roark; she was preparing for battle.

She found Roark on the veranda, sitting with his back to her at a little bistro table they must've moved outside from the restaurant. An empty chair sat on the other side of the table, facing the mountains and an imminent sunset.

"This is cozy." She put her things down and joined him. "Romantic" was the word echoing in her brain, but she knew better.

Firstly, she worked in the industry of everlasting love and romance, so she was immune to fanciful stuff like this. Secondly, Roark was admittedly jaded himself. She recognized a kindred cynic when she met one and, most importantly, there was no reason for him to try to romance her.

Roark crossed a leg to rest his ankle over his knee. "I thought you might want to get the full experience. Like you said, see what the guests will see if they're sitting out here for a wedding. I brought snacks as well."

Madison noticed a plate, covered with a cloth napkin, on the center of the table, and two steaming mugs of coffee with a little tray of cream and sugar.

"That better not be what I think it is under that napkin."

"Depends. What do you think it is?"

"Some of those cookies from the kitchen."

"In that case, it's absolutely what you think it is. Wright put some aside and made fresh coffee. You said maybe later, and now it is later."

"You're not going to seal this deal on the virtues of some cookies."

Roark leaned an elbow on the table and grinned. "That's what you think, but you haven't had these cookies yet."

She swore her chair tipped toward him with the pull of that playful look. All day long she'd fought the draw. It was wearing her down. They had a deal to make, and flirting with Roark was not the way she did business. She rolled her eyes to play off his effect. "Fine. Unveil the cookies. Let's get this over with."

He turned toward the table and moved one of the pottery mugs closer to her. "Okay, but you can't have any cookies until the color starts."

"Color starts what?"

"Oh." Roark whipped the napkin off the plate with a flourish. "You'll see."

Underneath the napkin lay ten—no, twelve—cookies. Six different frosted, two chocolate chip, two oatmeal raisin, and two of the Pumpkin Pleasure Rolls.

It was all she could do not to whine at the sweets. "I can't eat six cookies." Though she wouldn't mind trying.

"Who said we're splitting them evenly? I'm thinking ten for me, two for you."

She laughed, realizing she'd done so more today than she had in years. She was rusty at it, but still as loud as always.

"Here we go. Now you can have a cookie." He moved the plate closer to her. She chose a pumpkin one, only because she hadn't stopped thinking about them since she first saw them.

Roark grabbed a chocolate iced cookie in one hand, his mug of coffee in the other.

They turned toward the horizon to see the first shades of orange and yellow stain the sky. "Lovely," she noted. She wasn't one to swoon at nature, but the view was pretty.

"It gets better." He bit into his cookie and brushed the crumbs off his chest.

She refocused on the sunset and slowly, quietly, the colors went from a bright orange to burnt, to crimson, to a deep wine color. The color bled and paled, to violet and pink, until all that was left was a soft lavender with the navy blue of midnight chasing it across the sky.

A soft breeze caressed her skin, the uneaten cookie still in her hands. Madison blinked at the evening falling softly around her and realized her mouth was hanging open a little. "Is it like that every day?" Her voice was breathy, barely a whisper, and she didn't like the sound.

She sipped her coffee, now lukewarm. How much time had gone by since she'd joined Roark out here? And why was she waxing poetic over a setting sun when that was just the sort of ridiculousness she'd never entertain?

"Not every day." Roark reached for another cookie. This time a strawberry frosted. "But we do get a lot of them."

"It's spectacular."

From the corner of her eyes, she could see Roark turn toward her. "Isn't it? It's nothing magical like people say, but that doesn't make it any less beautiful. Our cleaner air, plus the high clouds we get this time of year, light scattering through particles in the atmosphere, *that's* the secret to our sunsets."

Yes, Roark was a kindred cynic, for sure. It didn't ruin the quality of the view for her though. In fact, it enhanced it. He made the sunset real, something she could rely on.

"So the climate is perfect for pretty sunsets in September?" she asked.

"Some of the prettiest."

That meant she'd have guests at least ten times as wowed as she was, because she wouldn't tell them about the atmosphere and particles. This location was perfect, and she'd make sure she got it without a sky-high price tag. The bride and groom's grumpy manager would be satisfied with not spending a load of money and, more importantly, the wedding couple would have the location of their dreams.

Then Madison's name would spread through the entertainment industry like A-list gossip and she'd be the It woman for fabulous weddings and events. She wasn't working this hard for anything less.

She envisioned patting herself on the back and bit into the cookie. "Oh . . . my . . . god."

The cookie's name was 100 percent justified; her eyes really did roll back into her head. When she got it together, she looked over at Roark.

He was smiling the smile of a man who'd told her so. "I know."

"What's *in* this thing? The soul your chef sold for it to taste so good?"

Roark slapped the table. "I'll have to tell Wright you said that, but I don't know what's in them. A cheesecake-type something or other? He won't tell me details and I'm not sure I want to know. Probably enough sugar to warrant a ban by the FDA. We don't question perfection." He grabbed one of the pumpkin ones too.

"No offense, but how can you eat these cookies and, first of all, not have diabetes, and second of all, still look . . . the way you look."

He grinned and she knew, this time, she was the one busted. "How do I look?"

"You know how you look. Answer the question."

"I limit myself to one a day. Usually," he added before she could point out she'd seen him have at least four today. "Today I'm giving a tour, so it's special. I haven't had dinner yet either, so I'm starving. I tell Wright that he's the reason I run every day. If I didn't run, I'd have to cut these out of my life completely, and that's just not going to happen."

He was a runner. She ran too, but not because of cookies. Running was the only time she was clearheaded and free. Now would be the time any normal person might mention they also ran. Share commonality, open up a little, bond over personal details.

Madison didn't do personal details.

She looked at the half-eaten cookie in her hand. "I'm keeping you from dinner. We should probably wrap this up."

"I'm not that hungry. Had about a half dozen cookies, after all. Besides"—he tapped the table with his finger—"we need to talk about your decision. You've had the tour, the view, and the cookies. What do you think?"

This was it. He'd either work with her on this or laugh in her face. "I might be interested in booking Honeywilde for this wedding, but there are a few . . . stipulations."

Roark turned his chair into the table and slid forward, both elbows propped on it. "I'm listening."

Madison turned her chair too, matching his posture. "I would need to book the inn for longer than just a weekend."

"That can be arranged."

"We're talking a big event here."

"How big?"

"The entire inn and the restaurant. No other guests allowed in or out for the extent of the booking."

Roark lifted his eyebrows. "Which would be . . . ?"

"For a week."

His eyebrows stayed up. "You want to book the whole inn, for a week?"

"Restaurant too. You won't necessarily have people staying here that entire time, but they want it booked up and blocked off for setup and privacy."

"Privacy? Who are they, royalty?"

"Let me worry about who they are. What I will tell you is I'm definitely interested in Honeywilde as the location."

"That's good to hear."

"But there's a catch."

"And that is?"

"I need it in three weeks."

Roark didn't exactly laugh in her face. First he stared at her, slack jawed, looked up to the sky, and *then* he laughed. "Are you nuts? Our inn isn't available in three weeks. You book this sort of thing months in advance."

"I don't have months of advance notice. They're getting married at the end of September and they're getting married here."

"We already have guests booked that weekend."

"How many?"

"I don't know."

"Yes you do. How many?"

He glanced away. "Ten rooms."

"I can compensate the cost or pay for their visit any other weekend they'd like to stay. Done. Next issue."

"You cannot throw together a wedding and have it here in three weeks."

"It's actually less than three weeks. And watch me." Madison reached for her portfolio and slid it over in front of her. "Now, I'm going to write down a figure, payment for the whole week at Honeywilde. You can tell me what it will take to comp the displaced guests and we'll tack that on to the end."

"Before you go writing down any figures, be aware that I know how reasonable our rates are. Don't start out trying to lowball me when I know you normally plan events for clients with means. They can afford us."

She narrowed her eyes at him. "You don't know who my clients are."

"How do you know? We have resources here too."

"I'm sure you do, but all the resources in the world wouldn't tell you whose wedding I'm planning."

"No, but it told us the *kind* of weddings you plan, and they're not the cheap kind."

A flash of heat, not entirely uncomfortable, shot through her body and fired her mind. Roark wasn't playing around.

"But I'm out on my own now. I could be planning for a conservative affair."

He grinned. "Or it could be a huge affair and you're playing it cool. I imagine you play it cool very well."

She concentrated on writing down a figure rather than holding his gaze. She tore the paper from the notepad and pushed it over to Roark.

"What do you think?"

He winced, shaking his head. "I think you're trying to hurt my feelings. And after I gave you cookies and everything. This won't cover us, and even after you comp a few guests, word will get out that we cancelled their plans. You and I both know the price tag on this event has to be worth risking our reputation."

She kept her expression carefully blank and waited. A man like Roark could probably sniff out weakness or desperation if she so much as flinched.

Roark sat back, studying her. He kept staring, his jaw locked into place, gaze unwavering.

How many people buckled under that stare? He probably used it on his brothers and sister all the time.

Roark grabbed the paper off the table. With her pen, he wrote down another number, but kept it close so she couldn't see. "As much fun as it is having a staring contest with you, I'm willing to write down an amount that is as low as I'll go, still make a profit, and feel good about the risk to our name."

Her pulse jumped. She loved the rush of the deal, the high of getting what she wanted. If his number was in any way a reasonable amount, she'd win.

Roark put his fingertip on the table again. "*But*, I'm only going to offer this rate if you can offer something to me."

A foreboding rush hit her like vertigo. She shook it off because surely Roark wasn't like *that*. "Offer what?" Madison managed to ask without clenching her teeth.

"This couple getting married has to be in the public eye, right? I mean, they must be somebody if they need the whole place and the privacy and all that."

She nodded, torn between relief that he wasn't being the pig her former boss had always been and the niggling feeling she'd given away too much information.

"Then the inn could potentially get some publicity out of this."

She opened her mouth to argue and he shook his head. "I know it might be a hush-hush thing until the wedding is over. Top secret, all that jazz, I know how it works. After the fact though, I want a few bragging rights. That's all."

"I'm not going to sell out a client. Ever." She balled her hand into a fist.

"Who's selling them out? I'm talking about some sentimental, romantic pictures for publicity after the fact. Not paparazzi type crap, but . . . a tasteful editorial on their nuptials.

"I don't want a little article in the local paper either," he said. "I'm talking a piece in *Southern Living*, *InStyle*. Magazines do wedding issues. Something in color about this great wedding and how it all took place at *the* Honeywilde Mountain Inn and Resort. See how charming? Look how unique. *People* magazine wedding feature. Everybody flock to the inn, right now, and book in for a week."

She bit at the inside of her cheek to keep from smiling. "How do you even know about wedding spreads in *People* magazine?"

"I go to the grocery store. I know things."

Madison shook her head. "This is their wedding, their celebration of love, and you're trying to use it to your benefit? To make money?"

"You aren't doing the exact same thing?"

She wasn't answering that. They both already knew the answer.

He propped his elbows on the table again and leaned forward, but his shoulders relaxed tenfold. "Look. You and I, we don't bullshit, right? The publicity of a high-profile wedding like this, even if it comes out after the event, is invaluable to you as an event planner. Why not get some value-added for Honeywilde? I'm only looking out for me and mine, same as you."

He was right. She'd be the total opposite of mum about this wedding once it was over. It'd be the first thing listed in her portfolio and the bomb she'd drop when trying to attract new clients.

"You're a tactical businessman, I'll give you that." She'd be lying if she said she didn't admire it. And find it extremely hot.

"I'm not *that* tactical." He shook his head and gave her that same guilty grin like when he'd been caught eating cookies.

The laughter that catapulted out of Madison shocked even her. She couldn't help it. A giddy high from working this deal took over, and she was riding it.

"You know you won't get any other inns on such short notice or at an insider price," he added.

"Oh, I'm an insider now?" She looked at the number again and then at him.

"If you get us a spot in *Southern Living*, you're a VIP for life. All I want are a few pictures."

"You know I can't guarantee that now. I have to talk to my client."

"I know. But the wedding is three whole weeks away. Influence. I know you have it."

She shook her head, trying to think. Whitney and Jack would be easy. All they cared about was getting the place. If it involved a few extra photographers and a quote, they'd jump on it.

The turnkey was their manager. He'd been a sour pill about the whole wedding from the get-go. Anything that wasn't his idea was a piss-poor one.

Madison straightened. That was it. She'd have to make him think the whole publicity thing was his idea.

She broke off a bite of her cookie and popped it in her mouth. "I may be able to work with you on this deal you've laid out, *if* their manager is in agreement."

"Manager?"

"He's a piece of work, but any publicity has to be approved by him. You'll have to charm him. I'll have to charm him. We'll all have to be a big ball of charming, but a lower price tag is a good place to start."

"I believe you're trying to manage me." Roark smiled.

"You're the one who threw out this rate along with wanting my client's participation. For that, we need to get their manager on board and that means knocking a grand off this price. And, for the week of the wedding, I'll be running the inn right alongside you. Will that be an issue?"

Roark looked down at the number and back up. "A grand less than this and you'll get us the promo?"

"Regional, at least. *Southern Living, Southern Style*. Maybe even *People*."

He sucked his full bottom lip between his teeth before giving her a firm nod. "If you get us in a nationwide magazine, you can have us at that price and run whatever you want. Now can you tell me who's getting married?"

"After we sign."

He glanced at his watch. "I can draw up the paperwork within the hour, but you'll want to review it before signing."

"Working late isn't a problem. I'm staying over. My bags are in the car. I only have three weeks to plan a wedding, after all."

To his credit, Roark's only show of shock was a quick pop of his eyebrows. Then he smiled. He pushed away from the table and stood.

"Madison Kline, you have yourself a deal." He stuck out his hand to shake on it.

"And a wedding to plan." She stood as well, and slid her hand into his.

A shiver of excitement made her skin tingle, her blood sing. She told herself it was merely the thrill of closing this deal. It had nothing to do with Roark, the fire in his eyes or his warm hand wrapped around hers.

Chapter 4

"Are you going to tell us who's getting married here, or do we have to guess?" Devlin propped an elbow on the arm of the sofa so he could hold his head up. Eyes closed, he lifted a coffee mug to his lips.

Roark held back the smart-ass answer itching to break free. The day was too new to start sniping at one another. Last night included about two hours of paperwork and signing contracts, and finally getting Madison checked in.

Settling into one of the chairs by the great room's fireplace, he decided he'd rather ease into the day gently than dive in headfirst by taking on Dev. He took a long sip of his black coffee before he answered. "The lead singer and lead guitarist of the band Red Left Hand will be having their wedding at Honeywilde."

"Oh yeah? I've heard of them." Dev nodded.

Sophie slapped her hands together with way too much energy for seven in the morning. "You're lying!"

Beau woofed his accusation from a pile on the floor.

"I am not lying."

Dev barely tilted his chin in her direction, creaking one eye open. "How do you know them? That's not even your kind of music."

"Are you kidding? Everyone knows them."

Roark had heard of them too, he'd been proud to say. They were a sort of alt rock, indie group out of Georgia, who'd hit it big because one of their songs got picked up for a movie soundtrack. "The even bigger news is, we're going to get publicity from it, after the fact. I'm hoping something like *People*. Honeywilde is going to get some serious promotion."

Sophie bounced up and down on her end of the sofa, taking little note of what he'd said. "Their song was everywhere this summer. I think they're on tour right now. I didn't even know those two were dating."

"Most people don't know, and everything is hush-hush, for now. We can't go blabbing to anyone about it. It's on a need-to-know basis until it's all over."

Sophie's smile went from ear to ear. "I can't believe Jack Winter, lead guitarist of RLH, is going to be staying *here.*"

Dev leaned down the couch toward her. "To get married."

"I know." She smacked his arm with the back of her hand. "But he's still hot. I love the lead singer, Whitney, too. She's so cute. I can't believe they're getting married. And they're doing it here."

"It's way too early in the morning for your level of enthusiasm." His brother turned into his arm to yawn.

"But this is so exciting!" She bounced again.

Roark appreciated Sophie's enthusiasm, always, but he believed in celebrating *after* they'd executed everything perfectly. "It won't be exciting until we pull it off, it's a huge success, and we can get our name out there."

Sophie leveled a look at him. "It's exciting now and the excitement only grows from here."

"All that we have to get done grows from here. We don't have a lot of time and a lot of the details will be on you."

Sophie waved off the pressure, like she always did. "I know Trev isn't here, but I'll get someone else on my team to step up. It's fine."

"Don't talk to me about Trevor."

"Of course. I wouldn't dare." She patted his arm.

His little sister helped keep the place running and, equally important, kept the Bradley brothers from killing one another. She wasn't only operations manager; she handled the overflow from Roark's mile-long to-do lists. She deserved help. She deserved a brother here helping them, like he'd promised.

Devlin sniffed, making sure to give Roark his most exasperated look. "This is good news, Roark. Don't be a buzzkill."

A ripple of warmth rolled down Roark's neck. If he were a dog, his hackles would be on their way up. "You were *just* yawning over this entire conversation. You don't give a rip about the wedding; you just like taking sides against me."

"I'm taking sides against you because you've got a giant stick up your ass."

"Boys." Sophie glared at them.

Roark saved his scowl for Dev. "This buzzkill closed a huge deal for us last night."

Sophie leaned over and gripped Roark's hand. "Exactly. So you can be a little happy about that success. You're not going to jinx it. Enjoy it. We can start the worrying later."

Maybe she had a point. "You're right. Yay." Roark put one hand in the air and wiggled his fingers in imitation of her.

"That's more like it."

"Now, we've got to come up with a game plan." He pulled out his phone and scrolled to his notes.

Devlin groaned and slumped as Sophie whined, "Not the phone. Let the coffee kick in first. We don't have to start planning now."

"I'd like to have some ideas ready before Madison comes down."

Sophie held both hands up, a look on her face as though Roark had said their rock-star bride and groom were here now. "Wait. Comes *down*? Did she stay here last night?"

"She checked in because it's time to start planning. The wedding is in three weeks."

"*Three weeks?*" Sophie's voice went up an octave.

"A little less than three, technically. I was getting to that part next. We're under a time crunch. That's why we need a game plan now."

"That's insane. It's impossible. You're both *insane*."

Dev leaned toward her again. "You get to meet Jack Winter," he whispered.

Sophie grinned. "I mean, I'm in. But it's still insane."

Dev propped his feet up on the bottom rung of the coffee table and leaned back. "You're all certifiable, but that isn't news. I'm on board."

Good. They were all on board, and enthusiastic in their own way, but where was Madison? If she wanted to take the lead on logistics, then they needed to start immediately. Early mornings were the time for Bradley meetings, mainly because once guests got up and the restaurant opened, they'd have no time to meet.

Roark was about to ring the cell phone number Madison gave him last night when Sophie popped up from her seat.

He turned to find Madison standing behind him.

She looked at each of them, her gaze hanging on his before it caught the coffee trolley against the wall.

Roark rose to his feet as well. "Madison. Good morning. You've already met Devlin and this is my sister, Sophie."

The greetings and handshakes were made when Sophie blurted out, "*How* do you look like a crisp million bucks this early?"

"Soph," he muttered, but she was right. Madison looked as good as she had the day before, maybe even better. More casual today, she wore beige slacks and a black blouse. Her hair was smoothed back into a clip, drawing attention to her high cheekbones and wry mouth.

As if more of his attention needed to be drawn.

Sophie got up to refill her coffee. "What time did you get up to look so put together?"

Roark cut his eyes at his sister, but she wasn't paying him a bit of attention.

"I wake up at six or so every day, but I'm a morning person."

"I'm a morning person too," Sophie argued, "and all I've managed to do is brush my teeth and put my hair in a bun."

Madison smiled, that little curl of her lips, before she poured herself a cup of coffee and sat in the chair next to Roark's. "But it seems I'm the one late to the meeting."

She crossed her legs toward him, watching him as she sipped her coffee. "No cookie cologne today?"

"Not today." He grinned.

"Sorry I'm late."

"I forgot to mention that if we meet, we meet in the morning."

"Yes. Welcome to the obnoxiously early Bradley-family meetings." Dev spread his arm out wide.

Roark bit back a retort. "We like to meet before the majority of the guests are up and about. Since we're a vacation resort, that's usually not until eight or later. A few hikers might be up earlier, but that's rare."

"Good to know." Madison tapped her foot in the air, the gold medallion on her black flats shining, her legs long enough that her calf came half an inch from brushing his with every tap. Mesmerizing.

"And who is this?" she asked, just as Beau rose from his napping spot by the fireplace to greet her.

"This is Beau," he answered. "Currently the family dog."

"You're pet friendly? That's a nice perk for your guests."

Satisfied with her scratch behind his ears, Beau flopped back down in his usual spot.

"He's not a fan of Roark's morning meetings either," Dev added, grinning at him.

Good thing he loved his younger brother. That was the only thing that kept him from throttling Dev on a daily basis.

Roark turned to Madison. "I've told Sophie and Dev that the wedding is in just under three weeks. I thought we could tell you what people have done for events here in the past, things that did and didn't work."

Sophie smacked the couch cushion between her and Dev. "You mean like that time the reunion party wanted the buffet line outside?"

Dev chuckled. "And later, when they were inside dancing, a couple of raccoons figured they were invited and tried to nab some appetizers to go?"

They both laughed, but Roark never had found it funny. That guest had raised holy hell about the vermin problem, when Roark had specifically told her that leaving the buffet up until late at night was a bad idea. He'd had to refund part of their deposit to keep the peace.

"Oh, come on, Roark. It's funny." Dev raised his mug in salute. "Those were the happiest raccoons you'd ever seen."

Sophie nodded. "They looked like little burglars who'd hit the jackpot. Black masks and all."

Madison shook her head, her chin dipped to hide her grin. "There will be no uninvited guests at this event. Two-legged, four-legged, or otherwise."

"You think that'll be an issue?" Roark asked her.

She turned to him. "It might. The bride and groom have hit it big this year. When that happens, you get paparazzi, gossip magazines. We're keeping their wedding top secret until it's over, but there could be leaks. We'll want to get some local security at the inn's driveway and entrance."

Roark added that to the list on his phone. "I know of some cops who do security when off duty. They won't ask who and why, and they understand discretion. I'm happy to contact them and keep the name confidential."

"That'd be nice. Thank you." Madison sipped her coffee, looking at him over the rim again. It might be indecently early in the day for some people, but Madison's gaze was alert, her eyes a sharp green, honed right in on him.

"You're welcome," he said, immediately taking a sip of his coffee too.

In his peripheral vision, Devlin and Sophie looked at each other. "Roark already told you who will be getting married here?" Madison asked them.

Both straightened up like a teacher had suddenly called on them.

"He did. I'm a big fan of theirs actually, but I can keep that to myself," Sophie said.

Madison waved her hand. "It's okay to let them know you're a fan, but we'll keep it reserved and professional beyond that. The bride and groom, the band, and a small wedding party will arrive the Thursday before."

Sophie beamed at the prospect.

Madison turned to Roark. "What about you? Are you a fan?"

Devlin snorted. "Ha! Roark only listens to NPR and nineties rock. He wouldn't know modern music if it bit him."

"As a matter of fact, I have heard of them."

"Only because Sophie likes them."

Roark ignored his brother and focused on Madison. "I wouldn't say I'm a fan, but I do know who they are."

She shrugged and set her coffee mug down on the arm of the chair. She wrapped her long fingers around the mug. Her nails were clean and short, with only the gloss of clear polish, and she wore no rings. Madison kept things simple and classic, nothing to draw much attention, but Roark noticed anyway. He'd touched those hands, a couple of times, and knew their soft strength. He tried not to wonder about them beyond a handshake.

"I like their music, but I wouldn't say I'm a big fan of theirs either," she said. "It's just as well. That way we don't have any distractions from planning."

No distractions. Right. "So, security for the weekend of the event. What else can we help with up front?"

Madison wiggled her foot again. "Off the top of my head? Things I need to organize ASAP include a florist and a photographer. I have a photographer who can drive in for the event, so let's pray he's available. Jack said they have the music covered because two-thirds of the guests are musicians. That covers the most urgent items on the list. For everything else, I'll need my portfolio, laptop, and something in my stomach."

He wanted to kick himself. He was acting like the mule-headed taskmaster his family accused him of being. Madison was only halfway into her coffee, it wasn't even 8:00 a.m., and here he was, already bombarding her with business.

Roark shook off his faux pas. "Of course. Work can wait until after breakfast."

"The restaurant serves until ten," Sophie suggested. "You guys could eat in there and go over anything else. I have no doubt Roark will keep us informed of our to-dos."

He waited for Madison's answer. She looked at him, indecision shifting through her gaze until finally, "Breakfast sounds good. I need to grab my laptop and portfolio from upstairs."

"Then breakfast it is. I'll take that." He took the empty mug from her hands, their fingers brushing in a brief caress that warmed him faster than any coffee, and had Madison glancing away. Roark didn't realize he'd stood as well, watching her go, until he turned to sit back down and found Devlin and Sophie grinning.

"What?"

They looked at each other.

"*What?*"

"I didn't say a thing. Matter of fact, I have to make a phone call, so . . ." Dev got up to refill his cup before making a quick exit.

As soon as he left, Roark stared holes into his sister. "What was that look about?"

She smiled sweetly, unfolding her legs from beneath her. "Nothing."

"You're a bad liar. Always have been."

"Well, if you insist, Dev and I were silently confirming our shared thought."

As they so often did. His brother and sister could have entire conversations without ever saying a word. Trevor too. He was the only one left out of the Bradley brain-wave loop.

"You and Madison." Sophie grinned. "There's sparkizzle."

"There's what?"

"You know, spark and sizzle. Sparkizzle. When y'all look at each other. Then you start talking to each other, and only each other, like Dev and I aren't sitting right there across from you."

"We didn't . . ." Roark let the sentence go. They'd done exactly that.

"Uh-huh. Sparkizzle." Sophie got up and smacked him good-naturedly on the shoulder. "Don't worry about it. We also silently confirmed that we think it's a good thing."

No, not a good thing. He wasn't going to deny his attraction, but the fact remained, he didn't have time for any sparkizzle and he sure as hell didn't need to be sparking and sizzling with their most valuable business partner to date.

"There's no sparkizzle." Roark stood, tucking his phone away. "We see eye to eye on how to handle business. That's all. We're both organized and . . ."

"Frustrated overachievers? You know what they say is good for frustration?"

"I'm walking away now." He turned to do exactly that.

"Okay, but I have to meet with the head of housekeeping, so you two can talk business over breakfast alone."

Roark stopped. If his brother and sister didn't think he could see straight through their little strategy, they were deluding themselves. "You're intentionally skipping out on me so Madison and I will have breakfast together."

"No, I'm not." Sophie's voice went up to that octave again that meant she was either fibbing or flabbergasted. "But I *am* skipping out on Beau. My meeting with Rose is in ten, so you can take care of his morning doggie time. It's your turn."

"C'mon, Soph. I don't have time."

"Then you better hurry before your breakfast date."

"It's not a date."

But Sophie had already traipsed away, leaving Roark with a not-date and a dog to walk.

Chapter 5

Madison drummed her fingers on her laptop bag, biting at the inside of her cheek as the elevator descended from the third floor. She'd gathered her things from her room, brushed her teeth, and given herself a much needed talking-to.

She was here to work.

With the booking of Honeywilde checked off her list, now was the time to line up all critical pieces of the wedding puzzle. Her career was everything, the only thing, and this wedding was vital. If the good word spread about her among the who's who of the highly affluent, she'd be secure for life. No more stressing from month to month. Even though she'd made a name for herself, no jobs were guaranteed. After Charleston, she'd still had to hope the next gig was a good one, and that it'd pay. Luck brought her Whitney, but hard work was going to bring her success.

Which was precisely why she did not need to pause her day to have breakfast with the hot innkeeper.

When it came to Roark Bradley, she would keep it polite and professional. Nothing could distract from this rock-and-roll wedding. Not even a man who oozed competence, confidence, and sex appeal—the combination of all three promising mind-melting bedroom times.

"Nope. Not going there." She smoothed back her hair. All of that was secondary.

Too much to do and a limited time to do it in. Breakfast with Roark, even a breakfast meeting, was an indulgence she couldn't enjoy. A protein bar and coffee on the way to visit florists, that's what she would be doing this morning.

She'd tell Roark to never mind about breakfast. They could meet briefly and then she'd be off to work on her own agenda.

The elevator doors pinged open to reveal Roark standing there, thick red leash in his hand, big, woolly brown dog sitting next to him. "Oh. Hello again." She tilted her head at Beau, his hair falling over his eyes. He was adorable, and safer than looking at the man beside him.

"I have to take Beau out really quick, and then we can do breakfast. There's a table ready in the restaurant. I wanted to let you know in case you were looking for me."

She should insist that she would not be looking for him, she was fine left to do her own thing, and he could do whatever he needed and didn't have to let her know anything. In most cases, that's exactly what she'd say, and this was the perfect opportunity for her to cancel.

But saying that to Roark would be rude. Not that she had any issue being curt and to the point, but he'd been so polite and hospitable. Even if being nice was his job, he seemed sincere.

Fine. She'd have one breakfast with him, and that was it.

She grabbed at something to say so she wouldn't have to stand there, watching him look irresistible with the giant walking hair ball. "So . . . is the dog yours or everyone's?"

"Beau is the family dog, though technically Trevor bought him."

Trevor. The brother with the suite downstairs. The one she'd only seen on their website and never met. He was supposedly the inn's recreation supervisor, whatever that meant.

"Is Trevor out or . . . ?"

Roark glanced down at Beau, sitting obediently by his side. "Something like that. A vacation of sorts, I guess. Sophie, Dev, and I are dog-sitting while he's off doing whatever it is Trevor does."

Madison nodded, tapping a finger on her bag. Of course the Bradley siblings were taking care of their brother's dog. While they'd stared daggers at each other a couple of times when they thought she couldn't see, they were clearly a close family. Close enough to communicate nonverbally and give each other hell.

She couldn't imagine having a couple of brothers and a sister, able to read her mind, always on hand to do whatever she needed.

Watch the dog for me, refill my coffee, run a resort inn with me.

Part of her envied Roark, the other part knew she'd get hives from having someone in her business like that.

Roark tugged on Beau's leash. "Go ahead and order if you'd like. I'll be back in a minute."

"Okay." She shifted the strap of her bag farther up her shoulder and watched him leave.

When he turned back, he caught her gaze with a smile. "There's Wi-Fi all over the inn, by the way, including the restaurant."

"You gave me the password at check-in."

"Oh, that's right . . . okay, cool. Back in a bit." He tugged the leash and the dog bounded after him.

Madison took a steadying breath and headed to Bradley's. "Cool."

The hostess seated her at a table by one of the floor-to-ceiling windows, with a perfect view of the mountains and the lake. A waitress immediately showed up with a steaming cup of coffee followed by a small basket of biscuits and a lazy Susan containing butter, what looked like molasses, and honey.

Madison leaned over and inhaled a big whiff of biscuit.

"Oh dear lord," she said on exhale.

No wonder a world-traveling music star remained obsessed by this place. Whitney was from the Southeast, and Honeywilde provided all of what was best about the South: the food, the warm, welcoming environment, the relaxed atmosphere, the gorgeous weather.

Madison grabbed a biscuit, cut it in half, and slathered it with butter before Roark could return and see how much she'd put on each side. The temptation to hurry and eat one now, and pretend like a second one was her first, was immense. She took a sip of her coffee while the butter melted. Roark appeared in the restaurant doorway a moment later.

Damn.

Not because she'd missed her opportunity for biscuit scarfing, but *damn*.

He spotted her and strolled over, saying hello to a few of the guests. His face was full of color from the morning air, his dark hair slightly tousled from the wind. He was still put together, top to bottom, in dark gray slacks and what looked like a ridiculously soft polo shirt, but she could easily imagine him less cleaned up.

Ruffled from the outdoors, his hair mussed up even more, smelling like sunshine and evergreen, and a day or two of scruff on his jaw. He was the kind of man who could work a bit of stubble. The kind who made your lips pink after kissing him, and rubbed deliciously against you in . . . other places.

Madison jerked her gaze down to her biscuit. Work, work, work. Job, job, job. She was not here to salivate over biscuits and Roark. She grabbed a menu, ready to fan her face when she caught herself.

"Hey." He pulled his chair out and sat down across from her. "Chillier than usual this morning, huh?"

She put the menu back down. "Yeah. Chilly."

He smiled at her, his little dimple and eye crinkles very close and undeniable. She hadn't girded enough for this meeting.

"These are unreal. Good luck eating just one." Roark reached for the basket of biscuits.

She bit into hers and her taste buds danced a can-can. "What is *in* this thing?" she asked, struggling not to moan and melt in her seat.

"Flour, eggs, the usual. But more buttermilk than you'd care to know about."

She took another bite. Maybe if she focused on the inn's other attractions, she could ignore the one sitting across from her at breakfast.

Time to put her train of thought back on the tracks. "I was going to say, a biscuit is all I have time for. I need to find a florist, *today* if possible."

He shrugged. "Eat and run. I understand. But if you're only having the one biscuit, you have to try it with our honey." He turned the lazy Susan so the little pot was in front of her.

She twirled out a bit and let it slowly swirl over her biscuit.

Roark smiled at the waitress as she came over to pour him coffee and top off Madison's. He told her they were only having coffee and biscuits and waited until she walked away to lean forward. "You mentioned florists earlier."

"Yes, Whitney wants a specific style, so I need one who's willing to work with me on being untraditional."

He kept his voice pitched low. "I know a great florist in town. We use her for the inn and she's open-minded about whatever we have in mind. There were some crazy lantern-flower things that Dev wanted last Halloween, and she managed to find them. Anyway, she'd work with you on whatever you want, won't ask a lot of questions about who's getting married or blab all over town about anything."

"Sounds promising. Did she do the gladioli in the reception area?"

"She did." He grinned. "And the arrangement over there." He nodded to a magnificent natural spray with greens and browns that flowed perfectly with the restaurant's rustic yet classy feel.

"Nice." Madison bit into her honey-covered biscuit half, and immediately gawked at Roark while reaching for the little honeypot. "The food here is ridiculous. You know this, right? The honey is . . ." She drizzled more in lieu of more gushing.

"That's why I said you had to try it. It's our honey too. We keep the bees right here. My grandpa was a keeper, hence the resort name. Honeywilde was his baby, from the ground up."

"Kudos to your grandfather." She closed her eyes, toes curling in her shoes. The butter was the right saltiness to compliment the honey's sweetness, and the biscuit was out of control. All of the food so far was out of control. No wonder the restaurant had a steady flow of patrons, even if inn traffic was slow.

"Anyway, flowers." Roark chuckled, probably because she looked like she was having a religious experience. "The florist I mentioned, Brenda, she's the one who suggested Honeywilde have a signature color too. Apricot. I'm telling you, she's your top choice in town."

"What's the name of her shop?" She was tempted to leave the biscuit stuck in her mouth as she leaned over and pulled her portfolio from her bag.

"Brenda's."

Naturally. No fancy flower shop names for Windamere, North Carolina. "I'll call her for an appointment. Maybe I can speak with her later today."

Roark laughed, shaking his head. He ate his biscuit and kept shaking.

"You don't think I'll be able to speak with her today?"

"You can speak to her all you like, but with less than three weeks' notice, she's going to show you the door when it comes to getting flowers. She stays booked up."

"Then why did you—"

He held up the other half of his biscuit. "*But*, since she does stuff for us all the time up here, I could talk to her. She likes me."

Madison bet she did. "You'll call and put in a good word?"

"Things will go more smoothly if I go see her with you. I need to talk to her about our fall arrangements anyway, and Brenda is . . ." He broke off to look out the window, amusement toying with his face, his dimple dipping in, fine crinkles at his eyes. "She's a lot more likely to cut you a deal with me there."

This was not part of what she'd had planned. Roark was a big, tall glass of distracting, and she needed to focus. Less time around him, not more. She didn't want to rely on him more than she already did, but if it got her a deal on the best florist in town, she'd be crazy to say no.

One of his dark eyebrows eased up. "Unless that's a problem."

Why would his help and accompanying her be a problem? If she made out like his joining her was an issue, then it would be. And she was the one with issues, not him.

"I only want to make sure this wedding is the best it can be, for both our sakes," he said.

"I know. It's not a problem."

They ate their biscuits in silence, Roark glancing at her like he wasn't quite convinced. True, spending the morning with him was a complication she hadn't counted on. But it wasn't his fault she wasn't prepared to partner so closely with him on this event. She knew the wedding was going to be a concerted effort, but knowing a thing and actively doing the thing were two different things.

He squinted over at her again, and Madison jumped to a topic to stop him from trying to figure her out.

"Did you leave Beau outside?"

He shook with an exaggerated shudder. "No. Beau is an indoor dog. He's up at reception now. Our woolly welcome wagon."

"He does have some wild hair." But she liked it. Beau's hair was disturbingly similar to hers if she got out of the shower and didn't do a darn thing to it.

Roark chewed and nodded. "That's because he's a Double Doodle."

Her laugh was a half cough of coffee. "A what?"

"Labrador retriever, golden retriever, and standard poodle mix." He cocked an eyebrow as if to say *I know, right?*

"I never knew such a thing existed."

"My sister found him when Trevor *had* to have a dog. The mix doesn't shed and he's as laid-back as they come. Perfect inn dog."

She eyeballed another biscuit, decided what the hell, and doused half of it in honey.

"What about you? Any pets?"

She almost choked again on the absurdity. "No. I—no. I travel a lot with my work. I can't even keep a houseplant alive."

Roark drank his coffee, barely making a sound, his quiet consideration making her skin tingle. It took every ounce of her control not to fidget under his gaze.

As quickly as she could, Madison finished the rest of her coffee and half of her biscuit. "Are you ready to hit the road?"

"I'm set." Roark stood, pushing his chair in before helping to pull hers back. "I can drive us into town."

"You've got the Southern gentleman routine down pat, huh?"

"What do you mean *routine*?" He sounded more amused than offended.

"The pulling out of chairs, holding of doors."

"Manners and social graces were big with granddad. I was about twelve when he passed, but by then, he'd already drilled into me how I was to behave around guests and grown-ups."

"Do you hold doors for male guests and offer to drive your male business acquaintances around?"

"I might." He wrinkled his brow, but with a playful tone in his voice.

"If it's all the same, I'll drive," she told him.

He shrugged like it didn't matter to him either way.

That's how she ended up with Roark in her Audi, his broad shoulder nearly touching hers, his arm taking up all of the room on the center console.

"We should've taken my truck," he muttered, shifting in the seat. "Not out of some male power-trip thing, but your car is pretty damn small."

"There's plenty of leg room." Madison fluttered her hand around her neck. "And did you just say damn in my presence?"

Roark rolled his eyes. "Stop it. And yes, I did."

She took in the way he filled up the bucket seat. The sight of his long legs and thick thighs assuaged any guilt over his discomfort. "I need to know where Brenda's is located so I can get there alone. And if I drive somewhere once, I know it."

He leaned over.. "Do you know how to get into town?"

Madison hadn't a clue.

Roark stared, waiting until she quickly met his gaze. Those gray-blue eyes were too near, too striking. She kept her eyes on the road. "Down the mountain?" she tried.

His puff of laughter was so close, the warmth brushed her cheek. "Yes, down the mountain, smarty-pants. And after that?"

"No." But he'd called her smarty-pants, like they'd been comrades for months.

Madison didn't know if the familiarity was merely Roark's nature or because he was accustomed to siblings, but he had a casual way of joking, teasing her as though they knew each other. The truly strange part was it didn't bother her as much as it normally would. If anything, it eased her self-doubt.

"Then a right onto Main Street and Brenda's is on the corner. Got it?" he asked.

"Got it." She hadn't heard a single word of his directions.

It didn't matter though. He ended up repeating all of it; precise, detailed instructions on where and how to go as they reached each turn. Something told her that his brother and sister never agreed to drive him anywhere.

A strip of brick stores took up the corner of Main and Broad Streets, and Madison parallel parked a few doors down from the shop. Brenda's Flower Shop had a glass front, the window filled with trendy décor and gift items, artificial wreaths, and arrangements in unique combinations.

"Roark!" a voice cried out as soon as they got in the door. A woman, maybe in her midfifties—with her impeccable caramel skin, Madison couldn't tell—standing not much over five feet tall, floated toward them with outstretched arms. "What on God's green earth has made you drag yourself all the way into town?"

Madison made it her business to study the refrigerated cases along the wall, all filled with the usual roses and arrangement fare, along with seasonal flowers and unusual greenery.

Roark hugged the lady, their reflection filling the glass door. "It's not that far. You act like I never leave Honeywilde."

"You don't!" Brenda exclaimed, her voice sharp in the small shop filled wall to wall with wares. "It takes a force of nature to get you down here. Nothing caught on fire, did it?"

"I came to talk to you about our next arrangements for fall. And to ask a favor."

"Anything for you, handsome." Brenda smiled up at him before turning to look at her. "And who is this lovely young lady you've brought to my store?"

Madison met Brenda's gaze in the reflection of the case. If she was capable of blushing, she'd be red from head to toe.

"Brenda, this is Madison. She's an event planner from Charlotte and she's planning a wedding at the inn."

Madison turned and smiled.

"And she is gorgeous. Look at you." Brenda fussed over her, taking Madison's hands and holding them out. "All put together, and I can tell you're smart. You look like you could be doing national news on CNN or something."

A pang of nerves bounced around her chest at the attention. Brenda seemed sincere in every word, and Madison wasn't sure if she was flattered or embarrassed or both.

"I bet you put on one fine wedding, don't you?"

"I . . ." She stumbled for a reply. Compliments directed toward her personally, rather than toward her events, were totally foreign. And she wasn't sure she'd ever met anyone who was as up front with them as Brenda.

She didn't know what to say. "I . . . think so. Yes."

Roark must've noted her struggle, because he got down to the reason for their visit.

"Wedding flowers in three weeks?" Brenda fisted her hands on her hips "Roark Bradley, have you lost your mind?"

"No, ma'am. And it's not all me. It's Madison's wedding." He thumbed toward her, trying to share the blame. "Please, Brenda. I need you to make this work. You can't say no."

"Did I say no yet?" Brenda put one hand out, counting on each finger. "I can make it work, but I'll need to order from my supplier by next week. Rush delivery. We'll need to make a decision this week on what and how much, to get it in time. I'll have to work nights to get the arrangements and bouquets done, along with what's already on slate."

"I can make it worth your trouble," Madison promised her.

She had to work with Brenda, and not because of the compliments or her welcoming nature. Her conviction behind all that warmth, the obvious dedication; when Brenda said she could make it work, the statement was fact, not fluff.

Roark was right. Brenda was *the* florist.

"If you're willing to work with me on style and getting the bride what she wants, you can name your price."

Roark cocked an eyebrow at the both of them. "I'll have you know, I did not get the same offer for the wedding location."

Brenda patted his arm. "That's because you're not me, honey."

"I know. I'll owe you for this. Please say yes."

Brenda considered him, hands still on her hips. "You most certainly will owe me one. *One* meaning you'll come into town more often. Last time I saw you was in the Italian place with that nice little teacher. What's her name?"

Roark lowered his chin and muttered, "Annabeth."

Madison gave the cut flower case another once-over.

"That's it. Whatever happened there? If you don't want to take Annabeth out again, take Madison here. A nice man like you should get out more." Brenda was on a mission, but then, Roark was the one who'd said he owed her.

He wrapped an arm around Brenda's shoulders. "I'll do my best, but who has time to date? Are you dating?"

She smacked at the hand on her shoulder. "We're not talking about me."

"I have an entire resort to run, and increasing business for me means better business for you."

"I know, I know." She patted the hand she'd smacked. "I'm mothering you. I can't help it."

Shadows suddenly passed over Roark's eyes, a sudden despondency that was too recognizable.

"I just don't want you to die up there, all alone on that mountain," Brenda cooed.

Roark burst out with a laugh, the shadows chased away as quick as they came. "You do have a flair for the dramatic."

"You bet I do." Her hand palm up, Brenda indicated her shop.

"Fine. If you'll do this job, Madison will pay you a mint and I'll do my best not to die alone. Happy?"

"Ecstatic." She took Madison's hands again. "Now you come see me tomorrow with what you have in mind and we will make this wedding"—Brenda snapped her fingers—"fabulous."

Roark fitted himself into the Audi once more. "Told you she was a handful."

Madison put on her seat belt and checked her mirrors before pulling out. "I like her, and she knows flowers. Thank you for the recommendation."

"No problem." He twisted around in the small space, trying to buckle himself in.

At the red light, she finally shooed his hand away and clicked the buckle into place. "You be sure to date so you don't end up on that mountain alone. And dead."

"Right?" He grinned, shifting around to attempt comfort. "She makes me sound like a secluded mountain man or a damn hermit. You'd think I never come into town."

"Do you?"

"Yes. As a matter of fact, I went out with that teacher again after Brenda saw us and *that* was the last time I was in town. I didn't have the heart to tell her we would not be going out again."

Madison sucked air between her teeth. "That bad, huh?"

Roark glanced over at her, a glint in his pale gaze. "The Southern gentleman routine includes don't date and tell."

She rolled her eyes.

"I will say, we came to a mutual agreement not to go out again." His voice was the same mellow rumble as always. In fact, she'd yet to hear him sound anything other than calm and collected, the occasional irritation at his brother Devlin not included.

Madison stopped for the last light on Main Street and glanced over, Roark's profile one of strong lines and dark definition. He was undeniably handsome, but the longer she was around him, the more he proved to be a genuinely decent man, the kind of man she had little experience with, the more enticing he became. The corner of his eye slightly lined with a smile.

"I apologize if I damaged your delicate sensibilities." She was teasing him. *Why* was she teasing him?

"I'll survive it. Somehow." Roark looked over and caught her staring, but did nothing to call her out about it.

Madison focused on the road as it opened up from the town's traffic lights into a slow climb up the mountain.

"This afternoon I'll reach out to the guys I know at the sheriff's department about security and let you know what they say."

"Good." She nodded firmly. "I'm going to visit a couple of bakers, run some errands, and should be back before dinner." She had no idea why she told him that. They weren't responsible to each other beyond work. They weren't even friends.

"I'll be there. Me and the biscuits."

Madison risked glancing over again. Roark regarded her with a smile, his eyes hypnotic this close-up.

Okay. Maybe she had some idea.

Chapter 6

R oark was extremely proud of himself.
Not because he'd gotten in touch with the deputy sheriff and already had some officers lined up for the weekend of the wedding—all without any of them asking for details—but because he hadn't been in and out of his office all evening, asking about Madison or checking to see if she had returned.

He'd been out of his office exactly once, for dinner, but beyond that he'd been hard at work on resort business. It was almost nine o'clock at night, well after dinnertime, but Madison's schedule was her own. None of his business. He was the picture of impartiality and responsibility, and his evening went along as though having Madison at Honeywilde didn't affect him at all.

All the while he wondered if everything was okay, if things had gone all right in town, and if so, what was keeping her?

He shook off the concern.

Madison wasn't his to worry about. He already did enough of that with his brothers and sister. They were adults now, sure, but his role as their guardian had never worn off.

He should focus on the task at hand instead of stressing about those around him. Namely, the figures on his monitor that needed his attention.

Madison and her big wedding deposit had arrived at Honeywilde just in time. He'd taken her check to the bank as soon as she dropped it off. He didn't always tell his brothers or sister how far in the red they were each month, because there was no point in *everyone* having sleepless nights. This time though, they'd gotten dangerously low on money.

Without Honeywilde, the Bradley family would be lost, and he wasn't going to let that happen. This place was the one thing that'd always been there for them, an anchor in the storm of their parents' marriage. They'd already come too close to losing Honeywilde once; he damn sure wasn't going to let that happen now.

Fall was western North Carolina's busy season, and with this wedding they were about to turn their luck around. A huge color-spread in a magazine could put them in the black for good.

If Madison knew the photographer she wanted for Whitney's pictures, he wondered if there would be additional photographers for the publicity part. He typed a note into his phone's memo pad, reminding him to ask her.

She'd seemed pleased with Brenda, which was to say, she wasn't so flinty-eyed.

He'd noticed that when things went well or Madison found something funny, her eyes flashed, making them seem impossibly green, and her mouth curved up at the corners. It wasn't much, but she wasn't the sort to make obvious gestures like huge smiles or boisterous laughter. Her hesitant reactions made him appreciate them that much more.

A brief smile was her response to his display of good manners, or . . . what had she called it? The Southern gentleman routine.

If she only knew how hard he was working to maintain propriety, keep everything on a gentlemanly level . . .

He'd probably get the wrath of Madison if she knew how often he got distracted by her lips or that thing she did with the inside of her cheek.

Roark tilted his head, the numbers on his computer screen going blurry. Her ferocity wouldn't be such a bad thing, under the right circumstances and channeled just so. Someone so composed had to let loose sometime, right? She was probably a wildcat in bed.

"Not helpful," he growled. Madison wasn't here for him to fantasize over.

Significant effort might be required not to do so, but he was up to the challenge. His mother may not have given them a lot of affection and attention, but she made damn sure they all knew how to behave.

His constitution reaffirmed, he went back to the matter of Honeywilde's outstanding bills.

A second later, his office door burst open. Madison rushed in until she reached his desk, slapping both hands down on top of it.

"He is going to be here tomorrow," she ground out, her eyes wide.

"Who?"

"*Him*. Whitney and Jack's manager. Phil Troutman."

Roark leaned forward and clicked off his monitor. This was the most emotion he'd seen from Madison yet, and it wasn't the type he wanted to see. "And this is a bad thing?"

She looked at him like he'd questioned what was wrong with having rabies. "It's a *very* bad thing. Where do you think I've been all night?"

Pushing herself away from the desk, she paced. "First I was on the phone, trying to talk him out of coming here, and then Whitney called and I had to calm her down. She's afraid he's going to monkey-wrench the whole thing. I know I told you we'd have to charm this guy, but let me warn you. He's a jerk. Evidently he's one hell of a business manager, I mean their band is huge right now, but he's unbearable when it comes to everything else."

"I don't get why a business manager cares about their wedding arrangements."

Madison stopped midstep. "He cares about their *everything*." She took up pacing again.

"Okay. Then how do we deal with him?"

She stared down at her hands and didn't answer. "I knew he'd do something like this," she muttered to herself.

"How awful do you predict it will be?"

"He called me when I got back from town and he was raising hell about the PR on the wedding. Whitney must have told him we'd talked magazine spreads. She's easily excitable and loves the idea. And she's too young to realize you keep a guy like Troutman out of the loop until it's too late for him to screw it up. He is *not* excited and does not love the idea."

"Why?"

"I have to make him love this idea."

Roark moved directly into her path and she came inches away from walking right into him.

"Stop for a second," he tried. "You're muttering and pacing and I can't help you if you don't clue me in."

Madison blinked up at him. "Help me do what?"

"Whatever it is you need help doing." He shrugged. "You said this Phil guy coming here is a bad thing. Tell me why."

"He's pissed that Whitney and Jack have done all of this without including him. The wedding, the publicity, all of it. Phil is going to try to nix the whole thing, especially the press."

Hell no, he wasn't. This wedding and the press were going to happen. "He already got the special pricing on the inn. He's not nixing a damn thing. Why would he want to do that?"

"Who knows with this guy?" She threw her hands up.

Madison was flustered. He hadn't been aware she got flustered. "Let's think. There has to be a reason he'd come all the way to Windamere to be a party pooper."

"Probably because he's a control freak and he's pissed that he's not in control of this."

"Exactly." Roark pointed at her. "He's not in control. You are. So what do we do to shut him down?"

"Appease him somehow. He insists that I—and I quote—fill him in on what the hell is going on, and do it quick."

"He sounds charming."

"Just wait. The bride- and groom-to-be are great, but I'm telling you, Troutman is a nightmare. You're going to get some firsthand experience, because if he has questions for me, he'll probably have an inquisition for you." Madison flopped down in one of the chairs by his desk.

"I thought people like him lived in New York or L.A." Roark went to the credenza behind his desk.

"I have no idea where he lives. The band is on tour right now, so god only knows where he's coming from. All I know is he's on his way here."

"Then he can bring on the inquisition." He opened the far right cabinet, grabbing two tumblers and the bottle of whiskey.

"I wish I shared your attitude." Madison let out a huff of air. "Normally I do. I'm usually the picture of control, but for some reason this man—this one freaking a-hole—wrecks my nerves."

"Maybe because he has a lot of power?" Roark sat in the chair beside her and put the glasses down on the desk.

"I've dealt with plenty of power over the years."

"Then maybe it's because he's a muckity-muck in the music industry? He's not like normal people you meet every day. Add to that he's an asshole and it stresses you out."

Madison eyed the glasses as he poured a finger of liquor in each, one corner of her mouth curling. "Did you just call him a muckity-muck?"

"Never mind that. Is it why he wrecks your nerves?"

She tossed a hand up and let it flop down on the chair of the arm. "I don't know. Maybe? Probably."

He didn't want her to be anxious, but her reaction was somewhat comforting. Madison was human and capable of doubts, same as anyone else. And for whatever reason, she was letting him see that.

Another splash in each glass for good measure and he slid one toward her.

"I need—I mean, I'd like for this high-profile, high-end event *not* to be my last, and when I took on the job, I'd met only Whitney and Jack. Working with them was a no-brainer. Nice couple and they were so happy to have me handle this for them. If I make a name for myself doing these types of events, then I can pick and choose what I do next. No more killing myself from job to job, eighty-hour weeks to pull it all together."

She picked up the tumbler and her gaze shot to his. "Shit."

"What?" Roark turned his glass in his hand.

"I . . . I didn't mean—Forget I said all that. I'm venting because Troutman messes with my mojo. I'm fine. Really."

He clinked his glass against Madison's. "I know you are. We all have someone who makes us nuts."

"What is this, anyway?" She swirled the amber liquid around.

"Homemade whiskey. Grandpa called it nerve tonic. A little dab will do you. But sip it."

Madison stared down at the drink and then tossed it back.

Roark watched her over the top of his glass as he slowly sipped his.

To her credit, she didn't hack and cough, but her eyes watered up. "Damn." She fanned herself.

"I did say sip it. It's not a shot."

She put the glass down and leaned back in the chair. "We need a plan for tomorrow."

"I'm down with a plan. I like plans." Roark grabbed his phone off the edge of the desk and angled himself in the chair to face her.

Madison mimicked his posture. "Troutman will probably get here before lunch, but knowing him, he won't call ahead to say he's almost here. He'll pop up without warning, like a wart."

"I'll let our staff know. Warn them that there may be someone snooping around." He added a note in his phone.

"And let them know he's a piece of work too. It's best to not react. I think he feeds off of it."

"We call that a *very special guest*."

Some of the tension finally left her face. "Oh yeah?"

"Yes, *a very special guest* is code for one who is difficult and hard to please. A guest who wants pita for lunch is worse."

"Why is that so bad?"

"It's code for a pain-in-the-ass guest."

Madison popped with laughter, covering her mouth to drown out the sound. He wished she wouldn't. The sound was loud and great to hear.

Rather than tell her so, he said, "I'll let Sophie and Dev know as well." He hit Sophie's number in his favorites.

His sister answered. "What's up?"

"We're going to have a surprise guest tomorrow, the kind who likes pita for lunch. Whitney and Jack's manager will be here, inspecting."

"For real?" He heard banging and a loud clank on Sophie's end of the line.

Roark would ask, but he wasn't sure he wanted to know. "For real. Will you let the restaurant and kitchen staffs know?"

"Yeah, I'm here now." More banging echoed through the phone.

"And buzz Dev to let him know?"

"No. I most certainly will not."

"Soph," he started. He didn't want to deal with telling Devlin about their pita guest tomorrow, especially not with Madison sitting right there. He could predict his brother's reaction, and all conversations that included him telling Dev what to do eventually led to Roark cursing and Devlin not speaking to him.

"Don't Soph me. Call your brother. I'm half hanging out of a broken dishwasher at the moment."

"What happened to the dish—"

"Call Dev." Sophie hung up on him.

Roark stared at his phone and then peeked at Madison.

She watched him intently.

"I have to call my brother and let him know." He rose from his seat as the phone rang.

"Yeah," Dev answered. The echo of voices in the background meant he was most likely in the game room.

"We have a surprise guest tomorrow, code pita. Our bride and groom's business manager decided to pop in and make life difficult."

"Managers have a way of doing that."

"Could you let your staff know, and anyone else you see? I'll let reception know."

"They aren't my staff, they're your staff, but yes, I will let them know."

Roark worked his jaw. "Thank you. We don't know what time he'll be here, but Madison says he's a control freak, so don't let him get to you."

Devlin's laugh was dry. "No problem. Got plenty of practice with that."

He was not going to respond or let Dev get to him. Roark ended the call and sat back down. "Now they know. I'll make sure Troutman is sold on Honeywilde, but I don't know how we'll sell him on the publicity or that his musicians want to get married."

Madison stared up at the ceiling, her posture less rigid than before. "He can't really stop them from getting married. They're adults. The publicity piece?" She tilted her head to the side. "If they're going to do what they want anyway, then it needs to benefit Troutman somehow. To get him on board with the promo, I need a strategy."

"I'm happy to be of assistance."

She straightened in the chair. "No, no. I'll manage. I need to think. If you'll make sure the inn and all of the staff are at peak levels, I'll take care of the rest."

The woman was bound and determined to handle this problem herself, and he couldn't force her to accept his help any more than a business manager could force his musicians not to get married.

Madison pushed herself up from the chair. "I'm going up now. I suggest you do the same. You'll need the rest to deal with Troutman tomorrow. Trust me."

"Good idea. Mind if I share an elevator with you?"

"I've seen you squeeze in much smaller spaces with me."

"Har-har." He grabbed the bottle off the desk and put it back in the credenza.

Keys in hand, he followed Madison out, but she stopped before the door, turning to him.

"Thanks, by the way. For the drink and . . ." Her gaze drifted around the room like she was lost for the right words. "Listening and the . . ."

"Help?" he offered, wondering if this was some kind of new experience for her. "Any time. That's why I'm here."

"I just need to sleep on it. By tomorrow I'll have a plan in place and we'll be set."

Roark wasn't sure if she was trying to convince him or herself.

She nodded once, that flinty look back in her eyes, as if her decision had been made and it would happen, if only by sheer force of her will. "Everything will be fine. Troutman will leave here the biggest fan of weddings, ever."

Chapter 7

"I'm not a fan of weddings," Troutman proclaimed, clasping his hands over the curve of his round belly.

Roark had to bite his bottom lip to keep from laughing at the expression on Madison's face.

Phil Troutman was of average height, round in the middle, and damn if his appearance didn't fit his name. His face was full, but curved to a point, the tip being his nose. His brown eyes bulged slightly as he stared, giving Roark the feeling he was being watched by a fish.

Madison gave the man a smile like she'd just finished sucking on a lime. "I'm sure you'll feel different after you hear what I have planned and see Honeywilde for yourself."

"Hell of a curvy road you've got coming up to the place. People get car sick a lot, I bet." Troutman frowned at Roark as though the roads were his fault.

He wasn't sure if such a comment warranted a response, but he was going to give one anyway.

"Actually, no. We don't get any complaints about the roads."

Madison bumped him with her elbow, a warning glint in her eyes.

"I'm complaining. That's one right there. Didn't you hear me?" Troutman jerked a handkerchief out of his pocket and turned away to scrub at his nose.

Roark took the opportunity to shoot a look back at Madison. *Nightmare* was a good way to describe this guy.

He moved closer to Troutman. "Can I get you some tea or anything else to drink before we look around? That might help if you don't feel well after the drive up."

"I didn't say I don't feel well. I said the roads are too damn curvy.

You ought to have someone look into that. Now, show me what's so great about this place. You've got until eight, because I have somewhere to be tonight. Everyone decided to cut me out of this decision, so I'm cutting myself back in."

Madison cocked an eyebrow at Roark. Without saying a word, he got the message loud and clear. Today was going to be a long day.

"I believe Mr. Bradley has a tour mapped out for us, if you're ready."

Roark clapped his hands and pivoted toward the great room. He went through the usual main floor tour, but about halfway through, Troutman turned to Madison, his face on full glower. "*This* is where you want to have the wedding?"

Madison stiffened. "It's where Whitney and Jack want to have their wedding. They want the ceremony on the veranda, and I'm going to make that happen."

Troutman tromped toward the French doors, garnering alarmed looks from a few guests who were reading quietly. He yanked on the scroll handles, which of course didn't open the doors.

"Here . . ." Roark caught up to him and turned the handle down to open the door.

They filed out onto the veranda, Troutman heading straight to the railing.

"It's kind of big," he grumbled over his shoulder.

"It's roomy enough so that a party of fifty won't feel claustrophobic," Madison called as she caught up with them.

"You don't think this will be dangerous? A lot of people drinking and dancing after a wedding? Someone could fall to their death, and who will they try to sue? My clients."

She shook her head, her voice tight. "There won't be drinking and dancing out here, Mr. Troutman. Only the ceremony takes place out here. We'll have the dinner, open bar, and music inside."

Troutman sniffed, turning to glare at the mountains. "I still think it's an accident waiting to happen."

Madison inhaled long and loud through her nose, her gaze locking on Roark's as if she was thinking of tossing Troutman over the railing.

She pinched her eyes closed. Slowly she exhaled, her face relaxing as she wet her lips. She breathed in and out again, and finally opened her eyes.

He had no idea what had just happened, but he wanted to see it again.

Madison pasted on a smile that was clearly false, but only slightly less attractive than the real thing. "Mr. Troutman," she sang, stepping closer. "I do not want the ceremony to be dangerous; that would be awful. I'd love to hear your ideas on how to make it safer. You know the last thing I want is to cause you or the band any trouble. I'd be happy jot down any wedding suggestions you may have."

Her voice was shy of a coo, the politeness too syrupy for anyone, let alone Madison.

It took him a moment to figure out what the hell was going on. She'd talked about the need to massage Troutman's ego, and how everything had to be his idea. The magic she was trying to spin on him had a purpose.

Troutman turned around to look at her too. "My ideas?"

"Yes. You're a brilliant businessman. I'm sure you have ideas to make this wedding absolutely perfect. We would be honored to have you involved."

Roark stood there, more than a little surprised at how good she was at playing sweet. She was anti-schmooze, so this had to be killing her, but if it got Troutman on board, he was all for it.

Then, as she all but batted her lashes at the fish man, he damn near passed out. He much preferred the tart version of Madison Kline, but he respected her spin skills.

Troutman crossed his arms to rest on his belly. "Well I-I don't . . ." He stammered, searching for the words. "I don't have time for all that nonsense. I don't mess with weddings and . . ." He waved his hand dismissively.

"We could always rent a tent and have the ceremony in the field below," she suggested, acting dead serious, as if that was anywhere near a good idea. "Of course that'd mean hiring out the tent and tables, because Honeywilde isn't equipped with a full outdoor arrangement." She looked at Roark, batting her lashes in the same way she had with Troutman.

It took a second to shake off the shock before he caught it was his cue.

"Right. We don't have *any* of that, but there's a place in town that rents it. I think it's weekly though, so you're probably looking at several grand? I don't really know. Then there's the drainage issue. If there's rain, even a few days before, there's sogginess."

"Yes." Madison winked at him. "Sogginess is a big issue in the mountains."

Roark cleared his throat to keep from breaking into a grin. He and Madison were joining forces to get fish-face to bite the damn bait, and he liked the feeling of being on her team.

"That sounds like a lot of bullshit hassle if you ask me." Troutman shoved away from the banister. "Let them get married out here. Get drunk if they want. I can get nondisclosures and waivers signed beforehand if need be."

How did this guy manage to *help* anyone's career?

The rest of the tour went exactly like the start. Troutman grumped about everything, pointing out liabilities and issues around every corner, only for Madison to lay it on thick, and Roark backing her opinions. With sugary-sweet manipulation, she offered to have Troutman involved in even the tiniest detail, until he buckled and went along with everything she already had planned.

"Well . . ." Madison turned and focused on Troutman once they returned to the great room, hours later. "What do you think of my plan?"

Fish-man probably didn't detect the challenging tone threaded through her coquettish demeanor, or see the steely look hidden by her thick, flirty lashes, but Roark saw it all. Madison had strength of will that shined through her doubts and overshadowed her cool reserve. He saw it in her posture, heard it in her voice, felt it in the air.

And damn. He was into it.

Troutman grunted and cleared his throat, wiping at his nose again with his handkerchief. "If you really want to know, the place seems fine if someone wants to get married. I don't think these two idiots should be getting married at all. *That's* the problem."

Madison's gaze locked with Roark's in what looked suspiciously like panic.

"I . . . I don't see a problem," she tried.

"It'll kill their chemistry on stage. Have you seen 'em? They've got *it* and they've only got it because it's new, it's a secret. The young fans like virile, available idols. They're going to end up a couple of useless saps who write the same old drivel as everyone else. I've told them as much, but you see who's still planning to get hitched. I'd make them call it off if I could. Unfortunately, I don't have that kind of power."

She stared at Roark, her lips slightly parted, but no words came out. "You know how these fall-in-love-hard, fast-wedding stories go. Sure, they'll end up divorced in a few months, but that doesn't help. Then they'll hate each other's guts and break up the band. Then what've I got?"

It was a horrible thing to say. Roark had barely survived his parents' divorce and here was this asshole wishing it on his clients.

Madison swallowed, her gaze darting about, but she said nothing.

Roark didn't want to convince Troutman of anything. He wanted to throw him out of the inn, headfirst.

"And that mess Whitney said about magazine coverage? *Absolutely* no. I don't want it turning into a media circus up here."

Roark took a step toward him at that, getting his attention. "It won't be a circus. We're keeping the entire weekend top secret."

Madison finally spoke up. "Right. But it's a wonderful opportunity for post-event public relations. To help their careers."

"No."

Her response was calm. "Mr. Troutman, a lovely feature in a magazine like *Southern Living* won't cause overexposure."

"What part of *no* do you not understand?"

It took every ounce of restraint Roark had not to step in and call out Troutman for being the unbearable prick he was.

"I've handled high-profile weddings before. We aren't talking about the paparazzi here," she argued.

"Are my words not getting through all that blond hair? I said no."

"Hey," Roark snapped. "We both heard you say no, but you're not listening. Your clients chose Madison because she knows what she's doing. She knows weddings and how to get the most out of them. She knows how to be discreet. I've seen her portfolio. She's the best at what she does, if you'll just listen to her."

Madison placed her hand on Roark's arm, her eyes wide before she regained the serene façade. "I'm sorry. I believe what Mr. Bradley is trying to say is that I'm *suggesting* the publicity because it's in the best interest of your clients."

Roark swallowed hard against the bile that rose in his throat. That was *not* what he was trying to say. Troutman was an ass and he didn't deserve her apology. The publicity was Roark's idea. Madison having to haggle with the likes of Troutman was his fault, and it made his stomach turn.

"How would advertising their sap status be in the best interest of my clients?" Troutman leaned back, his hands over his belly again, eyes shiny with greed.

"Well . . ." Madison looked around.

Roark blurted out the first thing that came to him. A lie, but he had to fix this. "I'm a big fan of theirs and the two of them getting married is intriguing. It won't hurt their chemistry; it'll make it better. Particularly if there are only rumors that they are an item, but no one really knows. Most fans love that kind of stuff."

Troutman cocked his head.

Madison piped up. "Plus, you've still got a few weeks. You could always work that angle of things. Rumors get out, fans get into the 'are they or aren't they?' chemistry. They're in a band together, but they've yet to confirm their relationship status. If you spun it the right way, I don't think a wedding would ruin their chemistry, I think it would amp it up."

"You don't tell me how to do my job. You're a wedding planner. I manage careers. You organize chocolate fountains."

"Hey." Roark clenched his fists with the desire to shove that handkerchief down Troutman's throat.

Madison waved her hand through the air. "I was merely . . . thinking out loud about how amazing this wedding will be. Gorgeous location, beautiful couple. You know, romance and luxury, but edgy. Women get carried away with stuff like that. Female fans especially love it."

Troutman looked like he was about to roll his eyes, but he stopped. "Wait . . . they do. It's stupid, but they do."

Madison clasped her hands in front of her like a hopeful little girl. If it wasn't so bizarre coming from her, Roark would've laughed out loud.

"I know *I* love the big weddings they put in magazines. The pictures of the dresses are always my favorite. I save them. I think we all have dreams of our own big day, you know?" She shrugged, false wistfulness pouring off her.

Roark shook his head, feeling like he'd just done a round of dizzy bats.

Troutman wrinkled up his already wrinkled forehead. "Women save those magazines?"

"They do." Madison kept it up, spinning a web of wedding magic for Troutman. She made the post-ceremony publicity sound so enticing, Roark was ready to go out and buy all copies of the magazine right now. And she did it all while making it sound like it'd be Troutman's idea.

He scratched at his round chin. "Let's say I convince Jack and Whit to do it. I don't want it in some cheap, B-list magazine. I want big-time. I want the cover."

Madison nodded. "Of course."

"I need to make some calls. Make sure this is going to take off like I need it to. Those two are going to get married whether I like it or not. Might as well make it work for me."

"I think it's a brilliant plan. Why don't we arrange a time to talk next week to see if there's anything else I can do?" She stepped closer to him with a smile so sweet it'd cause cavities.

Roark blinked to keep his eyes from popping out.

"Yes. I'll have my people call you."

"And I will walk you out." She stood right at Troutman's side and cut her eyes at Roark as they turned to go.

He watched them go, shooting daggers at the Trout the entire time. Who did that jackass think he was? The Trout was definitely fish-man's new name.

"Asshole," he muttered. His stomach rumbled, reminding him that dinnertime hunger wasn't helping his sour mood. He tromped toward the restaurant but paused at the bar near the entry. "Y'know what?" he said to no one.

"What's that, sir?" The bartender, Steve, stood up from where he'd been bent behind the bar.

"Jesus. Don't do that." Roark leaned on one of the chairs before slipping his jacket off and hanging it over the back.

"Sorry, sir."

"You've got to stop calling me sir. Roark is fine."

"Okay. Sorry, Roark. What can I get you?"

"Something to cure confusion and an asshole headache?" He rubbed at his eyes.

"What's that, sir?"

"Nothing. What've you got that you can make fast and it'll kick in even faster?"

"I'm trying out a new pomegranate drink. Have the fresh mix ready to go. Could I interest you in a taste test?"

"Tell you what, you pour me some of that pub mix with the sesame sticks and peanuts, and I'll test a double of whatever."

Steve hurried about, serving up a snack bowl and rattling a shaker of whatever the hell Roark had ordered.

Madison would find him as soon as the Trout was gone. He'd done a good job of not jerking Trout up by the ears, but she'd still looked miffed on her way to the door. What was that about?

Either way, surely she'd find Roark in the bar. Then he'd find out what the hell just happened. The need to see her alone gnawed at him worse than Beau with a chew toy. But only so they could discuss the afternoon's events, talk about tomorrow, talk business, and gripe about Trout being a jerk.

That's what he told himself, anyway.

Chapter 8

Madison found Roark in the restaurant's small bar. Even from the side, with his shoulders hunched in exhaustion, the man struck a figure that halted her steps. She kept going though, because she needed a drink and they needed to talk.

"Vodka martini, up with a twist," she told Steve, sliding into the seat next to Roark's.

"That bad?" He turned to look at her, his tie loosened, hair ruffled as though he'd scrubbed his hands through it a few dozen times. His gorgeous, crinkly-eyed grin made her consider ordering a double.

"You've met him now. You tell me."

"The guy's an asshole."

"I know."

Roark sipped on a dark pink concoction served up in a martini glass. She did a double take but was too tired to say anything. They sat in the empty restaurant as the bartender shook her drink in a martini shaker and Madison tried to soak up the calm.

She eased back in her chair and closed her eyes.

Troutman was exhausting. Dealing with him and finally resorting to playing the harmless female was grating. All of that smiling at stuff that wasn't funny had worn her nerves to a frayed edge. But sitting in a cozy bar, the lights dimmed, Roark quietly drinking his mysterious pink drink . . . this was nice.

She rolled her head to the side, keeping her eyes mostly closed so she could peek at him between her lashes.

He sat leaning forward with his elbows on the bar. His posture made his dress shirt pull tight across his broad back, his loosened collar and tie revealing the tan skin of his neck against his dark hair.

He kept his hair cut notably shorter in the back. She bet it'd feel great to rub against the grain. Soft but a little bristly.

Madison rolled her eyes. It'd been too long since she'd been with someone if she was ogling the back of a man's head. Thank goodness he couldn't see her, because she was undeniably mid-ogle.

"What is that thing you're drinking?" she asked, needing something to say.

"I have no idea. Steve, what's this thing I'm drinking?"

"Pomegranate martini."

"Pomegranate martini." Roark turned in his chair, holding up his pink drink.

"It takes a real man to be comfortable drinking a froufrou cocktail."

He laughed, his shoulders relaxing. "It only looks froufrou, doesn't taste it. It's good. Try it."

"No, thank you."

"C'mon. Try it." Roark set the pink drink in front of her and waved her forward.

"I don't want—"

He silenced her with a scowl. "You're going to sit there, give me crap about my drink, and then refuse to even taste it?"

After that whole dog and pony show, a little mercy was probably warranted. ". . . No?"

"Then get up here." He waved her forward, the damn eye crinkles on full blast.

"Is this your usual?" She sat up and raised his cocktail glass.

"No, smart aleck. I'm trying this because Steve is testing it out. Isn't that right, Steve?"

"Yes, sir. Roark is my guinea pig." Steve served up her vodka martini.

She took a sip of the pink drink and handed it back to Roark. "There, I tried it. Happy now?"

"Ecstatic."

Madison sipped her drink and hummed, letting her lids flutter closed. "Now *this* is a drink." She opened her eyes to find Roark staring at her. "What?"

"Nothing." He turned and sat forward again.

"Not nothing. Clearly something. You want to try my drink?"

He huffed with a laugh. "Uh, no. That's not it."

"Sure it's not." She put her drink down next to his hand. "Go ahead. You can try it."

"No, thanks."

"Hey. I tried yours. Fair is fair."

He slanted a look at her, scooped up her martini and took a sip. Both of his eyebrows shot up. "'S good. Strong, but good."

Madison took her drink back, allowing a triumphant grin. "This from the man with the hooch in his office? You'll have to try one of these next. Isn't that right, Steve?"

Steve looked back and forth between the two of them. "Yes, ma'am."

"It might be a good thing we don't have to drive anywhere after two of these. Isn't that right, Steve?" Roark leaned on the bar again.

"Yes, sir." Steve grinned at both of them. "I put in an order for the hot wings you like, in case you two are peckish."

Roark grinned over at her, a hint of color in his cheeks, his martini clearly already taking effect. "I know I'm peckish. How about you?"

Madison hid her smile in a sip of martini. "Peckish sounds about right." Among other things.

Hot wings did sound pretty perfect right now. Messy and mannerless, and strong enough to get the taste of obnoxious sweetness from sucking up to Troutman out of her mouth.

Speaking of . . .

"I'm sorry you had to deal with Troutman in full nightmare-mode," she told Roark.

"It's not for you to apologize for him."

"No, but he's certainly not going to do it."

"I bet he's never apologized for anything."

She nodded and took another sip. "Hell no, I know he hasn't. But he *is* the type to take credit for everything. To hear him tell it, *he* is Red Left Hand. Forget that Jack writes seventy-five percent of the songs or that Whitney writes the other twenty-five and *sings them.* No. Phil Troutman is the real star." Madison huffed and sipped until the hot wings arrived.

Steve set the plates down. "I did the large order in case—"

She'd already grabbed one and had it in her mouth.

She and Roark didn't say another word as they ate. The wings were spicy enough that she finished her drink to keep her mouth from catching fire. Steve delivered two more ice-cold martinis as they ate, and Madison was on her fifth wing before either of them made a sound beyond eating.

Roark's bark of laughter made her jump at first. Then, the settling sound of it relaxed her a little more.

"So . . ." He grabbed another cloth napkin to wipe his mouth and fingers. "I forgot to tell you, I decided Troutman's new name is Trout. Or rather *the Trout*. Because that guy looks like a fish."

Madison set her drink down so she wouldn't spill it as well as choke on it. She coughed and leaned against Roark's arm. "Oh my god, he does! I knew he reminded me of something, but I couldn't think what. He's got a fish face."

They laughed loud enough that poor Steve shook his head and walked to the other end of the bar.

"There are a few other names I'd like to call him too," she added.

"Like jerk? Asshole? We said that already."

"No no." She wiped her hands clean. "He's more than that. What's worse than being an asshole?"

Roark made a show of thinking. "*Is* there something worse? Horse's ass? I got nothing."

She grabbed his arm, giggling so hard she couldn't answer.

Roark was chuckling too, but studied her with a look that was way too serious.

She was rather enjoying the silly name-calling and the buzz she was sporting. Warmth spread through her limbs, a welcome change from the tension and the tight way she'd held herself all day.

"What?" She stared back at him.

"I . . . Okay, part of me knows I shouldn't call you out, but I've got just enough of a buzz to do it anyway."

She sat up a little straighter, noting the deepening color in Roark's cheeks and realizing these drinks were even stronger than she thought.

"What was up with your stellar sucking-up to the Trout? I didn't know you had it in you. You were never that nice to me. And all that stuff about wedding dresses and saving magazines and . . . just, *what?*"

"I was too, nice to you." She pointed a finger at him.

"Yeah, but it took a whole lot of me being charming first."

"Oh, you were being charming?"

"Damn straight, I was."

She laughed again, her body light and fizzy, as if champagne bubbles filled her blood instead of a little vodka. Madison lifted a shoulder. "Sometimes you have to play into people's expectations to get them to hear you. He had a bunch of preconceived notions about me, women in general, and trying to do serious business with him wasn't working. I have a lot of experience with that. Unfortunately. It was *never* going to work, not with a guy like that."

"True."

"The Trout sees this as some frivolous joke. If I have to tell him what he wants to hear, I can turn on the sugary coating. No choice. I couldn't get through to him otherwise."

Roark was quiet a moment, sipping his drink. "I see what you mean, and I caught on to it pretty quick. I thought you'd panicked there for a bit, but you bounced back."

Hell. She thought she'd covered that pretty well. "Who panicked? I did not panic."

"You looked a *little* panicked."

"I do not panic."

"If you say so." He shrugged it off. "Regardless, your strategy worked. The Trout is all into this wedding now."

"Only because he'll make money off it. That's all he cares about."

Roark took another sip of his drink. "You actually batted your lashes at him at one point."

"You didn't like that?" She laughed.

"It was disturbing."

Madison dipped her chin and raised both eyebrows.

"No, I mean, not . . . You batting your lashes is not disturbing. Directed at him, *that* was disturbing."

"You're not jealous, are you?"

"No."

She kept her gaze locked with Roark's as she took another drink. "Why? . . . Do you want me to be jealous?"

"No."

Roark sipped his drink, his eyes sparkling.

"I don't know. Maybe?"

He grinned, looking away as he put his glass down. "The way he spoke to you though, mocking your job and basically calling you a ditzy blonde, I wanted to kick his ass through the front door. Have him land headfirst."

"Yeah, about that." She set her drink down as well. "You weren't real smooth in hiding your opinions on the matter. That doesn't help us. Dial it back a notch next time."

"What's that supposed to mean?"

She turned in her chair to face him, her knees brushing against his leg. "Look, I appreciate your attempt at sticking up for my honor, or whatever, but I'm a big girl. I can take care of myself."

"I was trying to have your back."

"Did you also want to run off the biggest job either of us has ever had?" She understood his intent, but intent didn't matter to guys like Troutman.

Roark clamped his mouth shut, his posture stiff. "No."

"Then let me deal with a guy like Trout underestimating me and being a jerk. I can handle it."

With a sigh, he ran a hand over his hair, mussing it up further. She itched to touch the dark strands, smooth them back into place, see if they were as soft as they appeared to be.

"I guess my blowing up at him wouldn't have won him over, but you shouldn't have to put up with shit from guys like the Trout."

"I have plenty of experience putting up with shit. Trust me."

He took a swig off his drink and muttered, "That doesn't make me any happier about it."

He was offended on her behalf, and it was nice. She'd never had someone indignant for her. Roark was righteously angry in such a way that rather than ruffling her feathers, it was . . . endearing. Attractive.

"You did kind of blow up at Trout like an angry bear." She smiled.

He laughed. "I find it hard to stand there, not saying a damn word, when he's talking about getting through your thick blond head."

"You curse more when you've got a buzz on."

"I'm aware."

"You're less buttoned up. I like it."

"Thank you. And I didn't mean to come off like a bear. It's not that I don't get why you did the whole over-the-top-sweet act, but it pisses me off that you had to. That's not who you are."

"Oh, and you know who I am?"

"Hell yeah, I do. You're demanding and driven and you shouldn't have to apologize for that. I like it."

Madison blinked. No one liked her bossy ways. Her whole life, the fact that she had ideas and did something about them had drawn criticism and side eyes. But Roark didn't see her nature as negative. He got her, he liked it, and more than anything, he treated her with respect.

"Well . . . you're overbearing and kind of a know-it-all, but . . . I don't mind."

Roark's smile warmed her insides more than any martini ever could. "Thanks. You're also prickly and fine as hell. I mean that with the utmost respect."

Her pulse jumped at his compliment. His appreciative gaze was one thing. Expressing attraction out loud . . . that was a whole other level.

Screw it. If he was bold enough to go there, so was she. "And you're built like a brick house. Also respectfully."

Roark slapped the bar, laughing.

"I think we're a bit tipsy."

"Yeah, we are." He draped an arm over the back of his chair, facing her. His legs pressed against hers, his mouth close enough she could smell the sweet pomegranate on his breath. His eyes were the sky on a misty day, his jaw slightly darker this late at night, and, again, she wanted to touch. Reach out and run her hand over his jaw, down the strong line of his throat and into his shirt to see if he felt as warm as he looked.

"I should go to my room," she choked out.

"Me too. I mean—"

"But first, I'm finishing this drink because it is not going to waste."

They finished the last few wings and downed the rest of their drinks, with Steve cleaning up and sneaking glances at them. She caught Roark leaving a tip for Steve when they were finished. He grabbed his coat off the back of his chair and waited for her to slide out of her seat.

"'Night, Steve." Madison waved and followed Roark out of the restaurant, keeping her gaze intently on the back of his head.

She might be 'tini tipsy, but she was *not* going to check out his ass again. Not going to happen. Her first day here, she'd noticed it— kind of hard not to. He still had the butt of a college baseball player. No need to be reminded of that fact, especially because right now she lacked her usual professional polish.

Tipsy Madison was 100 percent more likely to be obvious about checking him out and 200 percent more likely to say something about it.

"Hang on." Roark stopped in front of the reception desk to grab his keys.

She dragged her gaze up to his face, just in time for him to catch her. "Why don't you live off-property?" she asked, before he could mention her checking him out.

"I like living here. I'm close if some minor emergency happens, which it always does, and I know what's going on around here."

Madison studied him once they got inside the elevator. "You mean you like to be close by so you can keep your nose stuck in everything and everyone's business."

"I do not keep my nose stuck in everything."

She laughed in his face. "Don't be ashamed. I'd be the same way. All up in everybody's business so they don't screw up. Or in case they do, you're close by to fix it. I know how it is."

"I'm sure I annoy the hell out of them."

"Like I annoy the hell out of you."

He turned to her as the doors opened to the third floor. "You don't annoy me."

"I annoy everyone."

"Hey." He followed her down the hall. "You don't annoy me."

"Maybe not yet, but you do realize I'll only be more in your business, the closer this wedding gets."

"So you've told me."

"And you're sure you're going to be okay with that?"

"I'll manage somehow."

She peeked over to gauge his reaction as she spoke. "It's been my experience that men, particularly male owners and managers of anything—inns, hotels, bars, restaurants, barns, gazebos—all have a hard time relinquishing even half of the reins to anyone, but especially to a woman."

"Have you met my sister? Do you think she waits for me to relinquish anything? When I don't relinquish, she snatches it out of my damn hand. I think you and I will work together fine."

"This is different. I'm not family."

"I know."

"I'm not your baby sister. I'm a stranger. Taking over your hotel for a few days."

"But that was our deal. I'll have to adjust."

"I probably won't remember to say please and thank you a lot. I'm not always nice and sweet like that."

As they reached her room, he stopped and turned to her. "Well, you *are* nice to the Trout."

She shoved playfully at his arm.

"Maybe you're not normally sugary sweet, but so what? You don't have to defend your disposition to me. I like it." Roark glanced down to where her hand had landed, still resting on his forearm. His gaze caught hers and she knew the look—heat growing, darkening his eyes.

She was playing with fire. They'd openly admitted they found each other attractive. The chemistry was pretty damn obvious.

Two mature grown-ups could say, *Hey, I think you're hot and you think I'm hot, we obviously both find each other attractive and stimulating, but we've got shit to do. Important shit that affects both of our careers. So we are not going to complicate matters by hopping in the sack together and getting naked and sweaty. Because that would be unwise.*

Roark leaned heavily against the doorframe of her room, his gaze hooded like maybe that pink drink was having some lingering effects.

She wasn't sure what she was supposed to say here. *You're right, I'm not sweet. Want to find out how much?* That wasn't even in the realm of possibility.

Okay, it kind of was, but not in the realm of wise. She could not hook up with Roark Bradley while putting together the wedding that would make or break her. Enough to-dos sat on her plate right now, and they weren't about doing Roark.

It would be the height of stupidity to take a situation, currently rolling along fine, and muck it up with something complicated. She was a smart woman. No matter how delicious he looked right now, all relaxed, his jaw a little softer, finally some freaking stubble making itself known so that his lips looked that much pinker . . .

"You're staring at my mouth." Roark's voice came out low and gravelly.

"What?" She pinched her lips together, jerking her gaze to his eyes.

"My mouth. You keep staring at it."

"So?"

"So. I wanted to kiss you *before* the staring. You keep looking at me like that and I will."

Madison swallowed back a whimper, her heart hammering in her chest. She wanted him to kiss her. Then it could be his fault. She wasn't the one stepping out of line into the land of unprofessional liaisons. Roark was.

She looked away and counted to ten. Her door was right there. Turn the key, go inside. It would be so easy to be a good girl right now.

Madison licked her lips, slowly dragging her gaze to Roark's, before intentionally staring at his mouth.

He said something on a harsh whisper, something like *thank god.*

Then Roark grabbed her and pressed his lips to hers.

She didn't bother with hesitancy. Who was she kidding anyway? Madison curled her fingers around Roark's tie and dragged him closer. He kissed the same way he looked, strong and smooth and in control. Oh, how she longed to make him lose control.

She licked against his lips, an invitation for him to do the same. A low growl rumbled in his chest and he turned her, moving until her back hit the door. Roark opened, licking his way inside her mouth to kiss her fully. His mouth was hot, the late-night stubble the perfect burn against her skin. Again she imagined it rubbing against her elsewhere and gasped.

The small sound from her spurred him on. His hands in her hair, making her shiver. He shifted one hand around to the small of her back to bring her closer to him.

What's more, she wanted to be closer to him. She wanted to feel him against her, curl into his body and hide from the world. Let him shield her from everything while he touched her. Have him protect her and take her apart all at once.

God, she was in over her head. Lusting for him was one thing. Liking him was another. But she couldn't stop.

Sliding her hands down until she found the firm curve of defined abs, she curled her fingers in again, dragging them lower until Roark shuddered against her.

"Damn." The word was a rush of heat against her lips before he pushed into her, anchoring a hand on the door behind her. He kept the other in the small of her back, curving her into him.

The hold on his control was shaken, his kisses needier, and it only made her want him more.

She tilted her head back, hoping he'd get the hint and rub that stubbly jaw along her neck, down her chest. Oh god, maybe she'd have the pink burn to show for it tomorrow. She could only hope.

Then the elevator dinged with a new arrival to the third floor.

Roark pulled away from her at the exact same moment she pushed.

"Shit," he muttered, smoothing down his shirt with hands as shaky as Madison's.

She tucked her hair back and touched her face. Thoroughly kissed. That's how she felt right now, and surely how she looked.

Another step away from her to be at a decent distance, and Roark turned to say hello to two couples returning from a late night in town.

"Evening." Roark nodded.

They all said hello, smiling at him and Madison, and studying both of them. They went into their separate rooms and Roark sighed, his shoulders slumping. "That wasn't awkward."

Madison slipped her key in the lock and turned, easing it open.

"Probably not a good look to find the owner in the hall . . ." He turned, but she was already in her room, blocking the doorway with her body.

"That . . . that was my fault," she said, her grip on the door tight enough to make her hand ache.

"Fault implies that there's a problem. I was right there with you, if you somehow missed my enthusiasm."

She stared at the plush cream-and-chocolate carpet and hardened her resolve. "I know. But I . . . we can't jump into some . . . You know what, it's late, we've both had drinks—"

"We're not drunk. You can't brush this off like it's the alcohol."

Her gaze locked with his. "I know. It's not the martinis or the hour, it's us. But we—I . . ." *Can't do this.*

Wanting his body, she could handle. But she liked Roark for more than just his looks, and that was way too much for her to cope with. She couldn't trust her feelings. They'd been wrong too many times before. She absolutely could not screw up her big opportunity here. And that's exactly what getting involved with Roark would do.

"I know." He scrubbed a hand over his hair, messing it up even more. "That went from zero to sixty really fast, but I don't regret kissing you."

Speed wasn't the issue; she was. He was the kind of man she'd always wished existed, but life had proven time and again that men like him weren't real. If she let herself believe, allowed the hope in, she'd only be disappointed.

She couldn't make herself regret their kiss either, but she could ensure it wouldn't happen again. "Good night, Roark."

He blinked, moving forward, his mouth open as if to argue. Then he stopped. "Good night, Madison."

Her grip still tight on the door, she closed it rather than watch him walk away.

Chapter 9

"It's fine. It won't be awkward." Roark slipped on his shoes and rose from the couch in his room. He'd face Madison, if not first thing this morning, then sometime today. Surely they could both carry on with their jobs like consummate professionals, but a little self-pep talk never hurt anybody.

"We're both adults, we can go about our day without this getting in the way or causing a problem. It'll be okay. I'm talking to myself, but other than that, it's okay."

Beau woofed at him, visibly offended.

"Sorry. I'm talking to you. Even better."

He grabbed his keys and Beau's leash, and locked up behind him. The feeling wasn't exactly relief that he didn't bump into Madison in the elevator, but he'd file it under the same category. He wanted to see her, but he needed time to think of the perfect, casual, every-thing-is-cool-like-before line, and time to practice not reacting to seeing her. He didn't want to run into her first thing in the morning.

So he ran into her *second* thing in the morning.

Madison sat in the great room, on the couch nearest the fireplace, in what Roark considered his favorite spot. Her laptop sat open on the coffee table, and she stared intently at the screen.

He strolled by without engaging. It should be her call whether she wanted to talk to him or do the avoidance thing for a while. Last night had amped up fast. His intention was a kiss good night. It'd turned into them all but grinding on each other, up against her door.

And it was awesome.

"Roark," she called out, flagging him over.

He cleared his throat and walked over. She was not quite smiling as usual, and the sight was oddly reassuring.

"I'm glad you're here," she said. "Sit down and I'll introduce you."

"Introduce me?"

"To Whitney and Jack."

He must've been scrunching his face, because she scrunched hers in return, jabbing a finger toward her laptop.

"Hello?" The sweetest voice came out of the laptop, making Roark start. On the screen was Whitney Blake, strawberry-blond hair in a sloppy bun, wearing an oversized sweatshirt, curled up next to a guy who looked like he could've been brought in for questioning about an armed robbery.

Jack Winter wasn't all skin and bones like a lot of guitar players. He wasn't Roark's size, but he kept in shape. He had jet-black hair, a ring in his eyebrow, a few in each ear, a tattoo peeking up over the neck of his stretched-out T-shirt and flowing down along his arm.

The two of them couldn't look more like opposites, but their happiness oozed through the laptop.

"Hey." Roark waved at the laptop, feeling silly. Web chatting, or whatever, was not his thing.

"Sit down." Madison moved over and jerked her chin toward the spot next to her.

He sat, the leather still warm from her body as she scooted in close so both of them could be seen through the computer's camera.

Whitney smiled into the screen, her teeth perfect. With her button nose and round cheeks on her slender face, she was cuter than a box of puppies. "We were just telling Madison thank you for whatever you guys said to Phil. He's done a complete one-eighty on us."

Jack chimed in, his arm slung behind Whitney. "Yeah, he was in a piss-poor mood when he left here yesterday, but he rolled in late last night going on and on about the wedding. I don't know how you convinced him, but thanks. We sure as hell couldn't."

Whitney laughed, smiling at Jack as she leaned further into him. "We tried."

"Lot of good it did. Grumpy-ass bastard upset you." Jack puckered up, accepting the pop kiss from her.

Beside him, Madison shifted.

The future bride and groom were head over heels in love, not quite to the point of being obnoxious, but enough to make him want to look away and give them some privacy.

"And thanks again for letting us get married at Honeywilde." Whitney flashed that smile into the webcam again.

"You're welcome." Even though he wasn't *letting* them. They were paying for every bit of it.

"I'm sure Madison told you, but I love your inn. I used to visit there as a kid."

Madison shifted again, more this time, her leg pressed warm against him. Roark glanced over from the corner of his eyes. She'd never mentioned a damn thing about it. The pressure against the side of his body was likely a silent plea not to sell her out, but it reminded him of last night: the firm length of her body, the softness of her curves, her pliant, welcoming mouth that gave and then took with equal enthusiasm.

"I love Honeywilde," Whitney was saying. "And the town, Windamere, is adorable, but kind of boho. It's perfect! I was ten years old when we were at the inn one summer, and a couple got married. The ceremony was the most beautiful thing I'd ever seen. I haven't been there since I was . . . oh gosh . . . eighteen?" She looked at Jack and he nodded. "Anyway, it's always been special. And so romantic. I told Jack there is *nowhere* else. If I'm getting married, it has to be there."

This time, Roark did look over at Madison and waited until she met his gaze. She had the decency to look chagrined.

He turned back to their rock-star couple. "It means a lot to us that you guys want to get married at Honeywilde. We're thrilled to have you." He could call Madison out, on camera, for not saying a word about Whitney being enamored with Honeywilde, about how this was the only place she wanted, and how he probably could've slapped an absurd price tag on the place and still gotten paid—but to what purpose?

The last thing they needed was to rock the boat with clients who, right now, beamed with satisfaction and expectation. He'd also negotiated a damn good deal for the inn. Nothing to bellyache about there.

Madison slid forward on the sofa, fingertips on the laptop. "We should probably go now. Still lots to do for your big day, deciding on the menu and photographers and such."

"And you're clear on what we want?" Jack sat forward as well. His expression said this was one aspect of the wedding he had a strong opinion about. "*No* bird food. No servings the size of a quarter with compote anything or little-ass vegetables." He ran a hand over his bed head. "There has to be real food."

"I know exactly what you're looking for," Madison assured him. "And trust me, this place doesn't do little-ass food."

"Yes! Thank fuck!" Jack sat back, tugging at his shirt.

Whitney nudged him in the ribs with her elbow. "Sounds great. Thanks again. We'll see you both in a couple of weeks." She waved into the camera, much like Roark had earlier.

He waved back as Madison ended the call. She closed her laptop and slid back on the sofa, canting her posture to look at him.

Roark turned as well, propping his elbow on the back of the couch. She did the tapping thing with her foot again, waiting. Whether her quiet was for him to crack and say something about Whitney's comment, or to be the one to bring up last night, he wasn't sure.

Either way, he wasn't talking first. Call him stubborn, but this time she needed to break the silence.

There were no shining gold medallions on Madison's shoes today, but little straps over the arch of short black boots, the silver buckle winking at him as she tapped. Fitted black pants wrapped over the miles and miles of her legs. How would it feel to have her legs around him, heels digging into his back? Or better yet, straddling his hips as she bore down on him, her pinned-up hair finally wild and loose, falling over his skin.

"Go ahead and ask. I know you want to," she said.

Roark about swallowed his tongue. "Wh-um, what?"

Madison lowered her chin, the daring back in her green eyes. "About what Whitney said. How much she loves Honeywilde and it's the only place for her."

He was determined to find out the full truth there, but that wasn't what was killing him at the moment. He shifted in his seat. "There was never any competition for Honeywilde, was there?"

"No."

"Then you played me to get a better rate?"

She bit at the inside of her cheek, her focus just over his shoulder as she nodded. "Troutman would've balked at your original price and I knew I'd have to get past him to make the deal. Sorry. I wasn't actively trying to manipulate you, but . . . I had to do what I had to do."

He thought about how she'd been with Troutman, spinning whatever tale was required to get the job done. Her client wanted Honeywilde and, by god, she'd gotten them Honeywilde.

"All's fair in business. Don't ever apologize for being good at what you do." Roark patted the back of the sofa and rose to his feet. Madison stared up at him, wariness etched between her brows. "Wait. You're not angry about it?"

"Why would I be angry? Yeah, I could've named my price and you maybe would've paid it, but then again, it could've been too high to appease Troutman, and then Honeywilde loses altogether. Plus, maybe now I can guilt you into a little extra promotional contact. Seeing as how you played me and all." He smiled down at her, half kidding, half meaning every word. Particularly the part about her not apologizing for doing a successful job.

"Oh, I see." She smiled back and rose to her feet. "Do a little extra to assuage my guilt?"

He shrugged. "Sure. If you feel like it. Sophie found out about an annual issue that a publication called *Carolina Style* does. The best weddings, parties, and social events of the year. You should check that out."

"I will, but I don't get you."

"I know. I'm an enigma like that. An enigma who needs some coffee." Roark stretched, craning his neck to spot two coffee carafes on the brass trolley. "Wonder if Wright made the Harvest Blend today."

"Normally, if I one-up a man I'm working with, he's pissed. For days. Possibly forever."

"It's not like you bled me dry. I'm still coming out of this smelling like . . . cookies."

She rolled her eyes, but he could tell she wanted to smile again.

He headed to the coffee trolley and Madison followed him over. "Business is business," he told her. "My feelings don't get hurt over it. I don't know what kind of people you're used to working with, but if the Trout is any indication, I hope you recognize that *I* am not like that."

Roark filled a mug and refilled Madison's. He took a sip of his coffee while Madison warmed her hands around hers.

"So . . . are we going to talk about last night or pretend it didn't happen?" she asked.

His sip went down as a scalding gulp. "You've gone and brought it up now, so, yeah?"

She looked around the empty great room. "We're adults. We can discuss it."

"You shut the door in my face. I took that to mean end of discussion."

"I did not shut the door in your—"

"You made a swift exit. I get it, but I can't pretend it didn't happen. I know there's chemistry here and sparkizzle, but now isn't the time or place."

"Spar—*what?*"

"Hey! There y'all are." Sophie rushed toward them. "Heads up. Wright and Dev are on the prowl. Wright wants to talk wedding and weekend food, Dev wants to talk parties, and you know how they get when on their respective topics, so if you don't have time to get into it, you better get out now while the gettin' is good."

"Take a breath, Sis."

"I'm serious. You know how they are. These boys corner you and your marshmallow is toasted."

"Roark," Devlin shouted across the great room.

"Too late." Sophie stepped past them to get to the coffee.

Devlin came over, Wright beside him with his hand out, ready to greet them. "'Morning. Nice to finally meet you," he said to Madison. "Don't get out of the kitchen too often for too long."

"I'm a big fan of your work already."

Devlin poured himself and Wright cups of coffee and handed one over. "We wanted to talk to you about the food, the rehearsal party, and any other entertainment you want for the weekend."

"Yeah." Wright nodded. "If you have a couple of minutes this morning."

Madison looked back and forth at both of them, then at Roark. Yesterday she'd been busy from sunup to sundown. He could only imagine what was on her agenda today, but he bet it didn't include this powwow.

Roark tried to help. "I'm not sure there's going to be other entertainment that weekend or that now's the best time to discuss it."

Devlin cut his eyes at him. "We need to talk about it sometime. Why not now?"

Roark opened his mouth to respond.

"Now works." Madison stepped in with the slightest touch on Roark's arm. "I have a few minutes, and if Wright has a moment, I'll take advantage of it."

"I'm all yours until someone shows up for breakfast." Wright held his arm out toward the seating by the fireplace. He took the chair nearest Madison's laptop and portfolio, leaving Roark to sit with her on the couch again, and Dev in the opposite chair, his long legs stretched out.

Sophie half sat on the arm of Wright's chair. "If I see any guests stirring, I'll yell."

"Do you have an idea of the menus you want for the weekend?" Wright leaned forward, elbows on his knees.

Roark laughed. "No tiny food was a pretty clear vote."

Madison leaned toward him. "Exactly. No tiny food. I'd like the menus to be the antithesis of the usual wedding food." She opened her portfolio and clicked her pen.

"Our clients are artistic and eclectic; their friends and families are as well. We'll need a vegetarian option for every meal."

"Not a problem. We keep vegetarian items on every menu."

They went on to discuss each menu in detail, debating the pros and cons of items and when to serve.

Madison wrote in her portfolio, her elbow bumping against Roark with every word. He caught himself watching her write, the quick strokes of the black pen, her long, slender fingers. When he jerked his gaze up, he caught his brother and sister watching him.

Sophie smiled and looked away, but Devlin studied him, his expression fathomless, as he spoke. "What about optional entertainment for the guests? They'll be here for two or three days. If they want to do more than sit and read all day, we could have some options available."

"And add to our list of things to get done?" Roark countered. Because it wouldn't be Devlin organizing the tiny details, it'd be him or Madison or Sophie.

"Do you want a bunch of bored wedding guests on your hands?" Dev cocked an accusatory eyebrow at him. "Because that's what you're going to have with a bunch of big-city businesspeople stuck on top of a mountain for three days. All we need are a few specially arranged activities available."

"I think we have enough to arrange."

"I'm not suggesting we plan the Olympic Games, Roark. I'm talking trips into town to the shops, maybe set up a visit to the winery down the road, a tour of the Astor estate."

"Who has time to arrange all of that and make it happen?"

"Am I the hospitality manager or not? I am capable of doing my damn job, you know."

"Devlin," he said. That was it, just his name, but his name was enough to bring wrath to Devlin's eyes.

Madison put a hand on Roark's forearm. "I think a couple of optional outings sound nice. We don't want bored guests on our hands." She jotted down a few notes. "Devlin, why don't you check on the cost of the things you mentioned, what it will take to make them happen, and get back with me on the details? We'll decide what works best and go from there."

"I'm happy to." With a special icy glare just for Roark, Dev pulled out his phone and tapped at it.

Wright, either oblivious to the tension or so accustomed to it that it no longer fazed him, went back to talking about food. "Why don't we do the same for the food? I can work up the dishes we talked about and you can try them. Pick the ones you like best."

Madison glanced up from her scribbling. "I won't say no to taste testing." She flipped to another page in her notepad and wrote some more. "Let's try these." She tore off what she'd written and handed it to Wright.

"Soph can get whatever ingredients I might need on the fly. Can't you?" Wright looked up at her.

"Let me see the list before you go committing me to finding a blowfish vendor." She leaned over, playfully snatching the list out of his hands.

"I'll need to try these dishes and make a decision pretty soon," Madison told them. "I want the menu set before we go into next week. I can leave other things to the last minute, but food I want planned and sorted so there are no issues."

Wright spoke to Sophie, his voice low, but not so low that Roark couldn't hear him listing off vendors he'd prefer to use.

His sister took out her phone, typing away as he spoke, and a burst of pride made Roark smile. Dev might resent the hell out of him, but he'd grown more committed over the last few months than he'd ever been before. And Sophie would probably run rings around all of them someday.

As they spoke, Madison turned to him, angling her body so that her knee bumped his thigh. He could've shifted to move away but didn't. He should've. Her leg pressed against his khakis and he swore that side of his body was about fifty degrees warmer than the other.

"You okay?" She mouthed the words silently.

"Yeah. Why?" He mouthed back.

She barely tilted her head toward Devlin.

Roark formed an O with his lips and shrugged it off. That whole exchange with Dev may seem like an issue to most people, but after all these years, Roark had accepted this was how they communicated. He didn't like it, he'd even tried to change it, but he was damned if he could fix it.

"It's fine," he whispered. "You okay?" He tapped his watch. "Time-wise."

Madison dipped her chin, her delicate earrings swinging, before she met his gaze again. "I don't meet with Brenda until ten, then I go in search of bakers, but thanks for asking." Her tone wasn't the sarcasm she'd used with Troutman. This thank-you was sincere.

"I spy, with my little eye, some meandering guests." Sophie nudged Wright, and they got up to head to the restaurant.

"I'll go with." Dev got up to leave with them, even though it was doubtful his presence was needed in the kitchen.

"Thank you. See you guys later," Madison called after them without looking up.

As soon as they were gone, Roark turned to her. "I—" He took a deep breath to keep from venting all of his frustration. "Sorry about that, if it made you uncomfortable. My brother and I, we don't always see eye to eye, but we . . ."

He worked his jaw, thinking. But we, what? Haven't gotten along since Dev got old enough to think for himself, so everyone else is used to it? We used to be best friends and now he resents my very existence? Sure. Madison was dying to hear all about the family shit show.

"It won't be a problem," Roark said instead.

"What won't be?"

"My brother and I." And their baggage. "You have brothers and sisters?"

"No." Madison immediately looked away. "It's just me."

"I'd say you were lucky, but I do love my family. I can't stand them sometimes, but mostly, I love them."

She stared at him for what seemed an endless moment, before she got up with her coffee mug. "About what I was saying earlier, about last night, I'm not going to pretend it didn't happen either. That would be childish. But I have a lot riding on this wedding and we need to focus on the task at hand, not . . ."

"Each other?"

"Yes."

He joined her, refilling his coffee. "You're not the only one invested in this event. I know now isn't the time for . . ."

"Distractions?"

"Right."

"*But* I was thinking, what if we made other arrangements?"

He wasn't sure where this was going, but he liked the general direction. "Arrangements are good. Go on."

"When the wedding is over and Troutman is off our backs, then maybe we could get together after the reception to . . . celebrate."

Roark quirked an eyebrow. "I'm amenable to celebrating."

She was trying not to smile, and mostly failing. "That's good to hear. It's just, I'm not interested in having *a thing*. I don't do . . . that, but last night was nice."

Roark was quiet for a moment. He knew what she was getting at. His mind normally operated the same when it came to relationships. Not having "a thing" meant there was no commitment between them. This was not a suggestion that they hook up after the wedding and then they'd date. This was he and Madison getting together when this was all over and having a night of what promised to be the hottest sex ever, and they'd leave it at that.

Maybe it'd happen again, maybe it wouldn't. No promises. One night was all he'd get from her, and normally it was all he'd offer in return.

"I can do 'not *a thing*' once this event goes off with a bang."

Whereupon they'd get it on like bunnies, because if he wanted her this badly now, he could only imagine how bad it'd be in three weeks.

Actually, less than three weeks. Good thing too. Because working with Madison, seeing her every day, the wry curve to her lips, legs that didn't quit, and eyes that promised all kinds of wonderful trouble, there was *no way* he'd make it that long.

Chapter 10

She wasn't going to make it a week. After not quite forty-eight hours of ignoring the buzz beneath her skin, the jittery high every time she got within ten feet of Roark, Madison reached the point she had to do something to channel the excess energy.

The plan was to deal with her desire for Roark, after the wedding. Work first, play later, then she'd leave. No muss, no fuss, and no reason to open herself up any further because she'd be gone from Honeywilde. The plan was solid and safe. With so much to do, she ought to be able to bury herself in one of a hundred tasks. Instead she kept thinking about Roark, the sensual assuredness of his kiss, the way his smiles melted her defenses, how his hands would feel on her skin while he was buried deep in—

Madison whimpered, knotting her running shoe tighter than necessary. It was barely six o'clock in the morning and she'd have to run for however long it took to put Roark, and about half a dozen deviant thoughts, behind her.

Her laces tied and her room key secure in the small pouch in the lining of her running pants, she snuck downstairs and past the reception desk, hoping no one would see her. Most of the inn was still asleep and no one was standing sentinel at the front desk.

She walked, but kept her pace swift as she stepped through the inn's front portico and out onto the paved walkway. It wound around to the side, leading to the main road. On her way up the mountain, she'd seen a dirt road about a fourth of a mile down that looked like it cut across the mountain. Such a road would make for a promising run, so she followed her instincts.

Sure enough, the road was worn smooth, probably by ATVs and service vehicles. She also dodged the evidence of a few horseback riders. The road curved and bent, with gentle inclines and valleys, a strenuous enough run she had to work for it, but not so much that she couldn't get lost in the zone.

Time passed, finally meaningless. Her mind began to clear of the what-ifs and worry, the way it did when she ran. In the solitude of running, she'd always found solace. Maybe because being alone was what she'd grown used to. So many times, being alone was better. Better than a bunch of backstabbing coworkers, better than some lying boyfriend, better than a belligerent mother who made it clear you weren't worth her trouble.

When she ran, she was strong. She wasn't wrong or needy; she didn't have to be someone she wasn't to gain approval. She was free.

The sun climbed higher in the sky, but one side of the road remained shaded. Birds sang a chorus of different tunes as her pulse climbed and her breathing came short and quick. She swore a deer darted across the road about fifty yards ahead. The forest came alive around her, and her with it.

Running in Charlotte didn't come close to running here.

She'd just hit her second wind when she heard the rhythmic patter of another runner coming up behind her. She eased right, the same way you do when driving, to let them pass.

"Hey." A low, breathy voice panted beside her.

Madison glanced over, her pulse skittering.

Roark.

"Hey."

"You said you ran. Wondering if I'd see you out here. On the old emergency road."

"Yeah?" She was breathing heavy too. What the hell? She'd come out here to avoid the Roark issue, not run with it.

"Best run you'll have all year. I bet. Enjoy." He nodded, and passed her.

She ought to let him. Her runs were her sanctuary, her time to process, her way of coping. She didn't want to talk to him right now. Not that there could be much talking this far into a run.

Roark moved ahead of her, pumping his sculpted legs, his baseball-player butt round in his basketball shorts.

Yeah. This was not going to work. She didn't want him showing her up, but mainly, running behind him would be unbearable.

Madison increased her pace and, after a minute, came up beside him.

His glance skated her way before he went back to watching the road.

Madison shifted into her highest gear and ran past him. She led the way for all of about five minutes, and then he returned to her side.

"Taking it up a notch?" His chest heaved with the effort of talking, his footfalls pounding.

She couldn't even manage a response and focused on keeping up her pace.

"Okay," he said and matched her.

If he edged forward at all, she pushed herself to do so as well. By the time they reached a sharp bend in the road, she was running full out, as fast as she could. He'd better be running at his top speed too, because she'd kill him if he wasn't also about to die.

"This is . . ." Roark flung a hand out in front of him, gesturing something to her that she couldn't comprehend.

This is exhilarating? This is insane? Both.

"This . . . That's . . ." More hand gestures as he started to slow.

Ha! Success. She would win the race.

They took the curve too fast, but the dead end around the corner was what drew her up short.

What the . . . ! She yelped.

The road just . . . ended.

A long, low, swinging gate stretched out across her path, blocking the way to an endless expanse of forest beyond. A narrow, worn path eased around the sudden obstruction, and veering onto it was the only thing that saved her from going headfirst over the top of the gate.

She ran a few feet, skidded to a stop on the stretch of the trail, and ran back toward Roark.

He slow-jogged around at the end of the road, shaking out his arms.

"What the hell? You couldn't point out the road was about to end?" She moved to stand in the way of his jogging.

"I tried. Couldn't get the words out. You were running at Mach two."

"*We* were running at Mach two. As I recall, I was not alone, but I was alone in not knowing the road was about to freaking end!"

Roark slowed to a walk and went around her, panting for air. "I tried. I swear. That's why . . . I was waving . . . my arms around. Why are you . . . so upset?"

"I'm not upset," she shouted. "It's just . . . I could've broken my neck." Her physical health had absolutely nothing to do with her frustration, but what was she going to do? Tell him she was aggravated because he'd showed up? Looking all hot and sweaty and yummy—and like something she couldn't put off for two more weeks.

He turned and came back toward her, standing there, staring, until he caught his breath. His hair was wet at his temples, darker, his face flushed from the run, making his eyes stand out, shining like fire through ice. "First of all, I'm not going to let you break your neck. There's a way around the gate. Obviously you found it."

"Gee, thanks. You've got an answer for everything, huh?"

A dark eyebrow quirked up. "Are you okay?"

"I'm fine." She looked away and began walking, shaking out her legs. "The dead end startled me, that's all. But maybe, instead of racing me next time, you should favor safety and let me know what's around the corner."

Roark laughed.

"Excuse you. Why are you laughing? I could've died. What if I'd gone over that gate? It'd be your fault and all because you had to win?"

He kept laughing, eventually waving a hand at her, helpless.

"Great. You think that's funny. My injury humors you."

"No," he managed to pant.

"Then why are you cackling?"

Roark bent over, holding himself up by planting both hands on his knees. His back shook with the last of his laughter, the damp T-shirt clinging to him, accentuating the dip and line of his spine, the rise of muscles along both sides, accentuating the narrow waist that flared up in a perfect V, all the way to his broad shoulders.

Madison jerked her gaze away and began to pace.

"I'm not laughing at you almost falling."

"Oh no?"

"No. I'm laughing because you are so jacked up right now. I like it."

"What?"

"The only time you let loose is if you've had martinis or run for miles, otherwise you're all . . ." He waved a hand at her again. "Composed."

"I'm composed? You've worn dress pants and a tie almost every day I've been here."

"So have you. The pants anyway."

She huffed and kept walking. Her composure or how he dressed didn't really matter. What mattered was Roark had caught her off guard. Again. He was here, in her sanctuary, and even though she was frustrated and had almost flipped over a fence, she still wanted him here.

That was the problem.

She could tell him to go ahead and run back toward the inn, and he'd probably do it. He'd leave her in peace if she asked.

The thing was, she didn't want him to leave.

He chuckled again, swiping a hand over his hair. "Your hair is finally messed up too. It's awesome."

She considered the benefits of shutting him up with her tongue in his mouth.

"I don't know if it's the adrenaline from almost crashing or the endorphins from running, but you look wild."

She marched right up to him. "I do not."

"I wish I had a mirror."

"That doesn't even make sense. Why would you need a mirror in the woods?"

He smiled. "So you could see yourself. Hair all out of place and your eyes dilated. It's damn—" Roark clamped his mouth shut and turned away, walking to the road's end again.

"What?" She followed. "It's what?"

"Nothing."

It wasn't nothing. Now he was the one pacing and refusing to look at her.

Madison stepped into his path, making him jerk to a stop. "It's damn *what?*"

"Hot. You look so fucking hot right now, with your hair all messed up and your eyes wild, all while you raise hell at me so fast I can't understand half of what's coming out of your mouth. I'm trying to—I don't know. But you said let's wait till later so we'll wait till later, but *damn*. Waiting is *not* what I want to do right now."

Madison kissed him.

She was sweaty and jittery and yes, riding an endorphin high and a sexual frustration roller coaster. No planning on her part, no seduction. She just laid one on him because she wanted Roark's mouth on hers again.

His lips were as hot and hard as the rest of him. She'd said later was better, but what the hell did she know? She needed a taste. One little taste to last until the wedding was over.

She pulled away, wondering when she'd grabbed onto his shirt, her fingers digging into his pecs. His shirt was warm and damp against her palms, his chest rising and falling as fast as hers.

"Wait." Roark reached for her, his hands spanning her lower back. "Where are you going? Why'd you stop?"

"I—I don't know."

"Then don't. I don't want to stop." He leaned forward, meeting her halfway, their lips crashing together.

And mother of pearl, the kiss was delicious.

It should be gross and sticky after running more than five miles, but kissing him was perfect. Hot and needy, his kisses made everything else disappear. He hadn't shaved yet and his overnight stubble rubbed the corner of her mouth, brushed against her chin, even better than she'd imagined.

This time she didn't fight the fantasy or the sound of need as it rose in the back of her throat.

"I know. Me too," Roark murmured.

She curled her fingers into his shirt, gripping his chest again. God, he was a solid wall of slick man.

Roark's kiss took her breath more than any run ever had. His lips were smooth but firm against hers. No slobbery lips, no licking her face off. He brushed and sucked her lips, sending currents of need through her body. She gasped with the force of it and he took the opportunity to nip at her bottom lip.

"This is such a bad idea." She didn't even pull her mouth from his as she put forth the weak protest.

"Yeah, but let's do it anyway."

She backed toward the side of the road, pulling him with her.

"Where are we going?"

"I have no idea." Her feet carried her backward, to the other side of the gate, to the small clearing she'd run past, hidden off the trail. She wasn't thinking ahead, or clearly. It just *felt* like the right place to go.

A patch of grass and moss sloped up to their right, and Madison maneuvered Roark until his back was to it.

He dipped his head, kissing along her jaw, the curve of her neck. She arched against him, even as she knew their current situation was ridiculous. What were they going to do, dry hump on the side of the road?

She tugged him closer, tilting her head to give him better access. He kissed and nibbled, his mouth and stubble leaving an indelible mark on her deepest desires.

Yes. Dry humping was precisely what they were about to do, ridiculousness be damned. Madison wanted him. On the side of a dirt road, in the middle of the woods—she wanted him, and she was tired of being composed about it.

Her hands against his chest again, she gave him a gentle push.

Roark glanced back, getting the message, because a sly grin danced over his lips. He eased down onto the slope of grass and took her with him. "At least it's been dry lately."

She didn't even care. Later she might. Right now, all she cared about was this.

Looping her arms around Roark's neck, she rolled and pulled him closer, their bodies flush, some of his weight against her. The ground was uneven but soft beneath her, sweet smelling and fresh. She turned her face, inhaling deeply, giving Roark the other side of her neck.

Roark kissed his way down to her collarbone, covering her breast with one hand, teasing it to a peak that had her arching against him, before making his way back up. He angled himself over her. Capturing her mouth once more, he licked his way inside, a low rumbling of want in his throat, and she had to hold back a whimper.

Madison tucked into him, brushing her thigh along his until he was cradled against her. His body heat was like a furnace on full blast, and she wanted more.

He broke the kiss long enough to inhale with a hiss, his chest pressing into hers. She clutched at his back, dragging him closer, needing the weight of him, the heat, the feel of him covering her.

God, she was hungrier for him than ever, with no logical explanation why. Maybe because she could do this to him, have the same effect he had on her. The buttoned-up, well-behaved business owner, rolling around on the ground, needy and desperate, looking as wild as he insisted she did.

She put her hands under his shirt, tracing over the plane of his stomach, the dip of his hip, before dragging her fingers down his back. Tilting her hips, she rubbed against him.

He ground against her until he was muttering curses, his kiss rougher than before. "I . . . I don't have—"

"Touch me." She managed to get out the words.

He nodded, his mussed-up hair brushing against her chin. He cupped a hand over her breast again, teasing her nipple before sliding his hand down and putting his mouth in the vacated spot.

His mouth was hot and damp, a clamp she felt on her flesh, even through her shirt and sports bra. He sucked before gently nipping at her with his teeth.

"Mmm." She made a noise of approval, touching his hair, the back of his head, before threading her fingers through the longer strands and holding him in place.

His big, warm hand pressed between her legs, through her running pants. She moved against him, encouraging, and he cupped his hand against her, possessive. Sliding his hand up and down, he taunted her until she was pressing back, a hairsbreadth from begging. Or demanding, more like.

"Touch *me*." Her grip on his shoulders turned into digging her fingers into his flesh.

Roark knew exactly what he was doing though. He gave her a lazy grin as he dragged his hand up and toyed with the hem of her shirt.

A wash of cool air brushed her stomach as he lifted her shirt and reached for the waistband of her running capris.

"Yes." She arched again.

He looked up, dark and hungry, the intent clear in his clenched jaw and the steel resolve in his gaze, enough to make her want to come right then. He held her gaze, never wavering, daring her to look away when he slid his hand down, inside her pants, beneath the fine woven cotton of her panties, to brush teasingly at her clit.

She couldn't look away. Something told her she should. Like looking into his stormy-sky eyes would only make things more complicated. With that expression on his face, the vision of him would be forever burned onto her brain, and was it worth the pain? Was he worth the pain?

But no matter how beautiful their surroundings, she only wanted to see one thing.

"There?" Roark asked, his gaze on hers, looking deep within, to places she didn't want anyone to see.

She jerked her chin in some semblance of a nod.

His touch was first a tender caress over her skin, seeking, teasing. With two fingers, he slid his hand lower, over her lips, to the cleft of her sex. He rubbed gently against her, back and forth, before he dipped a finger in and out, until they were both slick. With the lightest of touches, he brushed against her, in a quest, until he found the bundle of nerves, and her hips jerked, body as tight as a bowstring.

He lowered himself, a long, slow kiss on her lips, as he continued to touch her. A gentle pass over her clit, the slightest pressure upon return, he circled and coaxed, until she gave up and moved beneath him in counterpoint.

Roark leaned up, watching her, as if soaking up her every reaction. A flick of his fingers, almost a pinch, heated her body, her muscles tightening.

He murmured something, an encouragement, a compliment, she wasn't even sure, but the meaning reached her. He was there with her, in this moment, swallowed up by the insanity. Two people who didn't do this type of thing, doing exactly this thing in the middle of the forest.

Roark increased the pressure, moving his thumb over the tender nub and using two of his fingers to slide inside her.

"Oh—" Madison half cried out before clamping her mouth shut. She tilted her hips, moving with him, helping him find the right rhythm.

"Yeah. That's it. Damn, you're . . . you're beautiful like this." His words came out on a breathy exhale.

Farther in the trees, crickets chirped, a bird screeched. She was in the middle of nowhere, with Roark, and what grew inside her was wilder than the woods surrounding them. This wasn't what she did. Letting go, no control of the world around her.

"Yes." She tossed her head back. "Faster. I'm . . ."

He rubbed faster, turning his fingers inside of her to just the right—

"God . . . oh god. . . ." Madison's hips bucked up once, twice, of their own volition. Current after current of consuming sensation shot from her core, where he touched her, through her, her hips flexing, legs tight. She grabbed onto Roark's arm, burying her face into his shoulder, anchoring him there through her orgasm.

She imagined he kissed her temple at some point, or maybe he really did.

"Holy . . . hell," she finally said, collapsing back onto the soft moss.

Roark leaned down to one elbow, propping his head up, looking very content for the one who hadn't climaxed.

A dopey grin split her face, turning into a pop of laughter as she looked up into his satisfied gaze. "I'd just planned on going for a run."

He grinned, rolling forward. "Me too."

"You're a troublemaker."

"*I* am not the troublemaker here." Roark's laugh was a warm breath against her skin.

He reached across her to hold her hip, rubbing his thumb back and forth over the sensitive skin above the waist of her pants. "I should probably feel bad about the location and timing. Not ideal . . . or very gentlemanly."

The thing was, she didn't want gentlemanly when it came to what they'd done. "I'm pretty sure I jumped you, so the timing is on me."

"Okay. I'll let you take the blame." Roark rolled away to stretch, grimacing as he did so.

"Are you okay?"

"Yeah, just . . . need a second."

It took her a moment to catch on. "Oh."

He nodded.

"Or . . ." She cocked an eyebrow at him. "I have another idea."

His grin remained, color rising to his cheeks the same way it had when she'd caught him eating the cookies. How could a man be so off-the-charts sexy, and yet so adorable at the same time?

Madison pushed against his shoulder to make him lie back, just as she was attacked from behind by about a hundred pounds of hair and a slobbery tongue.

Chapter 11

"Beau! Beau!" Roark tried corralling the overexcited dog with both arms.

Beside him, Madison was of no help. She shook with laughter, trying and failing to get up off the ground.

"Dammit." Roark took a tongue, straight to the face. He rolled over to climb to his feet, Beau bouncing happily beside him. "Where the hell did you come from?"

Madison got up, swaying on her feet. "Did he get out of the inn and run away?"

Realization hit him all at once as he got up and made a grab for Beau with one hand, brushing himself off with the other. "His morning walk. I guaran-damn-tee you, Dev is on dog duty today. He's the only one who lets Beau off his leash to run ahead."

Madison's eyes went wide as she looked toward the path. "You mean, your brother . . . ?"

He nodded, shaking off the back of his T-shirt.

"Terrific. On a scale of one to ten, how much do we look like we just had a quickie?"

"Fifteen. You have twigs and moss in your hair." Roark reached over, plucking at her destroyed ponytail.

"Faster." She shook her hair. "We should get back on the road. Pretty suspicious if we come wandering out of the woods." Madison feigned a voice of innocence. "Oh us? We were just . . . picking blackberries. At daybreak."

Roark snorted with laughter.

"Don't laugh. That's not helping."

"Come on. Beau will follow if we go to the road."

They hurried onto the worn path and toward the gate, making it back onto the road.

"Do I look okay?" Madison walked ahead of him.

She looked more than okay; she was extraordinary. Hair a mess, clothes rumpled, skin glowing from exercise and sex, but he was pretty sure that's not what she meant. "You still have some stuff in your hair. Bits of . . . nature."

"Well, get it. Get the nature. I can't see it."

He laughed, picking at her ponytail, putting it in a worse state than before. "Hold still, I'm trying to get it all."

"Hang on." Madison reached for her hair tie, letting her hair down and shaking it out.

"Talk about not helping. Now all I want is to go back and get more nature on you."

She peered up at him. "Stop," she reprimanded, but she was smiling. Roark held her head still. "Wait. I think I see a baby spider."

She poked him in the side. "If I was actually scared of spiders, I'd kick your ass."

He finished picking the bits of leaf and grass out of her hair and threaded his fingers through the strands before pulling away. "Sorry. Just, your hair looks good down."

"Very good. I agree."

They startled at the sound of another male voice.

Devlin stood a few feet away, dressed in worn jogging pants and a hoodie. Beau ran around him, elated that now there were three humans on his walk.

Beau bounded toward Madison, making her take a step back.

"Don't worry," Dev said. "He won't jump. Just being friendly. Though, not as friendly as my brother."

"Dev." Roark knew he was using the voice his brother hated. But if he hated it so much, why did he insist on doing and saying things to bring it out?

"Roark," Devlin said, in perfect mimicry of his tone.

Madison quickly pulled her hair back and into a ponytail again. "Guess Beau needed to get out early today."

Dev hummed an affirmative, his gaze darting over both of them as Beau trotted over to sniff at a tree on the side of the road. "It's not that early anymore. Roark wasn't back, so I figured I'd better take him."

"You're perfectly capable of walking the dog too, you know." Roark knew he sounded childish, but he didn't have to be responsible for everything, all the time.

Dev's biggest gripe in the world was that Roark was overbearing and treated him like a delinquent instead of an equal. If he wanted to be treated like a grown man, he should act like one. Not some of the time or when it benefited him, but all of the time.

Plus, could a guy not even have a roll in the hay—almost literally—without somebody needing him to do something or interrupting him?

"And you shouldn't let Beau run off alone," Roark added, exercising his right to be sullen.

"He wasn't alone. You guys were here." Dev flashed his crooked grin, the one that won women and angered boyfriends countywide.

"You didn't *know* we were here."

"What can I say? I lucked out." Devlin clapped for Beau, drawing him back over from the fallen tree limb he'd been inspecting.

Madison eyed the both of them, shifting her weight on her feet. "I should . . ." She thumbed over her shoulder, up the road.

"You don't have to go." Devlin stopped her. "My brother is just ill because I interrupted the two of you."

Hell yeah he was, but he'd be damned if he was going to admit that Dev had interrupted anything.

"No, I'm ill because while Trevor is in Portugal, Beau is *our* responsibility, yet you always try to put it on me, same as always."

Devlin rolled his eyes. "Same as always, like you hate being in charge so much? And Trev isn't in Portugal. He's in Peru."

"Wherever. He took off and Beau is with us now, which means we all have to take care of him."

"Some of us don't mind taking care of him." Devlin reached down to scratch the dog's ears.

"Don't try to make it out like I'm the bad guy and you're a saint. Last week you were bellyaching and stuck me with taking him out in the rain."

Dev's gaze snapped up, eyes cold. "You like to run in the rain. I figured you might want to take him for a jog. Excuse the hell out of me for problem solving."

Madison shifted on her feet, arms crossed. "You run in the rain?"

"Sometimes." He glanced over, aware she was grasping at anything to change the subject and stop their bickering.

"Well, speaking of running. I'm going—" She nodded to the road again.

"No, it's fine, Madison." Devlin broke the stare-off with Roark. "I think we're about done anyway. You done?"

"Yes," Roark ground out.

"Roark stays pissed at me three times out of four, likewise for me. You'll get used to it."

Roark held in the growl of frustration that clawed to get out. No one in the world could push his buttons like Dev, and he damn well knew it.

As if the dog knew too, Beau lurched toward him, head-butting Roark's thigh in a demand for some attention.

Roark scratched at Beau's neck. "Hey, buddy."

Dev flung the unused leash onto his shoulder. "So what are you two up to?"

"Running," they replied in unison.

"Really? Because it kind of looked like you were playing with Madison's hair."

Madison cleared her throat and studied the ground at her feet.

"Don't be rude." Roark patted Beau's head.

Devlin laughed. "What? I'm just saying." He was the picture of false virtue, blue eyes wide with a big, sweet smile.

Dev knew what they were up to out here, and if not, he'd figure it out.

"Roark was picking leaves out of my hair." Madison went straight for the truth, making both of them turn to look at her. "You were. Can we head back now?"

"Um . . . sure."

Madison nodded a goodbye to Dev, but he stepped forward. "Before you go, Wright worked up the menus you guys talked about. I made a few suggestions and, anyway, if you want, you could try them tonight."

She lit up, uncrossing her arms. "Tonight is perfect. I hope to finish up in town before dinner."

"It will have to be later, after the restaurant is finished with the dinner crowd."

"I eat late anyway."

Devlin snapped his fingers for Beau again. "Good. Then show up hungry. We have a lot to choose from." He gave them both a wave goodbye. He and Beau were almost out of earshot when he yelled, "We'll go ahead and set an extra place for Roark too."

Roark sighed, shaking his head. "My brother. Never making my life easy."

Madison frowned, matching his brisk pace. "Are things really so bad? I mean, he is your brother."

He jerked his chin toward her. She sounded bothered by it and so serious. "What? No! I mean . . . we argue, we bicker, but like he said, it's what we do. It's not *bad* bad. We just . . ."

She glanced at him, her steps steady as she waited.

He and Dev were so different, yet shared so much. They both bore the brunt of their parents' issues, more so than their younger siblings, and for better or worse, it'd made them who they were today.

"I don't know. I try not to overthink it because it's never made things better, but our bickering is about more than—"

"Walking a dog?"

"Yeah." The word came out with a self-deprecating laugh. "A good bit of my moodiness may have also been sexual frustration, but I wasn't about to tell him that."

She smiled. "Thank you."

"I know Dev and I pick at each other like we're ten sometimes. I'm not proud of that, but I can't ever stop myself once we get going. He's so . . ." Roark growled and imagined himself shaking the shit out of his brother, because that was the only way he knew to explain it. "He's my brother and I love him, I do. But dammit, I want to boot him sometimes. I'm several years older than him, always more responsible, and now that I'm majority owner of Honeywilde, and kind of his boss, our relationship is . . . I don't really know. It bothers him, same way with Trev, but that's how my parents divided up the place when they left. We just don't talk about it."

"I doubt I'll ever meet Trevor, since he's in Peru, but I'll be sure to avoid the topic around Devlin."

She meant it as a reassurance, but Madison's words only reminded him how temporary her time at Honeywilde really was. Trevor would return like he always did, but chances were, she'd be long gone. This was not Madison's home, and their arrangement, regardless of how it may have changed at this point, was not long-term.

The back of his neck tingled and he glanced over to catch her staring at him. "What?"

"Do you think Dev will tell your sister about running into us? He's at least suspicious."

"I'm sure he knows what we were doing, or some version of it anyway, and he'll absolutely tell Sophie everything."

"Gee, I'm so reassured. Thanks."

"Welcome to life around a big family. Good luck keeping a secret. Dev tells Sophie everything. And Wright is his best friend, so I'm sure he'll bring it up to him too, but that's it. Dev doesn't confide in anyone outside of the family."

She ran her hands over her hair. "Your sister is going to give us that look as soon as she knows."

"*Thank you!* She swears I'm making it up when I say she does that."

"The look that's both suspicious yet encouraging?"

"Yes!"

Madison shook her head. "You're not making it up. She wields that look."

"She's the queen of looks and then trying to act innocent about it."

"If she's up front when we get back, we'll get all kinds of looks."

"We have five miles. Between now and then we can appear more respectable."

"We're walking the whole way, right? Because I can't run right now."

"Definitely a walk."

They kept up the pace on the dirt road, but remained at a walk. Every time he snuck a peak at Madison, she was looking at him.

Smiling, she waved her hand in the air. "What we did back there . . ."

"Was great." He grinned, veering over to walk closer to her.

She bumped her arm against his. "But I said we'd wait."

"We waited two days."

Her laugh cracked through the woods.

"We did," he insisted.

"We're the epitome of restraint."

"I don't know about you, but forty-eight hours took a hell of a lot of restraint on my part."

Madison stopped walking. "Oh thank god, me too. I know I shouldn't have jumped you like that—"

He stopped and turned toward her. "You hear me complaining?"

"No, but I meant to be better—"

"You get *better*?"

She swatted at his arm, smiling. "Stop interrupting me. I'm trying to say that the plan was to get through the wedding *first*. Take care of business before, you know, pleasure. I intended to stick to the plan."

"Do you think we can?"

Madison looked up at him, her green eyes still soft, skin radiant. Her gaze lingered on him for a moment before she groaned. "It's looking pretty doubtful."

"I mean, we can try." He had no intention of trying. Madison, wild and greedy with need, was the most spectacular sight he'd ever seen, and that included Honeywilde's sunsets. He wanted to see that look again, wanted to feel her in his arms, her fingers digging into his back, watch her face pinch tight before smoothing out in bliss. His plans included ruining her plans to wait until later. They could do later, but he also wanted them to have now. Over and over and over, for as long as they could.

"I don't regret what we just did," she said.

"Me either."

"But . . . moments like that, with your brother, could happen again and . . . I'm here in a professional role. Even though I know your family might not be judgmental, it's still . . ."

"Complicated?" Though what was so complicated about it, he wasn't sure. They could keep it simple, if that's what she wanted.

"Yes."

"Does this mean I shouldn't join you for dinner tonight?"

"No. No, I mean I want you to join me for dinner. I'd like your opinion on what they suggest and prepare."

"But I should go back to behaving? And we pause on the sex in the woods?"

Madison tilted her head, silent for a moment. "I . . . Yes? Yes. I think that'd be best. Err on the side of discretion."

"Then I will try." And by *try*, he meant try his best to make all of this happen again. The woods were optional.

Chapter 12

She didn't see Roark again until that evening. All day was spent in town, trying to find someone who would make her a freaking wedding cake. Flour and frosting. You wouldn't think it'd be a big deal.

But apparently it was.

Conflicts ranged from not enough notice, already booked, to not budging from the kind of wedding cake they typically made. One lady did white cake, buttercream icing, and that was all she'd do. One kindly baker told Madison he was big into fondant, and she ought to go that way. All very typical, very safe, and not what she wanted at all.

Madison smoothed back her braid as she walked to the restaurant. It would be fine. She'd find a damn cake somehow and it'd be the most unique, memorable cake in the world.

Just as well she'd decided to spend the day away from Roark anyway. Roark, and all that came with him.

The tiny dimples when he smiled, the storm of his gaze when he'd touched her, urging her toward orgasm, and those hands . . .

"Dear god." She shook her hands out before she reached the great room. Thinking about him would not be conducive to a relaxed, business-focused meal. She'd end up forgetting about the food and spending every second wondering how his hands would feel all over her, everywhere, holding her waist, her thighs, what it'd be like to be stretched tight beneath him . . . on top of him.

Madison stopped walking altogether and took a deep breath.

Dinner. Menus. Tonight was about finding the perfect food selections for Whitney and Jack and their guests. Tomorrow she had to find a freaking cake lady and a cake, and her lust for Roark Bradley didn't have a thing to do with any of it.

This morning had been a moment of weakness, and honestly, who could blame her? She'd felt selfish for not returning the favor, but perhaps their interruption was a sign. Get on with her responsibilities so she could get it on with Roark, later.

She found him in the far, windowed corner of the restaurant; only two other couples still dined. The lights were low, white candles inside hurricane lamps sat in the center of each table. She hoped like hell they weren't the only two eating tonight, because this was way too much like a romantic date.

She dated occasionally, but she didn't do romantic dates. It'd been almost eight years since she'd allowed for things like candlelight and long talks, opening up and sharing, making promises and trusting someone. That road had been traveled, and she'd thought it was love. She'd always thought it was love, be it with her family or boyfriend, simply because *she* felt it.

The catch?

Love isn't poetic and beautiful when you feel it alone.

If no one is there to love you back, or they refuse to, then love is destructive and painful. Love, believing in it, trusting the feeling of it, only ever brought her pain and grief.

So she just . . . didn't.

"I hope there's a lot to choose from," he said, getting up to pull out the chair next to him. "Because I'm starving."

She opened her mouth to tell him not to pull out her chair, but clamped it shut. Pointing that out would only make him think something was up. Plus, he'd had his hands in her panties. Pulling the chair out could slide. Her fear of having a quiet dinner with him was *her* fear. She could squash it with the expertise that came from years of practice.

"I'm hungry too."

"I feel like a glass of wine. Would you like some wine?"

She would love some wine, but it'd only make the atmosphere seem that much more romantic. "I don't like sweet wine."

"Not surprised."

Madison narrowed her eyes.

"Don't look at me like that. I don't like sweet wine either. I think tonight, given the mixed menu, maybe a cabernet. You probably like cabernet, right?"

She loved cabernet. "Sounds fine."

He ordered a bottle and gave her a knowing smile as Steve opened and poured. Roark sipped at the wine and nodded. "Let her try it too. We'll both decide."

Steve poured her a small amount, a knowing smile on his lips.

Madison took a sip. "Nice."

Steve filled their glasses and left the bottle for them. A great idea, for sure.

"I knew you'd like it," Roark said, raising the wineglass to his lips.

"You enjoy that, don't you? Being right."

He shrugged with one shoulder. "A little. You don't?"

"I plead the Fifth."

"How did it go with the cake bakers today?"

"Don't ask. And they don't like to be called cake bakers."

"Seriously?"

She nodded, taking a long, slow sip of her wine, smooth and rich on the way down. "It's a funny business I'm in; plenty of little quirks that don't make sense in the regular world. I once called a pianist an organist. I won't make that mistake again. Don't ever piss off the church lady either—if you happen to ever work with a church lady. She can make planning anything in the church a living hell. Then she'll pepper the earth with your ground-up bones."

Roark blinked at her. "Damn. Maybe we can make things easier on you. I've yet to grind up anyone's bones. Though I did threaten to throat-punch a marketing guy once. Tried to screw us over on advertising space and that wasn't going to happen."

Madison smiled, because she probably would've threatened the same thing had someone tried to pull one over on her. She raised her glass, suddenly feeling better about the vibe of the evening. She could talk about work, share war stories, and *not* look deeply into Roark's eyes. It would be fine. "Here's to not taking people's crap."

Roark picked up his glass and clinked it against hers. "And to finding you a cake. I bet we could help with that."

"How?"

Wright approached, with Devlin right behind him. Similar in

height, but beyond that, the two friends couldn't look more different. Where Devlin was dark, all intense blue eyes and angled jaw, Wright was bright, with sandy brown hair and soft brown eyes. If Devlin had an air of daring, Wright oozed comfort.

"I hope you guys are hungry because I've cooked a spread for you." Wright grinned and rubbed his hands together, his excitement contagious.

"I've tried some already," Dev added. "So good, you'll fall out of your chair."

Roark tilted his head toward Wright. "How do you feel about wedding cakes?"

Wright's brow furrowed. "They're okay, I guess. Usually pretty boring. No offense," he said to Madison.

"I'm not the personal protector of all things wedding. It's okay."

"Why do you ask?" Wright settled back on his heels as the penny finally dropped for Madison.

"Yes!" she exclaimed, loud enough to make Dev and Wright flinch.

Roark chuckled. "Madison is in the market for a cake . . . maker? Decorator?"

"I need a chef to make Whitney and Jack's wedding cake," she clarified. "Please say you'll make their wedding cake. No one in town is cooperating."

"I make *cakes.* Love making those. But I've never tried a wedding cake."

"That's perfect. I don't want it to be traditional anyway."

"I don't know. There are stabilizing issues with tiers. You don't want a lopsided mass for a cake." Doubt wrinkled his forehead.

"You could totally make a wedding cake. Come on." Devlin nudged him in the shoulder, enough confidence for both of them. "There's yet to be something you couldn't whip up. You'll figure out the tiers, no problem. At least give it a try. We've got time before the real deal is needed."

"Exactly," Madison agreed. "We could do a test run to be sure, and if it turns out great, then I'm in if you're in."

"I guess I could come up with a mini–wedding cake. Bake something up and let all of you try it. It's not my area, so I'd feel better if everyone liked it and agreed."

More family time, more food. She hadn't been this well fed or included since—ever. She'd *never* had someone look after her the way they did here.

"Then it's decided." Roark leaned back, stretching his legs out enough that they brushed hers. "Wright will bake a test cake, which I'm sure will be perfect, and we'll all try it and rave about it, and Madison will have her wedding cake."

"Okay, but let's get through the main menus first." Wright tugged Devlin toward the kitchen and they both reappeared with armfuls of food.

"This place is a foodie's wet dream," Madison muttered.

She didn't mutter quietly enough, because Roark shot her a look, mischief in his eyes. "Told you that's why I run."

Just mentioning the run made a little color rise in his cheeks. The sight sent tingles down her back, like a hundred tap-dancing fairies, reminding her of how irresistible Roark was.

"Oh *that's* why?" she teased him, making him blush more.

The man was ridiculous and he made her react without thinking. Sexy and strong, but without all of the arrogant baggage. It only made him hotter. She grabbed the first thing that was set down in front of her, stuffing it into her mouth to keep from telling him so in front of Devlin and Wright.

"What all do we have here?" Roark asked, the perfect gentleman as she chomped on some kind of crostini that had her salivating.

Wright went over each item, all of them some kind of finger food or appetizer. "I thought you could pick your favorite combinations and decide when you might want to serve them, rehearsal dinner versus wedding reception, or both. I'm open to other suggestions that come up too."

He stood back, arms folded over his broad chest, as Devlin stepped forward with two notepads and two pens. "To write down your opinions and votes."

Madison swallowed her mouthful of food. "You're so prepared. I'm impressed."

Dev smiled at the compliment.

Armed with taking notes about the food, the meal and the night felt less date-like and more like work. Work was better for her focus. "I don't know what kind of crostini that was, but it was delicious." She sipped at her wine.

"A tomato and olive bruschetta," Dev said.

Roark popped what looked like a stuffed date in his mouth. He moaned in appreciation while Madison tried one.

"Okay, well, we're going to leave you to this course." Devlin turned to go, but Wright lingered, watching over his creations. Dev nudged him and he dragged his feet as he followed, but turned back. "Don't forget to make notes so you can tell me what you think, exactly. And don't fill up; I have main courses for you to try next."

Madison watched them go before trying one of the dates. "I can't promise I won't fill up. It's all too good."

Roark nodded and chewed.

"I'm going to assume everything Wright cooks is delicious and go with what I think would be the best and most memorable. Something special."

"These dates are pretty special. I think this is prosciutto wrapped around them."

"That looks like bacon-wrapped something over there."

"Anything wrapped in bacon *has* to be on the menu." He speared one with his fork. "It's shrimp. Put it on the menu." He held the fork out toward her, waiting.

"You're going to feed me? Is this common practice at Honeywilde?"

He smiled, unfazed at her attempt to keep things strictly business. "Nothing about today has been common practice."

She buried her face in her wineglass, remembering his lips on hers, the hard heat of his body. Her pulse skittered as though he was pressed against her now.

"Why don't you just take the fork before you suck down all of your wine?"

Madison reached for the fork, her fingers brushing over his. A smile played on his lips.

Had his mind drifted back to their tryst in the woods and what he'd done with those fingers? Because her mind insisted on going back there, at least once every half hour.

"Mm-hmm," she managed. "You're right. Definitely putting shrimp on the menu."

Roark picked up his wine, tapping the glass. "And the stuffed dates. They're a must. Salty and sweet and creamy. Good combination."

Nodding, she put dates on her list.

"I can only think of one thing that might taste better," Roark added. His voice was low and rough, the tone spilling into her senses, his meaning clear enough that she felt the flood all the way to her toes.

She stubbed those toes against his shin. "Stop," she whispered, her body wanting him to never stop.

"What'd I do?" He grinned over another date.

"You said you'd try to behave."

"This *is* me trying. Turns out, I'm not very good at it."

"You used to behave quite well."

"That was then." He shrugged. "You're a bad influence."

"I'm a—" She gaped. "Aren't you supposed to be responsible?"

"I'm responsible for us behaving?"

"Yes," she hissed. Because if the responsibility was hers, they'd fail.

He lifted a shoulder again. "Then I think we're screwed."

The urge to look away struck, but she wasn't some blushing bride.

Fine. If he wasn't going to keep his eye on the task at hand, she would. She swallowed down the last of her wine and nodded, not trusting her voice at the moment. Anything she said was likely to come out all breathy and needy, and hell yes, that's how she felt, but she was a professional, dammit.

Roark refilled her glass. "You know, you're supposed to savor the wine."

"I'm aware." She bit off the words.

When Wright and Dev reappeared with main-dish options, Wright set down the first plate, announcing, "This is the stuffed trout special. In my opinion, a must-have."

Roark tossed his head back and laughed. "Oh, you *have* to serve trout to the Trout."

Madison was too busy trying not to choke on her wine to respond.

"Try these too, though." Devlin pointed to the other plates on the table. "The fillet is the best you'll have. That's my vote for the menu. Better than a chicken option."

Roark cut into the steak. "You would favor the priciest dish."

"Because it's the best dish," Devlin argued.

"I love steak too. It's definitely on the menu." Madison regarded Roark as she cut a bite for herself. She wasn't taking Devlin's side because she loved steak—she did—but to squash a pointless spat before it began.

She knew the two of them cared about each other, but she could also tell their constant competition was born of some need to be accepted and respected by the other.

Roark might not realize it, but the brotherly antagonizing didn't go one way. He pushed Devlin's buttons as much as Dev did his.

"See?" Devlin asked as they both chewed.

"We'll let you guys finish," Wright interjected, tugging at Devlin's arm.

They sampled a bit of everything, but her mind was made up and Roark agreed.

By the time Devlin and Wright returned she was full, and confident this wedding would have the most well-fed guests in rock and roll history. "Definitely the steak and trout for the seated reception." Madison pointed to the risotto and vegetable dish and a Portobello kabob. "The vegetarian options for sure. We'll need one both nights."

"And the hors d'oeuvres?"

Roark handed over both notepads. "Here's what we voted for."

"Any suggestions?"

"No." Madison was adamant. "Everything here is perfect, and whatever sides you choose to go with, I trust you."

Wright looked like she'd given him a Michelin star. "Are you sure?"

"I'm positive."

Dev elbowed him, looking delighted.

"O-okay. I'll jot down what I'm going to make though and give you the list tomorrow. Just in case."

"Can we get you guys anything else? Dessert? More wine?"

"No," they said in unison.

Wright and Dev cleared the plates away, leaving Madison, Roark, and the rest of the wine.

As Roark would say, *cool.* She could do this. All she needed was a work topic.

Roark provided the opportunity. "I don't think Wright grasps the concept that you're going to love whatever he comes up with. Including side dishes. He's insecure that way, so you'll have to approve his list."

"I will. And thank you for thinking of him for the wedding cake.

If that works out, then I'm down to just a few items and then it's all logistics."

See? No problem. All aboveboard, floating in safe waters.

"So, do you want to go for another run tomorrow?" Roark asked before taking another sip of wine.

Danger. Dangerous waters.

Madison held his gaze, refusing to let him win this little game he played. She was going to stick with her plan and ignore the thick, strong leg pressed against hers, the heat seeping through fabric to warm her skin.

"I don't know. Why?"

"It's good exercise. Actually, I was thinking, after all that food, I could use a walk. Tonight."

She wasn't sure if he meant a "walk" or a walk. Either way, she already knew, if he asked, she wouldn't say no. She didn't want to say no. Even with what this deal meant, as nervous as the prospect of letting him in made her, and as much as her career needed this wedding to be her total focus, everything within her wanted *him*.

"You want to go?"

Madison's chair screeched across the floor as she shoved it back to stand. "What do you think?"

Roark slid his chair back and stood, holding out his arm so she could lead the way out of the restaurant. Once out the door, he headed outside onto the veranda. She let him lead the way down the stairs and onto a path that wound around to the back gardens of Honeywilde. Her short heels wobbled on the pea gravel and Roark offered his arm. Madison stared at him rather than take it.

"I don't want you to fall. The last thing I need is you on crutches."

She tucked her hand under his arm, holding on to him. Roark had no idea how rare this was—as in, never—or what it meant that she was letting him *lead* her anywhere. Before, hell would've frozen over before she'd let a man lead her on a nighttime stroll. Now, here she was.

Roark slid his arm down to hold her hand, gently squeezing it before stepping off the pea-gravel path, in-between a row of lily greens, and onto the firm ground.

"This will be easier on your shoes," he said, but he didn't let go of her hand.

Sex was one thing, holding hands was totally different. One was straightforward and she could do it and focus on the physical pleasure and *only* the pleasure; the other led to an elaborate maze of emotions she wasn't equipped to handle. Messy and complicated and something she'd never succeeded in.

Why she was allowing this to happen, she had no idea.

They wandered about twenty feet off the path, to a clearing that led to the sandy beach and swimming area of Lake Anikawi. She glanced up to find the moon full and round in the clear sky, the light reflecting off the water in bright ripples.

"Wow," she breathed.

"I know."

The moon shone on them like a spotlight, like the universe shining a light on them, as if to say *Look what you're doing, Madison. You're doing the very thing you swore you'd never do again. And you're fully aware you're doing it. So don't get mad when it blows up in your face again.*

She was on a moonlit stroll, with a man who went from smelling like cookies to evergreens and earth. The kind of guy who could keep her warm in the middle of an ice storm, pulled out chairs, and liked to touch her hair. What the hell was wrong with her?

She closed her eyes and muttered a curse.

"What?" Roark turned, looking concerned. "You okay?"

"I'm fine." She wasn't fine, she was an idiot. An idiot standing there, studying his face, the straight nose, the strong jaw held tight, wondering how strange it'd feel to look around in a couple of weeks and not see him there. "You said you wanted to walk. We aren't walking."

He grinned, rocking back on his heels to glance at the ground. "Like you didn't know that was an excuse to get you out of the restaurant and somewhere private."

He finally looked down at her, that mischievous glint in his eyes.

"You're awful." She went to drop his hand but couldn't. Because she didn't want to. This wouldn't end well, it never did, but what if she enjoyed it for now? Being with Roark, however short the time might be, promised to be amazing in so many ways. What if she allowed herself at least that much? A moment to experience bliss.

"I told you I wasn't doing so great at behaving," he said.

"Are you even trying?"

Roark tilted his head. "Sort of?" His voice was a self-deprecating plea. Strapping guy, oozing self-assuredness but attempting to look pathetic. The tactic wasn't working.

This time, Madison tugged him forward. "You say that, but you attempted to feed me from your fork, rubbed your legs against mine under the table, and are taking me on a moonlit walk."

"No, see, when I say I'm trying, I mean I'm trying to seduce you. I'm no master of seduction, but rubbing my leg against yours and attempting to feed you are indications of my sexual interest, to emulate what we did this morn—"

Madison put her hand on his chest to stop him. "I know why you're doing it. You don't have to explain."

He dipped his chin, with a slow sweep of his lashes like he'd done the day they met, before he grinned. The devilish boy underneath the layers of responsible gentleman.

"Stop. Don't look at me like that."

"Is my attempt at seduction working?" Roark stepped closer.

"You're ridiculous."

"Answer the question. Is it working?"

It was working way too well.

He pulled her close, placing a hand on the small of her back, his warmth surrounding her, engulfing her senses.

"Are we going to dance now? I thought you weren't a romantic."

"Believe me, I am not trying to dance with you. Can't dance worth a damn. I was thinking about kissing you though."

Madison looked up at him. Playfulness lit his eyes. She wondered if the same light filled her, because giddiness was a good look on him. She liked seeing it there, some of the seriousness peeling away to reveal the heart of someone who wanted to be happy in the moment.

Her resolve was already in tatters, and Roark's longing look, the palpable need to throw everything into the night sky and live, finally broke her.

To hell with caution and to hell with fear stopping her from having so much as a taste of life.

Madison licked her lips. "Stop thinking about kissing me and do it."

Chapter 13

Roark kissed her and she opened to him immediately. Petal soft and as perfect as he remembered. He sucked on her bottom lip, releasing it long enough to murmur, "I thought about you all day. About doing this."

"Me too." She pulled him down again. This time, the rough slide of her tongue luring him closer. She tucked her body against his and looped her arms around his neck.

He took advantage, running his hands down her back, over her hips. Madison was tall, and firm with lean muscle. All softness reserved for her lips, the slight swell of her hips and curve of her breasts, her round bottom.

He eased one hand lower, brushing over her ass, murmuring his compliments.

"It's nowhere near as awe inspiring as yours," she said, smiling.

Roark chuckled, dipping his head, his mouth to her ear to whisper, "I beg to differ."

He cupped a hand against her face, stroking his thumb along her jaw until she relaxed, tilting her chin back. Down the line of her throat and over her skittering pulse, he followed the path of his thumb with his lips, leaving a trail of kisses. Low on her throat, he breathed her in and kissed the tender skin, before sucking and biting gently.

"Roark?" Madison dug her fingers into his arm, holding on.

"Yeah?"

"I don't want to wait to be with you."

He leaned away just enough to look at her. "Me either. What do you say we ditch that plan? Try for new and improved."

She laughed, the full one that she usually hid behind her hand, except this time she didn't.

"If we go back in through reception, we'll probably run into Sophie and get the look."

"And Devlin and Wright if we take the veranda," she added.

He shook his head, looking around. "I've got it." He took her hand and led her back through the lily rows and onto the pea-gravel path, until they stepped onto the inn's lower patio.

"The basement?" she asked.

"There are rooms down here, remember? And it's entirely vacated now that Trevor's gone." He tipped over every potted plant on the patio until he found the spare key.

Madison reached for him as soon as he was within reach, tugging him forward by the front of his shirt.

Roark leaned in, taking her mouth with his. Madison's soft exhale was probably the closest she'd ever come to acquiescence. The force of that will was one of the things he liked most about her.

He kissed her softly, meaning to keep it that way. Keep it light and playful, and easy enough to back away from, but then a little sound rose in her throat. The same sound as this morning, and it was his undoing.

Roark pulled Madison into him, pressing her to the glass door as he parted her lips and kissed her in all the ways he'd fantasized about all day. Her fingers curled into his shirt, clutching him close, her lips and tongue hot against his.

He managed to break away long enough to get the door open and they stumbled into the basement level of the inn. In the pitch dark, it should've been a bit drafty and creepy, but all he felt was Madison.

She clung to his arm, her body snug against him, the warmth from her kisses lingering on his lips. He stole one more kiss, something to think about while he tried to find the damn light switch.

He held on to her with one hand and patted along the wall with the other. His fingertips brushed the switch and he flicked it up, two floor lamps on either side of a huge sectional sofa slowly brightening.

"Welcome to the unused floor."

She stepped toward him, brushing her fingertips against the front of his shirt. "Aka, somewhere to go that doesn't include going upstairs and bumping into your family."

Roark reached up to touch her cheek, cool from the night air. He tucked his hand under her chin, tilting it up just that little bit more. "Think this will do?"

Madison pressed her lips to his. She tickled the seam with the tip of her tongue until tendrils of want, hot and thick like flame, licked through his body, making him groan.

She smiled at his reaction. Cupping the back of her head, he took her mouth, no tickling or teasing. He buried the promise of everything he wanted into it. All he wanted to do to her, everything he wanted her to do to him, searing her onto his brain so it'd be enough to last long after tonight.

He had to break away to catch his breath, and she leaned with him, breathing just as heavily.

"Is th . . . ?" Madison cleared her throat and tried again. "Is that an empty guest room?" She pointed to the door behind him.

Roark caught his breath. "Yes."

"Thank god."

He led the way, shoving open the door and turning on a floor lamp. The room was neat and nondescript, clean and never used. He hadn't even thought about this hideaway as an option until their moonlight walk.

Madison stepped around him and backed toward the bed, that provocative smile on her lips. "This is already better than a patch of grass."

He followed until they bumped against the edge of the bed. She leaned back as he kissed her, tugging him forward by his tie so they both fell. They bounced once, his heart thumping in his ears, his body buzzing with anticipation.

He eased his way up the bed, strong enough to scoot Madison up with him and kneel over her thighs.

"You look so pleased right now." Her eyes twinkled and shined.

He jerked at the knot in his tie. "You have no idea."

"Has it been awhile?" She sat up and moved his hand away, working the knot open so she could slide the tie from around his neck.

"I . . ." Roark shrugged as she started on the buttons of his shirt, her gaze intent on his. "Yes, but that's not why I'm so pleased. I'm here with you. That's why."

She glanced away, too fast for him to see the words register. When she turned back, her expression was carefully serene. "How is it even possible that it's been awhile for you?"

"Work, I guess, and life? I don't get out a lot? I don't know."

Madison reached for his cuff links, deft in unclasping them before pushing the shirt off his shoulders and down his arms. She tugged at his undershirt and slipped her hands beneath to brush at the sensitive skin low on his abs.

He flinched, bowing forward and capturing her hands to hold them in place. "That tickles."

"I know." She grinned. "I'll stop if you take the shirt off."

Roark tugged at the back of his undershirt, pulling it over his head.

"You're a hot guy though, and not a creep," Madison blurted.

He tossed his shirt aside and reached for the soft knit of Madison's sweater. "Thank you, but you know how it is. If you're busy, it's hard to . . ."

He had to tread carefully here. A phrase like *find someone* was the kind of heavy wording that'd make Madison shut down. Holding his hand on a night stroll had been a big step for her, he could tell. He wasn't going to push too hard, so he settled on warm but neutral. "Work makes it hard to meet someone you mesh with."

She studied him, looking deep into his eyes as he finally got the little bastard buttons of her sweater undone. "Yeah." She glanced away. "I don't mesh well in general."

"Hey." He touched the sharp line of her jaw until she looked at him again. "You mesh fine. Just have to find the right people."

When the tightness around her eyes finally relaxed, a soft smile curling her lips, he peeled her sweater away and she raised her arms, letting him pull the shell over her head.

Madison leaned back, unusually vulnerable and bare, fair skin in black satin, looking like something to be worshipped.

That's exactly what he planned to do.

He dipped his head, kissing gently over the swell of each breast. He placed his hand against her back to hold her up, then he went lower and, through the silky smoothness of her bra, sucked her nipple into his mouth.

Her breath was a sharp inhale, before she let it out, shuddering in his arms.

He sucked harder before gently closing his teeth over her. And she arched her back, pushing against his mouth, shifting her hips beneath him.

Roark moved to her other breast, giving it the same attention. He kept at it until her fingers were in his hair, gripping his scalp. The cool distance of her work demeanor broke apart when they were like this. To say he didn't love it would make him a damn liar. In fact, the difference between professional Madison and passionate Madison made it that much hotter.

He moved lower, kissing the soft skin of her stomach, working at the zipper of her pants and tugging them off. Her high heels fell to the floor.

He caught her hips and reached back, cupping her ass and lifting her up. Roark lowered his head between her legs, kissing her through her panties, breathing in her heat.

"*Oh. . . .*" Madison's hands moved helplessly through the air like lost butterflies, before landing on the duvet. She twitched and writhed in his arms, but he wasn't letting her go anywhere. He held her hips in place, licking and sucking at the satin until she was soaking wet and her legs were trembling.

"Roark . . . *Roark.*" She reached for his head.

He hummed against her core.

Her fingers curled into his hair, but suddenly she was wriggling free. He rose up, confused, until she shoved at her panties.

Roark slid the thin straps off her hips and down her legs, tossing her panties aside. She worked at her bra as he all but jumped out of his shoes and crawled back onto the bed, shifting Madison across the bed until the top of her head was at the edge. She was spread out and lovely beneath him, warm and wanting.

He'd wanted her since day one, spent days and days fighting it, and the last two trying to be patient. It would be too easy to rush this, give in to what he wanted, but the one thing he wanted more was to feel Madison fly apart against his tongue.

"Come here," he said, reaching for the band on her braided hair. "May I?"

She hesitated. Her hair was never down when he was around, except once in the forest. He knew there was some reason she kept it up, maybe for work, but he loved seeing the waves around her face.

Madison touched the end of her hair. "Okay."

Roark pulled the band free, threading his fingers through her hair, from the bottom to the top, until all of her hair fell loose in loops and waves, to brush the top of her shoulders.

Finally, he let himself look at the rest of her. From the flush of color in her face, the spark in her bewitching eyes, the pert tips of her breasts, down to the strip of hair between her legs, she was better than anything he'd ever imagined. Madison, laid bare for him to see, lit a fire inside of him.

He didn't want to just have sex; he wanted her to experience mind-blowing pleasure *with him*, because of him. If this was all they'd have together, then he wanted it to be unlike anything else.

Not just because Madison was beautiful and smart, but because—

"Looking at me like that, I swear to god, Roark, if you don't touch me soon, I'm going to die." Madison's voice shook with need.

Roark caressed the length of her body as he eased between her legs, nudging her thighs wider with his shoulders. He kissed the inside of each thigh, the smooth skin of her legs brushing over his arms, then against his sides. He brushed the tips of his fingers up and down the soft folds, finding her wet and pink. He hadn't seen her yesterday, only felt, but the sight of her stoked that fire until it became a twisting need.

She lay spread before him and he was at once humbled and really fucking pleased about being here with her right now.

He ran the back of his hand over her, brushing his knuckles against her cleft, up and down, until a shiver ran through her. He kissed her there, right at her core, and her thighs clamped against his sides.

He licked and sucked, Madison's body drawing tight around him, until she began to unwind with every brush of his tongue. He touched his thumb to the soft flesh, kissing and rubbing until her back arched and he knew he'd found the right place.

Roark covered her with his mouth, a growl of satisfaction at the taste of her, another when she flexed her thighs in his grip and went back to grabbing at his hair.

"More . . ." she ground out, tilting her hips, pressing herself against him.

Her body arched like she was trying to sit up. "Where'd you learn—oh God." She fell back against the bed and didn't try to sit up again. She reached for his hair again, fingertips pressed against his scalp.

He rumbled his approval against her flesh. She gasped and yanked his hair. "Yes. That."

Roark did it again. He did all of it again, over and over, sucking roughly at her clit. Madison writhed beneath him until her whole body tightened, legs squeezing him, fingers in his hair. She cried out as she trembled and pulsed against his mouth.

He held on to her, soaking up every sensation, every bit of her climax, until her limbs flopped down, as if boneless.

He eased up to see her face.

"What. . . ." She squeezed her eyes shut and didn't finish the question.

Roark crawled up, kissing the smooth skin of her legs and stomach along the way, enjoying how she flinched and shivered at the touch. He propped himself up and waited as she barely shook her head, eyes still closed. "Seriously. What just happened?" She turned her head to look at him.

"Was that okay for you?"

Madison pushed him over onto his back, only a quick flash of a smile before her lips crashed into his. He brought her with him, pulling her half on top of him, wrapping his arms around her to hold her naked body against his.

She leaned away, holding herself up with an arm on his chest. "You still have on too many clothes. *That* is not okay."

"Your fault. You didn't undress me all the way."

She leaned over, kissing him again as she straddled his hips. Roark held her, opening to her kiss, giving as good as he got, relishing the way that Madison didn't hold back. A little puff of frustration puckered her lips as she battled with his belt, getting it undone and tugging at his pants.

"Lift your hips." She slid back and jerked his pants down his legs, along with his boxers.

His erection sprung up, very happy to be free. In true Madison fashion, she didn't look away, lower her gaze, or bat her lashes. She didn't hide her approving grin or the carnal flash in her eyes.

It made him want her all the more.

Chapter 14

Roark pulled her down and kissed her again.

Madison's hesitations melted away, her earlier doubts gone; there was only him and now. She'd had her reasons for thinking they should wait, but those reasons were dust, blown away by the strength of what Roark made her feel.

Beautiful and accepted exactly the way she was. And it made her free. Free to enjoy him and everything they did.

She slanted her mouth over his and slipped her hand between his legs, brushing past the length of his cock to run her hand over his balls.

He sucked in a breath, sharp enough to make her lean back and look down at him. "That okay for you?" She parroted his earlier question.

As he managed to nod, she did it again, squeezing gently, and then wrapped her hand around him. She stroked the hard, smooth length of his cock, smiling at his every reaction.

The more she touched him, the more lost to her touch he looked, and the more the pleasure bloomed inside of her.

With her free hand, she reached for his face, cupping his jaw and rubbing her fingertips over his stubble.

"I like your scruff," she murmured. "It feels . . . nice. Especially just a minute ago."

Barely a huff of laugh escaped him, as she kept drawing pant after moan from him. She eased down his body and when she wrapped her lips around him, Roark went from breathing heavily to not breathing at all.

Peeking up, she could see him. He bit his lips hard, pinching his eyes closed.

"*Fuck.*" He exhaled.

She wasn't gentle or teasing in her touch or with her mouth. She licked and sucked and took. Roark quivered and shook beneath her, muttering encouragements until some choice profanity fell from his lips.

"You . . ." He waved a hand at her, attempting to sit up.

She stopped but kept one hand wrapped around him. "What?"

"You have to stop." He held himself up with one arm.

Madison tilted her head to the side. "You sure about that?"

He held his body so tight, he looked like he'd pop. "I'm—yeah. I'm not going to last if you keep doing that."

"Maybe, but you did this to me. *Twice.* I intend to have the same effect." Madison leaned to the side, her leg draped over his, brushing the fine hairs on his thigh with her fingertips.

He grabbed the hand she danced along his thigh and pulled her forward, kissing her. "You're having the same effect. Trust me." He rolled against her so his erection, the proof of her effectiveness, was trapped between them. "But I want to be inside you. I'm not eighteen anymore. You keep up with that and . . ." Roark gave her a knowing look.

She tucked her face into the crook of his neck. "God, I want to too, but I don't have a condom—"

"I do." Roark released her and rolled off the bed. He dug through their clothes and into his pants for his wallet. He stood, triumphant, a foil square in his hand.

Madison smiled at the view. She couldn't help it. Sex with Roark was amazing and titillating and everything sex should be. There was no undercurrent of pressure. She was free.

"Amusement is not what I'm going for right now." He attempted to look stern in all his naked glory.

She grabbed his forearm, tugging him back onto the bed. "You know I'm not laughing at you. It's just . . . I'm happy."

Roark knelt beside her on the bed and rocked back on his heels, studying her. With his stormy-sky eyes, he saw her. More than she'd shown anyone.

"I'm happy too," he said.

Her nerves buzzed with so much of what she kept hidden being slowly exposed. She didn't want him to know it all, but there was relief in his understanding a little.

She reached for him, continuously drawn in by the paradox of the no-bullshit businessman and the blithe, playful man.

Their kiss was languid, unhurried, like they had all night to explore. And in truth, they did.

Madison took the foil from his hands, helping him roll the condom on before pushing at his shoulder. She kept shoving until he lay down.

Roark stretched out on the bed beneath her, giant cat-who-got-the-cream smile on his face.

Madison stroked him once more before climbing up to straddle his hips. His hands were a warm, solid reassurance as he caressed her thighs, her hips, her waist.

She rose above him, using her hand to guide him against her core.

Roark's slow, contented inhale made her gaze lock with his.

"Damn," he said, reaching up to brush her hair back over her shoulder. "You're even more beautiful like this."

Madison eased down on him, inch by inch, pressing into him until he was deep inside her. The stretch was a tingling need for movement, for friction.

She leaned down to kiss Roark, rocking her hips back and shivering with the pleasure.

"Good?"

Madison hummed against his lips. She kissed his jaw, the slight stubble tickling her lips.

Roark tilted her chin back, kissing and sucking along her neck, just the way she liked.

She rocked back and forth again and again, searching for the rhythm and motion that would make her body sing.

Roark shifted beneath her. Holding on to her waist, he planted his feet, knees bent behind her, his hips tilted. He rocked into her, counterpoint to her movement, and the effect made her grab at his chest.

"Sit up a little," he said, his voice gravelly, sounding as needy as she felt.

She held herself up, just enough, with both of her hands on his chest, pressing back against him and rolling her hips.

With each roll, he thrust into her, the friction and force *exactly* what and where she needed.

"Dear . . . god." She moaned, curling her fingers into his flesh.

"Yeah." He ground out the words in response, gripping her hips tighter.

Madison tossed her head back, grinding down on him with all the strength her thighs and abs could muster.

He thrust into her, the bed shifting back and forth with their efforts. Madison held on, feeling the tension build once more in her spine.

"Yes . . . Like that."

Below her, the sweat on Roark's brow and over his body made him glow. Life was unfair, that he looked that good when sweaty. Mixed with the flush that crept over his cheeks and down his neck, coloring the top of his chest, he was absolutely edible.

How could he be so strong and capable but also so delicious that she wanted to devour him? "I'm gonna—"

Roark nodded stiffly, his jaw already clenching. "Fuck yeah, me too."

With his words, her orgasm hit her, fast and fully. No slow rise this time, but a blast of pleasure so unexpected she cried out, pinching her eyes shut.

In a haze, she managed to open them and watch Roark come. The line etched between his brows, the look of pure bliss on his face. Even as he rode the last waves of his orgasm, still pulsing inside of her, he pulled her down on top of him and kissed her long and deep and so thorough, she knew. One night with Roark would never be enough.

Roark went to the bathroom to clean up, then slid back in bed with her, curling on his side to mirror her position. "Hey."

"Hey." She tucked the blanket around her, snuggling down, reminding herself to relax. She wanted to be here with him and if he wanted pillow talk, she should be able to handle it.

Maybe.

Better to keep it light though. To talk about what just happened not only meant *talking* about what just happened, but what if it jinxed the whole thing?

What they had was too good to risk jinxing. They were happy, enjoying each other, and he still found her appealing. Too much talking, too much digging around in the life and times of Madison Kline, and all of that would end.

She was pleased they hadn't waited, but the possibility of this going further for longer, left her at a loss.

"I'm glad we didn't wait until after the wedding is over. I think another couple of weeks would've been pretty . . ." He didn't finish the thought.

"Yeah," she answered, unsure of what to say but knowing she had to say something. "And I . . . I don't think this will affect our work or anything." She was trying to convince herself as much as him.

"No. Of course not." He didn't sound so sure either.

"We've got a lot of the work out of the way, and stuff, and . . . we won't let this interfere." In truth, she wasn't worried about the work. The event would be spectacular. She was worried about them, and how she should behave around someone she was working with and sleeping with. This wasn't what she did. The few lovers she'd had over the years weren't men *in* her life. They were dates, easily compartmentalized and then brushed away if they wanted too much.

"Have you ever . . . ?" Madison slowly raised her eyebrows.

Roark mirrored her expression. "Have I ever what?"

"Have you ever had sex with someone you do business with?"

"No!" He shook his head. "I don't normally—this isn't something I—no. The answer is no."

"Me either. This isn't how I carry on." Her foot brushed against his ankle, and she left it there.

"Yeah. But like you said, it won't be a problem."

"No, of course not."

"And it won't mess with what we're doing. Daily operations and your planning, everything; it will be business as usual."

She stopped with her foot on his calf. "So . . . you think this is something we should continue to do, right" Anyone else might not have to ask, because they'd know. But she wasn't anyone. The casual confidence with which some people carried on affairs and even relationships was foreign. She understood doing everything for herself and being by herself. Navigating a tryst with a business partner? She didn't have a clue.

Roark worked his jaw. "Well . . . yeah. I want to. Don't you?"

She smiled, relief washing over her, warming her like sunshine on a cold day. She slid her foot back down to slip it under his ankle. "Very much."

Roark moved his feet to capture hers between his ankles.

She struggled to pull her foot free, and he laughed at her fruitless effort. "That's cheating. Let my foot go."

"Only if we're done talking. I can't concentrate with your knee rubbing up my thigh. *That* is cheating."

She let her mouth fall open. "I was *not* rubbing your thigh."

"When your foot is halfway up my leg, what do you think is happening with the rest your leg?"

Madison reached over and pinched him, giddy that she'd survived their talk without botching things up.

Roark cried foul as he rolled over and pinned her beneath him. "What if I pinched you?"

"Don't you dare."

He laughed, holding himself up on one arm.

"You're not going to move, are you?"

"Nope." He brushed her hair back over the pillow.

She never let her hair down in front of anyone, not anymore. But his reaction to it was unmistakable. "You like my hair like this." It wasn't a question, but she studied his face, waiting for his response.

"I like your hair, period. I thought the braid tonight was very hot, but then I wasn't sure if that was leftover horniness from this morning, or if braids were really *that* hot and I'd never noticed."

Madison bumped his leg with hers.

"I'm being serious," he argued. "I like it up too."

"Good thing, because I never wear it down while working."

He nodded, gazing down, giving her plenty of time to say more.

If he only knew how saying that much was difficult for her.

"I used to wear it down all the time, when I first started out, but I learned reactions were better if I didn't wear my hair natural."

"People react badly to your good hair? Maybe they're jealous." He grinned.

"No, not like that. It's . . . a lot of people wouldn't take me seriously or I'd get a lot of passive-aggressive attitude. I don't know. People assumed I was either a dingbat or a floozy. You saw Troutman. He's not an anomaly. Whenever I wear my hair up, or at least straightened and pulled back, people take me seriously. Men look me in the eyes. Brides seem to have more confidence in my ability to get their wedding planned. All-around a win, so I went with it."

He regarded her quietly before he asked, "Are you okay with it?"

Madison shrugged.

She'd never really thought about it, and no one had ever asked. "I . . . I don't know," she answered honestly. Perhaps she was revealing too much in the simple reply, but it was too late to take it back now.

Roark nodded, accepting her response. "Sometimes you have to go with what works. Do what you've got to do, you know?"

She nodded. Oh, how well she knew.

He smiled and the acknowledgment of her small offering eased her anxiety. "I don't think people would take me seriously with long curly hair either, so we have that in common."

After holding herself so tight, her laugh burst out. Somehow, with one little joke, Roark made sharing the truth okay.

She kept laughing, shaking her hair so it spread out, a mess around her head.

This wasn't a side of her that anyone got to see. This was something held in check, hidden, and she tried not to feel anything about letting him in.

She tried, and failed.

Chapter 15

"Yes, there will be other photographers at the wedding, but you will be *the* photographer. You're doing the portraits, the shots for their album." Madison paced the length of Honeywilde's great room, phone in one hand and a giant cup of coffee in the other.

"Three other photographers though? I heard one of them is from New York. You won't even need me."

Of all weddings, her favorite photographer had decided *now* was the time to be an insecure diva. "Frank, please don't do this."

"I'm not going to let them treat me like some hick amateur. I mean it. I'll walk."

"No one is going to treat you poorly. You know I'd never let that happen and I'll be in charge of the whole shebang. Trust me when I say you'll be fine."

"But what if she hates the shoot? What if it all goes to hell and she bad-mouths me on *Ellen*?"

"She . . . *what?* Whitney is not going bad-mouth you. She isn't even going on *Ellen*."

"She might. Everyone goes on *Ellen*."

"The bride loves your work and she will love you. She's from Tennessee. I've met her, she's lovely, and she doesn't want some big-city hotshot doing her bridal pictures. She wants personal photos, shot outside with natural lighting, foliage, and a distinct mountainous feel."

"Madison, honey. You know I love working with you, but I haven't met this girl. How am I supposed to connect with her and take intimate-feeling pictures if I've known her all of five minutes?"

"I trust your talent. You can do it."

"I've seen her on TV, of course. Did you know she was listed as one of *People*'s Best Dressed at the Grammys? The *Grammys*, Madison. She looked like a golden goddess."

"Then you have your work cut out for you."

"Annie Leibovitz would have her work cut out for her. I will be lost."

"Frank." She used the most calming voice she could manage.

He kept fretting, going on and on about *W* magazine and *Vogue*. This was going to take some ego stroking and another cup of coffee.

Madison let him continue spewing doubt, getting it all out as she refilled one of the inn's pottery mugs and headed for the front entrance.

Finally, Frank's ranting slowed to a murmur. She stepped outside onto the portico and continued her pacing there. Now she could raise her voice, just enough to get his attention. "Frank. I need you to come back to earth for a second and listen to me. Are you listening?"

"Yes." Frank's tone indicated he was also sulking.

"Whitney does not want a sleek, edgy editorial for her personal wedding album. These will be *her* pictures, not photographs sold to a magazine. She wants cozy and private. Something special. That is what you do. I showed her your portfolio and she chose *you*. Now, I need you to pull it together and remember how spectacular you are at what you do. Okay?"

"Okay."

"And there is no one from New York or Los Angeles who can shoot this area or a sweet Southern girl on her wedding day as brilliantly as you can. Got it?"

"Got it."

"She wants some black and whites of her soon-to-be husband too. He's more . . . let's go with rugged and handsome, and she wants lots of shots of him in a suit, because it will probably never happen again."

Frank laughed because it wasn't the first time they'd gotten such a request from a bride.

"Are you okay now?" Madison turned to pace down the walkway, just as Sophie walked out the front door.

"I'm okay."

"Good. I need to run, but I want you here next Thursday. If Whitney arrives early, I'll make sure you guys have coffee or something."

"That'd be wonderful. Thank you."

"Anytime. It's all going to be fine, Frank. Amazing. You'll see." Madison ended the call before he could argue about the amazing part.

"Hey." Sophie nodded to her, Beau pulling at his leash as they walked over.

He bounded up to Madison, nudging her hand with his wet nose.

"Sorry." Sophie tried pulling him back.

"It's fine. We made friends. Didn't we, Beau?" Great, now she was talking to the dog too.

"You did? When?"

"Um . . ." *Right after I made out with your brother in the forest and he made me scream so loud your other brother probably heard us.* "I was out jogging and ran into him and Devlin."

A slow smile curled Sophie's lips and she swung the handle of the leash around. "Oh, that's right. I forgot Dev told me he'd run into you and Roark."

That sly little grin meant Sophie hadn't forgotten a damn thing. Not in her entire life.

"Yeah." Madison nodded and glanced away.

"So, are y'all running buddies now?"

"What? No. I mean . . . we might run at the same time again, sometime, but we're not . . . we don't have plans to run together. Again."

Sophie studied her for the longest few seconds of Madison's life and then shrugged. "That's a shame. I think Roark would be more likely to run if he had someone to go with him. You know. A running buddy. Running is more fun with someone else, don't you think?"

Madison fidgeted with her phone and then clasped it between her hands to make herself stop. God, she hoped they were really still talking about running. "I do."

"I better take Beau before he starts whining. I'll see you later. Wright has some cake samples he wants you to try, and as long as you don't mind, I'm getting in on that action."

"Of course."

"'Kay. Bye!" Sophie waved before she and Beau bounded down the stairs and took off like they were trying to out-happy each other.

If people didn't realize that petite redhead was two steps ahead of them, they were in trouble. Luckily, Madison knew.

It made her like Sophie all the more.

"Was that Soph?" Roark stuck his head out the front door.

"Yes. She's taking Beau for a jog."

He stepped outside, coffee in hand as he scowled. "Damn. I needed to ask her something." Roark glanced at Madison, and his gaze softened. "'Morning."

"'Morning." She buried her nose in a long sip of coffee.

He strolled toward her. "You're up early."

"There's a lot I have to do today."

"I know. I've seen your lists. Did you try some of our Harvest Blend yet?" Roark nodded to her coffee.

"I have no idea. I think this is just black coffee."

He peered down into her mug. "No, Wright buys a Harvest Blend for fall and *finally* made some today, thank the lord. This stuff is the good stuff. Little bit of pumpkin and nutmeg. If you'd had it, you'd know."

She glanced over at his mug. He took his coffee black too, but a delicious, spicy smell wafted up in the steam. She took a deep inhale. Like autumn in a cup.

"Here, try it." He held his mug out to her.

"No, I couldn't—"

Roark didn't argue with her. Not verbally anyway. He held his mug even closer with one hand, his free hand out in offering to hold her cup.

"Okay." She passed over her plain black coffee and took his Harvest Blend, sipping it slowly. His coffee was hotter than hers and twice as tasty.

He might not be getting his coffee back.

"I'm not getting that back, am I?"

Madison shook her head and grinned into his cup. "Your sister thinks we should be running partners."

Roark choked on the mouthful of coffee he'd taken from her mug.

"She said Devlin had mentioned us being out for a run together and that running alone was no fun and that you needed someone to run with, and toward the end I wasn't so sure we were talking about running at all."

"Oh jeez. I told you. Didn't I tell you?" He rubbed a hand over his face.

"You did. And if she doesn't know we slept together, then she's very much in favor that we do so."

Roark's mouth fell open. "Did she say that?"

"No. But she distinctly implied. Your little sister is wise beyond her years and a hell of a lot bolder than her size would indicate."

He tossed his head back and grinned. "You're right about that. I'm actually kind of surprised she didn't come right out and tell you we should hook up."

"She'd say that?"

"Damn straight. In front of family, and you, now that you've been here awhile. In front of guests and vendors, she's all proper manners and behavior. You'd think sugar wouldn't melt in her mouth, she's so sweet. With closer acquaintances, she'll say whatever she wants, when she wants. If you're familiar, all bets are off."

"Then she'll probably ask you about it later?"

"I don't doubt it. As soon as she gets the chance."

"What will you tell her?"

Roark's gaze remained steady on hers. "What do you want me to tell her?"

Madison took another drink of Roark's coffee, trying to figure out if she wanted Sophie to know for certain. She pretty much knew already, and Devlin too; Wright would know soon enough.

Did it matter? She wasn't ashamed of sleeping with Roark, and she was fairly certain Sophie wasn't going to judge her or hold it against her. But was their intimacy something she wanted to be general knowledge? Other people wouldn't understand. They'd either judge her for mixing pleasure with business or they'd think she and Roark were *together.*

They'd get it in their heads they were a pair, and then there'd be certain expectations. The questions and pressure would come next. Were they a couple? Was it serious? She and Roark would be paired together before she even realized, and she'd start to care. Caring, followed shortly by him turning into the coldhearted bastard that every man became with time. Then he'd leave her behind with the wreckage of her feelings and she'd have to start all over. Again.

Her answer was a big *no, thank you* on everyone knowing the details. Easier and safer to leave it to speculation.

"I prefer you not tell her anything concrete. Let's not make a big deal of it. If that's okay?"

Roark nodded. "Sure. You think that will work?"

"I don't know. But I don't want her getting the wrong idea. You know? She might not understand like you and I do. Sophie seems very nice, and blunt, but she might be prone to think along more . . . permanent lines when it comes to people being together. Especially when it involves her brother."

"Right." Roark nodded again.

The end of her stay was already going to be problematic enough; his family knowing they were together, however temporary, would only make it harder. "I don't want her to think we're *together*, or have it cause any confusion later, when I leave."

And god forbid she become closer to Roark's family. She had about a week and a half left, and already, anticipating the end made sailor knots of her insides.

No. Better to keep it simple. A cut, no matter how deep, healed better than a gaping wound.

Roark took another sip of his coffee, looking toward the walkway and the path Sophie had taken with the dog. "You're right. We wouldn't want anyone to be confused on where you and I stand."

"Exactly." This was in his best interest too. More so than hers. After the wedding, when she went back to Charlotte, he'd be the one left with the questions. It'd be easier for him to wave it off as no big deal, versus a family inquisition. From what she knew of the Bradleys, it'd be quite the inquisition.

Though, now that she thought about it, being brushed off as no big deal had the coffee curdling on her stomach.

Roark kept staring off toward the walkway. "And even if she figures out the truth, because she's smart like that, I'll explain to her that you and I are just friends. She doesn't need to read anything more into it. It's not permanent and nothing worth discussing. Like you said, it's not a 'thing.' We're just enjoying each other's company."

Nothing worth discussing. Right.

Madison gripped her coffee cup until her hands burned, and she blinked at his profile, wishing he'd look at her. What he said were basically her words, and pretty much what she wanted. At least . . . what she thought she wanted.

Everything *would* be easier this way, safer for both of them.

"Yes, that's . . ." She had to clear the knot in her throat. "That's good. We're, um, enjoying each other's company. That's it." Even though, at the moment, she wasn't enjoying any of this.

Chapter 16

Roark stalked around his office, trying to accept what Madison had said.

Enjoying each other.

Is that all they were doing? On the one hand, damn straight it was enjoyable, but it was more than that. He *enjoyed* his coffee this morning. What he and Madison shared was . . .

"Damn," he murmured.

Being with Madison was invigorating, both in and out of bed. He felt alive and challenged; he could be himself and she wasn't put off or offended when he was insistent or straightforward. In fact, she was the same, and she dished it back with a little more on the side.

And the sex . . .

"Damn," he said aloud again. He didn't have words that would properly capture how he felt being with her.

Yesterday, on their run, was a natural high. Last night was a rush like jumping off Diver's Rock into the lake below. But with Madison, he had no life jacket. He dove in, thinking he could handle the depth. Then it was too late to question otherwise.

"Oh well," he mumbled. Pointless worrying about it now, he was already in midair. Madison's words were a needed reminder of how hard the landing would be if he lost sight of it.

Caring too much for someone who wasn't on the same plane was a disaster. He had flesh and blood family members who reminded him of that fact, daily.

No. Madison was right. What they did in their free time was their business and he needed to remember to keep it light and fun. Otherwise, people might mistake their camaraderie for something serious, a relationship that had a future.

Someone knocked on his door and he shook off his thoughts.

"Yeah?" he called out.

"You coming or not? Madison said you'd probably want to try these cake samples. You can stay locked up in there if you want, but it means more cake for me."

Roark opened the door to find Dev leaning against the frame. "That's a yes then?" his brother said.

They walked toward the kitchen, and he was just waiting for Dev to say something about Madison.

"Do me a favor?" Dev slowed his steps.

Here it came. "Sure. What?"

"Even if these cakes aren't the best you've ever had, be gentle about it. Wright has worked his ass off. We don't have to use him if the cakes aren't up to snuff, but don't be all . . . you know. Don't be too hard on him. Let him down easy if it comes to that."

Roark stopped walking. Dev looking out for Wright wasn't unusual. The two had been buddies forever, and Dev had always treated him like family—better than family in some ways—but this was about more than having Wright's back.

"I'm sure his cake baking is as great as everything else he does in the kitchen. In the unlikely chance it isn't, I wouldn't be hard on him regardless."

Dev pinched his lips together in a thin, straight line.

"I wouldn't. Come on, I'm not that bad."

His brother didn't say anything, his silence speaking plenty. Roark would admit he was sometimes hard on Dev, but that was because, after all that Dev had been through, he needed guidance, discipline. Roark had tried to keep his brother somewhere close to the right path since they were kids, and he'd failed, miserably. Now they were adults, and Dev was headed in a much better direction, but Roark struggled not to make suggestions and . . . guide.

"I'm cut-and-dried sometimes, but I know I'm not that bad."

Dev tilted his head, disagreeing.

"Fine. If the cakes aren't any good, I'll let him down easy."

"Thank you." Devlin nodded and they headed to the kitchen.

Wright, Sophie, and Madison waited inside.

"No one in this family is going to miss out on cake." Sophie smiled at them.

Madison said nothing but moved over to make room beside her.

"Can you blame us? Look at these." He stood next to her, close enough that their arms bumped together.

Along the prep table, normally used by the sous chef, Wright had lined up five single-layer, round cakes. He wiped his hands on the towel thrown over his shoulder. "I hope you guys like them."

"I'm sure we will." Sophie elbowed him before pointing to the first one. "Are both of those chocolate? Because I'm here for the chocolate."

Wright went down the line of cakes, pointing at each. "I put them in the order they should be tried, for the palate. I didn't bother with traditional wedding cake, since that was eighty-sixed from the start. This first one is caramel cake, next is hummingbird cake with cream cheese frosting, then just a few layers of the mile-high vanilla and chocolate cake, and finally bourbon chocolate cake with brown sugar and caramel frosting."

"That last one already has my vote." Sophie wiggled her fingers as Wright sliced a small piece from the first cake and placed it on one of their fine-dining plates.

"For the full effect," he explained.

They each got a plate and tried the first cake at the same time. A chorus of "mmm" and "yum" filled the air. Madison looked over at Roark as she chewed. She leaned in to whisper, her breasts brushing his upper arm. "How are we going to choose if they're all amazing?"

He'd be satisfied taste-testing the rest of the day and drawing out any decisions, if it meant cake on his plate and Madison pressed against him.

He cleared his throat. "I don't know."

Next up was the hummingbird cake; fruity, nutty, and creamy. They had a few bites of each until they'd tried them all. Roark was twice as high as the sky on a sugar rush, and firmly in the hummingbird-cake camp.

"Yep. I'm sticking with my vote for the bourbon and chocolate," Sophie offered, finishing off her slice.

Madison looked over the cakes, still picking at the hummingbird. She waved her empty fork in the air. "The bourbon and chocolate is my favorite too, but it's so rich for an entire cake. I like the caramel, but I'm afraid it would be too . . ."

"Boring?" Sophie ate another bite of chocolate.

"Yes."

Roark put his plate and fork down with a clang of finality. "The hummingbird cake. That is your wedding cake. It's delicious, textured, known as a Southern treat . . . it's the obvious choice if you want something memorable."

"I can't believe I'm saying this, but I agree with him." Devlin licked his fork clean. "The hummingbird cake is so good, makes you want to smack somebody."

Sophie paused with her fork on the way to her mouth. "Y'all would think that. Guys don't know cake."

"A guy baked these cakes!" Dev laughed and poked her full cheek.

She flicked a bit of frosting at him in retaliation.

"Guys," Roark said, calling them down. It'd been so long since Roark heard his brother laugh, he'd forgotten the sound, but they needed to concentrate on making a decision.

Madison leaned over to look at Devlin. "You make a good point though. Wright is the creator. Wright, which do you think is the best choice for a wedding cake?"

Wright studied all of the cakes before glancing at Sophie. "I tend to agree with Roark and Dev. You can't go wrong with a hummingbird cake. It's a crowd pleaser."

"Told you." Roark smiled at Madison, full of pride at his choice.

Sophie set her plate down. "But I don't like nuts in my cake."

Dev chuckled, so she dug him in the ribs with her elbow.

"Or what if someone has a nut allergy?" Madison tapped her fork against her lips.

"You could have both," Roark suggested. "Have hummingbird as the main cake and do the chocolate bourbon as a groom's cake. No nuts."

"That's a lot of work to put on Wright. He'll have enough to do as it is. I'm not sure two wedding cakes—"

"I don't mind," Wright insisted.

"Yeah, and besides, I usually help with events and catering." Sophie eyeballed the chocolate cake. "If it means having chocolate cake at the reception, I'll work overtime."

Madison worried at the inside of her cheek, sucking it in. "You don't think the two will clash? Maybe it's too much cake."

Sophie shook her head. "That sentence doesn't even make sense. Too much cake?"

Roark looked at the hummingbird and chocolate bourbon cakes beside each other. "I think they'll complement one another, in looks at least. Try tasting them, one right after the other."

Madison stared down at her empty plate. "I ate all of my chocolate."

"Here." Roark picked up his plate, still containing most of his slice. He cut off a bit with his fork, making sure to get the proper cake-to-icing ratio. "Try a bite of your hummingbird again, and then try my chocolate."

Madison cut off a bite of the hummingbird cake and tried it.

"Now, this one." Roark held out his fork.

Madison opened her mouth and he slipped the bite of cake between her lips. She smiled as she chewed, her eyes closed and her chin tilted back.

A vivid memory of her unfurled before him, from their run: her head tilted back, eyes closed before she met his gaze, tiny moans of pleasure, and then she cried out with her climax.

Roark cleared his throat and put his fork down. Between the sugar rush and erotic thoughts of Madison, he was going to need another run or a cold shower, or this could get embarrassing.

She finished chewing and opened her eyes with a sigh. "They're delicious together. Rich, yes, but these cakes say *unique, a one-of-a-kind wedding*. You're right. It's so annoying."

Roark smiled, reaching for her and touching her arm before he realized what he was doing. He dropped his hand and glanced around; the rest of the kitchen had gone silent. Three sets of eyes homed in on him and Madison.

"Okay." Sophie smiled, gazing over at them. "I vote for both. Two cakes are always better than one, anyway."

Wright slapped his hands together and picked up the dirty plates. "Perfect. I'll do three tiers of hummingbird and a double tier for the groom cake. Anybody want more before I wrap them up?"

Everyone groaned, but Sophie nabbed what was left of Roark's chocolate cake before Wright could get it. "Dev and I will help clean up." She winked at Roark. "I'm sure you and Madison have stuff to take care of."

Once they were outside of the kitchen and alone, walking toward his office, he leaned into Madison. "She definitely knows."

"I told you."

He opened his mouth to say he'd make sure she didn't get the wrong idea about what it meant, but he clamped his lips shut. "I have a serious sugar high right now," he said instead.

"I feel like a slice of cake with two legs. Two sugar encrusted legs."

"I'm not sure if that was supposed to turn me on, but it kind of is."

Madison bumped his arm. "No. I mean, I'm a walking sugar rush. What would you say your blood-sugar level is right now? Five hundred?"

"I don't know what you mean." Roark turned to her, making his eyes as wide as he could.

Her laugh washed over him, making him even giddier, riding high on the sweet wave. Then, brilliance struck.

"You know what would help burn off a sugar high?"

She cocked an eyebrow. "Maybe. But I don't think I'm capable of either right at this moment. Especially not running. The other . . . maybe later?"

"I wasn't going to say run."

The smile that crept across her face was a delight. "Do not say the other right now, because I'm too—"

"We should go swimming."

Madison blanched. "*You* should have your head checked. It's barely seventy outside."

"It's seventy-five degrees. Midday September is still warm. Indian summer. It's supposed to be almost eighty on Friday."

She shivered, even though they were in the cozy reception area. "But it's down in the fifties at night."

"This wouldn't even be a polar plunge, and those are good for you. Healthy. You're a runner. Come on."

"Yeah, but . . . cold. And I don't have a suit."

Roark arched an eyebrow. "Who said you needed a suit?"

With a giggle, she pinched her lips together, but she was giving him a yes or no answer.

"Unless you're too chicken to try it."

She lowered her chin, giving him that glare. "I bet you used the chicken challenge all the time growing up, didn't you?"

"Some." He'd used it on his brothers all the time. It always worked on Dev, never on Trevor, but it was worth a shot on Madison. As competitive as she was, a challenge didn't exist that she'd be called too chicken to try.

Madison looked around the great room, and then glared back at him, her mouth set. "I'm not going anywhere near water without four or five towels and blankets. And a heat source."

He grinned, even as inner doubt niggled. This was a lot of trouble to go through for something that wasn't a "thing." They didn't have to go swimming together. They didn't *have* to do anything together, and yet here he was, working to convince her that spending more time with each other was a good idea.

"Don't grin at me like you've won this battle. I haven't said yes yet."

"I can tell Sophie we've gone to . . ."

"Meet with Brenda, the florist, in town?"

"Yes." He snapped and pointed at her. "Good one. So, that's a yes?"

"No."

No was probably the smart option here. They should each take care of their ever growing list of responsibilities and spend all afternoon neck-deep in work. If they happened to fall into bed again later tonight, great. If not, that would have to be fine too. It shouldn't matter.

This was all going to come grinding to a halt soon. Why go through the trouble of a little day trip away, even if it did hold the possibility of some amazing outdoor sex? In the end, what was the point?

Madison glanced around again, chewing at the corner of her mouth. She was thinking about it.

Roark let another cluck build, low in his throat, before taunting her with chicken noises. There might not be any point to taking her away and spending a little extra alone-time with her, but he was still going to try his damnedest to do it anyway.

Madison clamped her hand over his mouth. "We're going skinny-dipping, just to shut you up."

He grinned behind her fingers. "I'll meet you at my car in fifteen minutes."

"Ten. And I'll meet you at *my* car."

"I've seen your car. There's no way it'll make it. We'll take my truck."

She opened her mouth to argue.

"But you can drive."

Madison eased her mouth closed and dropped her hand. "Deal."

Screw worrying about putting too much into this "not a thing" thing they were doing. So what if Madison would be gone in a week and half? That gave him more reason to soak up every moment now. If this was all going to end soon, he'd enjoy every bit of it while he could.

Chapter 17

She hoped she looked patient, waiting outside by Roark's truck, because she sure didn't feel it. Inside she simmered with the need to know where he was taking her, but more than that, why she'd agreed to go.

This wasn't her. Madison Kline did not go skinny-dipping, period, much less with a business acquaintance, in the middle of the day, *in September.*

It'd been over a decade since she'd gone swimming with a guy. At the time, it'd struck her as romantic. She'd thought it was love, but she was nineteen and still stupid as hell. Look where believing in love had gotten her. Once again, she'd been left, all alone in the world, nowhere to call home and no one to call . . . well, just plain no one to call.

This swimming trip was not romantic. It'd be fun and sexy and that's it. Even though it shouldn't be happening at all. Acting like a teenager again, giddy at the prospect of running off for a couple of hours together. She had work to do, and for her most important clients to date. What the hell was she thinking?

"You ready?" Roark strolled up beside her.

No. She was in no way ready for any of this. "I'm driving." She held out her hand for the keys.

Roark climbed into the passenger side of his big, black truck while she pulled herself into the driver's seat. A huge, olive-colored duffel sat between them.

"What's all that? Besides the requested towels." She nodded to the bag and started the truck.

"Some stuff. Don't worry about it. We're going to take a right out of the parking lot and head down the mountain."

Madison gave the mysterious bag and the bag's owner another look before backing out. "Dear *god* we're up high. Do you drive *over* other cars on a daily basis or is it a weekend hobby?"

"My truck isn't that high. You're used to sitting on the ground in your itty bitty sports car."

"I do not sit on the ground. I drive a normal car."

"Ha!"

She kept both hands on the wheel but turned her chin enough to glare at him. "What do you mean, *ha?*"

"You drive a convertible that tops out at over two hundred miles per hour. It's not a normal car."

"Normal for me then." Madison turned right and drove them down the mountain. She could do this. A little time away near the end of the day didn't mean there were any new expectations or added pressures between them. They'd be swimming, for crying out loud, and she was making something out of nothing.

The only real issue was taking the time away from work.

"I have about a million things left to do before I can call it a day." She came right out and said it.

"I know. Me too."

"Taking an hour off to go swimming isn't a good use of our time."

Roark shifted in his seat to look at her, his arm slung over the back of her seat. "Then I guess we'll have to make good use of our time."

She caught the mischievous look on his face. "In an hour? I was with you last night, remember? There won't be time to swim and—"

"Get frisky al fresco?"

She tossed her had back and laughed. "You're a nut."

He shrugged.

"I don't get it though. You like a good laugh, you obviously enjoy joking around, but you glare at your family if they cut up too much. Why don't you ever lighten up around them?"

Roark shrugged again. "I do sometimes, but when we're working, we're working. Joking is for later."

"But they're your family and aren't you always working? No one is going to judge you for joking around with them."

"I know, but . . . it's complicated."

"Must be. Since you think Trevor's irresponsible for taking a sabbatical in Peru, yet you're blowing off work, midday, to participate in an arguably illegal activity?"

"Kind of sounds like you're judging me," he quipped.

And maybe she was, but she didn't look down on him for being serious. She merely liked seeing the happy, freer side of him as well. She bet his family would too.

"Okay, first of all, Trevor took off to Peru months ago, with no indication of when he'll be back, *if* he'll be back, why he was going, or where else he's going. We haven't heard a word from him. He could be dead on the side of the road, and what can I do to help him way over here? Not a damn thing."

She glanced over. "Who says you have to help him?"

"You're kidding, right? With Trev, he'll need someone to bail him out of whatever he gets into, and who else is there?"

Roark sounded like a mother hen. His agitation about Trevor was from worry. He cared about his youngest brother and didn't like that he was off somewhere outside of Roark's reach.

She couldn't imagine having anyone worry about her like that. Her mother never worried about her when she was kid; forget fussing over her well-being as an adult. She'd showed Madison the door at eighteen and that was it from mommy dearest.

"Plus, there was no purpose to Trevor's trip." Roark lifted his hand and let it flop back down on the headrest. "He went for the hell of going. Our little day trip here will take all of a couple of hours and I know the purpose. I have a goal. That makes it a whole different ball game."

"You have a goal?"

"Yes, I do."

"And that is?"

He tapped his fingers on the driver seat. "I told you last night. Seducing you. I thought that part was self-explanatory."

She chewed on her smile. "That's what this is?"

He lifted his hand toward the road. "These are my keen skills of seduction. Take you off somewhere secluded and we both get naked. The chance of sex increases exponentially. Are you not swooning already?"

Her laughter filled the truck's cab. "Oh, I'm mid-swoon right now."

"Take a left at this stop sign." Roark pointed ahead. "And yes, I'd be annoyed as all get-out if Devlin took off for the afternoon and didn't tell me where he was going, but the difference is, I get all my shit done. No matter what, I do my job. Dev? Eh. It depends."

Madison flicked the turn signal and slowed to a stop. She'd told herself she wasn't going to say anything. To say something meant learning even more about Roark and who he was. Learning more about him would lead to liking him even more. But noticing a thing and not stating her opinion on the thing was not her style. "Then you're aware you're pretty tough on your siblings?"

Roark worked his jaw and pointed left. She took the turn but waited silently for the next mile or so. He could try to dodge her observation, but try was all he'd do. She'd sit quietly if that's what it took for him to answer.

"I'm aware," he finally said into the silence.

She kept her mouth shut, having learned long ago that if you wanted people to tell you something, the best thing you could do was shut up.

He sighed and shifted in his seat. "I guess old habits are hard to break. I don't know. Veer right up here."

"Old habits?"

"I'm their big brother." He said it as if that fact, in and of itself, explained him entirely. "I'm the oldest, by a good few years, so I've always been in charge of my brothers and sister."

"You're not that much older. You make it sound like you were an adult when they were born."

He propped his other arm along the passenger door and looked out the side window. "I was changing Trevor's diapers when I was five, teaching Dev how to dress, fix his own snacks and not wet the bed. Mom and Dad were busy. Doing other stuff. They couldn't manage it all. Couldn't do much, really, so I helped out with the usual stuff."

What he did was more than the usual stuff. At five, he was a kid himself. Helping out occasionally at dinner or bedtime was one thing, but it sounded like Roark took on a lot more than that.

"I'd guessed you were always the leader in the family, but at least you have one."

He shifted in his seat to face her.

She glanced over, and the intensity of his gaze made her face warm. A flash of heat streaked down her neck. She knew what he was going to ask before he even asked it, but she couldn't stop it. All of her silent hoping and cursing couldn't turn back the direction of this conversation.

"What about your family?" Roark asked.

Damn good question. She'd asked herself that about a million times. She tightened her hold on the wheel, staring at the road so hard it blurred. She'd told him before that she didn't have any siblings. As for the rest . . .

"Turn to the left here and follow the road until it ends."

"Sounds ominous." She tried to smile and change the subject.

"Not as ominous as you not answering the question."

"No family. It's just me." She could feel his grimace without looking over.

"I'm sorry. Did they pass?"

It'd be so much easier to accept if they had. Madison laughed, the sound icy even to her ears, but thoughts of her parents turned her cold. "Hardly. I'm sure they're both alive wherever they are."

He made a noise, contemplating what she'd said. "So were you orphaned or . . . put up for adoption?"

"I wish." She pinched her lips together to keep her mouth from crumpling. "Look. I don't want to talk about it."

"Okay." Roark was silent as they bumped down the road. "But it sounds like maybe you should."

"There's nothing to talk about." She spat out the words. "My dad took off and never looked back. My mom let me live with her until I was eighteen, and that was that. End of story."

But ten years later, she still didn't understand why no one wanted her, and it still hurt like hell.

"*Let* you live with her?"

"I said I don't want to talk about them." She bit off the words, right as she hit a nasty dip in the road at full speed, bouncing both of them around like basketballs.

"Okay, okay. We don't have to talk about them."

Madison clenched her teeth.

"But I'm here if you ever want to," he said. His voice was so soothing, so understanding and accepting—and something in her snapped.

No. She was not going to spill her guts for him to soothe and accept her, because no matter how good it might feel to let him in, at the end of it all, he wouldn't be around. People never stuck around.

Roark would always be *here*. Not with her if she wanted to talk about it two weeks from now. Not months from now, when she woke up from the same old nightmare of being lost and alone. She would always be alone and that had become just fine with her.

Rather than say anything, she put her foot down on the gas pedal. The road was half washed out, but Roark's truck was a four-by-four and could take it.

They bounced down another half a mile, Roark muttering next to her until one particularly hard knock worked him up.

"Seriously. I'm not interested in wrecking today. The road ends up here, by the way. I know how you like fair warning before you get to a dead end. Son of a—"

Madison jerked the wheel, skidding the truck to a stop. She hopped out of the truck before Roark could fuss, and started tromping toward the lake, about a hundred yards off the road.

"What the hell was that about?" Roark shouted, his words following her through the grass and copse of trees.

"Hey. Hey!" He jogged to catch up to her. "Where are you going?"

She flung her arm out toward the lake. "This is our destination, isn't it?"

"Yes. This is the secluded side of the lake."

"Then that is where I'm going."

His sigh was full of gruff frustration, and she didn't blame him. She was a frustrating person to know. Ask any of the people who'd known and left her.

"What was all that stunt-car driving? Do you seriously think that's going make me *less* curious about what's going on with you?"

"I don't want to talk about it."

"Okay," he said, the sarcasm so thick, Wright could've used it for frosting.

A shrill noise rose from her throat and she couldn't stop it. The Indian-summer sun beat down on them, making it feel like an August day in September. She hadn't even reached the water when she started stripping off clothing.

"I . . ." Roark turned back to watch the trail of shirt and shoes and bra she left behind. "Okay." He slung his duffel down once they got to a clearing at the water's edge. An old campfire site sat surrounded by rocks, the ashes from a fire not too long ago.

Roark had stopped talking and tugged his T-shirt up over his head.

Madison shucked off her pants along with her panties. She tossed her earrings on top of the pile. She knew, if nothing else, nudity always worked if you wanted a man to shut up.

Hopping on one foot, Roark pulled off one shoe and then the other. She was way ahead of him—completely naked, arms crossed, tapping her foot as she waited. When he looked up for the third time as he pulled his pants off, she snapped, "Let's go. This was your idea. Quit dawdling."

"I'm not dawdling," he snapped back. "I'm enjoying the view. You're stunning, even when you're mad as hell. Maybe more so, which is probably a messed-up thing to say, but I don't care."

"Thank you," she huffed.

"You're welcome." Roark flung his pants and boxers down on the ground like he was trying to break a plate.

She turned her back on him and went toward the tiny sandy area that might constitute a five-foot beach.

"You can't wade in," Roark called out. "You'll never make it. You've got to jump off the little fishing dock over here."

"Wonderful." She stomped over to the dock and reached the end of it before she realized she was alone. Roark was still in the clearing, messing around with his pack. "You're dawdling again," she yelled.

"Gimme a damn minute!" he shouted back, then continued to mutter something lost to the breeze.

She shivered as it blew, but she was so fired up it'd take a lot more than a little cool air to chill her out. Taking her anger out on Roark wasn't fair, she knew that, but thinking of her shitty excuse for a family did this to her. Getting to know the wonderful people surrounding Roark, the tight family and thoughtful friends, didn't help matters. Once again, she was small and helpless, worthless and resentful. Her past shouldn't have this effect on her. Not anymore. For years she'd been angry, at them, at the world, but she was over that. She'd moved on and her past didn't matter.

But being around Roark and his family meant seeing their affection, regardless of how they picked at one another. She'd witnessed Roark's concern for them and it brought the bitterness of jealousy along with the pain of loss.

She had no one, and something about the way Roark asked, so careful and caring, wanting to know more about her, she wondered if she should tell him why.

No.

It didn't matter. In less than two weeks she'd be gone. He didn't need to know all about her. Sure as hell didn't need to know about her family. No one did. She wasn't that girl anymore and she never would be.

"Okay. Ready." Roark stepped onto the dock, headed toward her. Even in her anger-fueled haze, she recognized a hell of a sight when she saw one.

Maybe because she was angry, and had pissed him off a good bit too, Roark stalked along the dock. His cock lay heavy between his thick thighs, his long strides showing off the rise and fall of every muscle, the broad shoulders blocking out the clearing behind him.

"We'll go on the count of three. On your mark." Roark grabbed her hand and held it.

She flinched, tempted to yank away. How could he bicker with her one second and want to hold her hand the next? This was when the yelling should begin, tempers becoming more venomous by the minute until everything got ugly. That's how things worked where she came from.

But Roark's hand was warm, his touch solid, and when he looked over at her, his gray-blue eyes weren't stormy. They flashed, but not with anger.

Madison swallowed down the flash of panic and opened her mouth.

"One . . . ?" he offered helpfully.

She blinked, knowing she either had to jump in right now or end up scream-crying about her history. "One . . . two . . . three!"

The water hit her like a wall. A big, cold, wet wall. She broke the surface, cursing like a sailor, and realizing this was *exactly* what she needed to snap out of the past.

"Jeeeeeeeeeeeeesus that's cold!" Roark yelled beside her, treading water.

Once she was done cursing at the lake, she turned to Roark. "We're both friggin' nuts. I hope you know that."

His head tossed back, he was laughing so hard he could barely stay afloat, let alone respond.

She fought not to laugh at how ridiculous he looked, almost drowning because he found this moment that funny. So she splashed him. "This was a stupid idea."

"I swear, the wrath is rising off of you like steam. This idea was genius."

Chapter 18

"Are you sure you want to start a splash war?" Roark wiped his eyes from the sheet of cold water she'd sent his way.

"No! You're just *so* proud of yourself." She splashed him again, and swam toward the dock.

He swam after her. "Are you cooled off now?"

"Yes. But as you might recall, I wasn't fired up until *after* you planned this little adventure. Can we get out now?"

He smiled at the way her wet hair clung to her face, her mascara a big black smear under her eyes. This version of Madison, unkempt and a little imperfect, was captivating in its rarity.

"Yeah, we can get out now. You did your first polar plunge. Of sorts. High five."

She eyed him suspiciously before slapping her hand against his. They both reached the dock's ladder and held on.

"There was no 'of sorts' about it," she insisted. "I legitimately plunged. Fair and square." She splashed him one last time before climbing out.

He wiped his eyes and caught a great view before following her out. "Nah, a legitimate polar plunge is anytime from November to March."

They both hurried down the dock to the blanket he'd laid out, the stack of towels and extra blankets sitting on it.

"November? Do people want to die of hypothermia?"

"There are places off the coast of Canada where they ocean plunge in the dead of winter. It's all about warming up after. Hence..." He held his arm out toward the extra blankets and the little fire, already burning.

"You brought all this?" Madison wrapped one of the huge towels around her, using another to dry her hair.

"It sure wasn't the skinny-dipping fairy. I had the stuff in my duffel."

"That's why you were dawdling."

"Yes. While you were riding my ass, I was making sure our warm-up plan was in place."

She fixed the towel over her hair, the other one around her, and grabbed a blanket. "And now I feel horrible for nagging you."

"Eh. I'll let you make it up to me."

Madison shared a smile with him as she sat on the blanket. Roark scrubbed at his hair, one towel wrapped around his waist, the other covering his shoulders. He reached inside the olive duffel bag and pulled out a bundle of firewood, laying the pieces of log over the fire, along with more newspaper for kindling.

"I brought plenty of blankets. You can go ahead and get under them," he said.

He poked at the fire with a stick until the logs were set up the way he wanted. Once the fire reached a good roar, he crawled onto the quilt and sat beside her, pulling Madison and the pile of blankets closer. She shivered a moment, huddling in, waiting for the fire and their body heat to warm them up.

"You think you're pretty smooth with these moves, huh?" She leaned her head against his shoulder. "Finally all toasty warm, yet naked under a bunch of blankets."

"I don't know if 'smooth' is a word that'd ever be used to describe me. Transparent in my ulterior motives, maybe?" He drew her closer, leaning his head on hers as they watched the fire grow.

He didn't know how long they sat there like that, but it was long enough for the fire to lull him into a hypnotic calm, making him brave enough to broach the subject again. "Do you not talk about your parents because that makes life easier? Pretend the past doesn't exist so then maybe it won't?"

Her sigh was still heavy, but it held less edge than before. "You're not going to let this go, are you?"

"You didn't let me off the hook about me and Dev. And I'm not really known for letting things go. Sorry."

She shifted against him. "I'll say this. I want to talk about my parents about as much as you want to talk about your relationship with Devlin and Trevor."

"That bad, huh?"

"Worse."

He nodded, rubbing his jaw against her hair but not pressing her for more.

Maybe she felt comfortable because of the campfire, or maybe she was secure being so physically close, surrounded by a cocoon of blankets. He didn't know why, but for some reason, Madison finally opened up, and her story fell out.

"My father left right when I hit an age when I *really* needed him, and he never looked back. I think it finally got to be too much for him, on top of my mother being . . . well, she wasn't maternal to me or faithful to him. But he was all I had and . . . he was gone."

Roark nodded, afraid to speak and stop her from sharing.

"Or maybe he figured I didn't need him anymore. Like I was old enough to get by and he could get the hell out of a bad marriage. I don't know. And I don't know why I'm even telling you that much."

Roark stared at the lake in front of them, the glassy surface looking serene and perfect, but cold underneath.

"So you've basically taken care of yourself since he left?"

Madison nodded, her head shifting beneath his chin. She wasn't going to do any more talking about herself. She didn't come right out and say as much, but he knew. If he wanted to fill in the blanks, he'd better start guessing.

"Were you completely alone after he left?"

Her weight against him grew somehow heavier, but all the more welcome. "I wasn't out on the streets or anything. Mom kept a roof over our heads, but . . . it wasn't because of me. We moved around, depending on who she was dating at the time. I was just in the way, but I suppose I was lucky. None of them ever laid a hand on me. My mom or her boyfriends."

Something inside him roared at what she said. Not just the truth of her words, but that she said them with such composure. He wanted to attack the injustice of what she'd gone through, fix the wrong that was her youth. But she held no more rage against her past, just wearied acceptance. It made him want to fight for her.

"I bet you got a job before you were even legal," he said, trying to fill in the blanks, knowing she wouldn't.

Madison hummed an affirmative.

The differences in their pasts, but the harsh similarities, curled a knot of pain in Roark's chest. He thought of his own parents. They never abandoned him and his siblings, but for as much as they were around, they had completely checked out of providing any sort of nurturing or emotional support.

They made sure the Bradley kids had a roof over their heads and food in their mouths, but Honeywilde's roof offered more stability than his parents'. They had nice rooms growing up, but if they wanted someone to hug them and tuck them in at night, they'd better do that for each other. If they wanted peace away from the battleground of their parents' marriage, they knew to stay away from them.

Madison, as distant as she could be, had given him a window into her life. The least he could do was open the door to his. If it was too much for her, he had no doubt she'd let him know.

"My parents were around for our childhood, and stayed married until I was in college. Though . . . I don't think they should've. To say their marriage was rocky . . ." He shook his head at the memories. "Gross understatement. I'm pretty sure they resented the hell out of each other by the end, but they stuck it out."

Madison eased away from him, turning to look him in the eyes.

"I can't say we were better off that they did. They were around, but miserable. And they weren't there for us. If that makes sense. I was the one nagging everyone to do their homework, brush their teeth, go to bed at night. My parents stayed up working and arguing. Mostly arguing."

"Is that why the inn didn't do well for so long?" she asked.

He nodded, swallowing hard. "It started then, all the way up to when they split. My father finally gave up and left Honeywilde to us kids. Said it was what his dad would've wanted. Regardless, it was the wisest business move he ever made."

She leaned against him once more.

His childhood was dysfunctional, his family life tumultuous, but he'd always had his brothers and sister. Even when things were at their worst, he knew he had Dev, Trevor, and Sophie to take care of. He had a purpose, people who needed him and loved him. Madison had been all alone. She had no one.

"I'm sorry." His words were muffled into her hair.

She sat up again, pulling the towel off her head and looking a little affronted. "What are *you* apologizing for? You weren't the one who was a crap parent. Besides, it taught me how to be independent.

I wouldn't be who I am today if I hadn't realized I had to take care of myself because no one else would."

"But you should've had someone to rely on."

She shifted farther away, her green eyes seeing way too much. "Oh yeah? Who did you have to rely on? I don't mean take care of; I mean who took care of you?"

He had to laugh, because even without him saying it, Madison knew they weren't so different. "Back then? The inn staff, occasionally. Sometimes Sophie, maybe even Devlin. On a good day, Mom was up for dealing with the inn and taking care of us. She'd eat dinner with us and stuff. On a bad day . . ." He shrugged. "All she could manage was keeping herself together. Never mind four kids."

"Then why have four kids?" Madison clamped a hand over her mouth. "Sorry . . . I know that's harsh, but seriously."

He'd wondered the same thing himself, many times. He was thankful for his big family, but he'd never understood why his folks thought having more kids would help. "I have no idea. I'm glad there are four of us now though. I can rely on Dev when he's really motivated. When Trevor was here, he was our outdoor rec guy, and I can always count on Soph. She keeps me on track, and when we start wanting to kill each other, she stops us. She's little, but she can be scary."

"She's definitely a paradox. And she looks nothing like the rest of you."

He leaned away to see if she was joking. She wasn't. "Sophie isn't my biological sister. She's adopted."

Madison blinked at him. "Oh."

"I'm sorry, I assumed you knew. Everyone in town knows our story; I forgot you might not."

"That explains the difference."

"She jokes and says she is literally the redheaded stepchild."

Madison smiled, but shook her head. "Then I *really* don't get your parents. If three boys was too much, why adopt another child?"

Roark took a deep breath, instantly back to being seven years old, when this tiny, fiery four-year-old girl came to live with him. Shame weighed on him, remembering his first, entirely selfish reaction.

Someone else I have to take care of.

"I don't think they had much of a choice; guilt being their overwhelming motivator. My folks were Sophie's godparents, our moms were best friends. When her parents died, my parents didn't want her going into a home or to live with an elderly aunt. They'd talked about being guardians for each other's kids, so . . ." He shrugged.

Why anyone would want Roark's parents to be the back-up parents for their kids was beyond him, but it'd made Sophie family, and that much had always felt right—once he'd gotten past that initial resentment.

"I remember the day she came to live with us. She was so small and scared; I thought she'd drown in a family as big as ours."

"I can't imagine her scared of anything."

"It took some time, but she came into her own. I never had to worry about her the way I did my brothers."

"But I bet you still did." She gave him a knowing look.

He shrugged it off. "Nine times out of ten, if I had to corral my brothers into doing their homework or coming inside to eat, she was right by me, fussing twice as loud, even if she was guilty right along with them. I think she liked bossing them around."

"I'm sure she did." Madison laid her hand on his leg and shifted closer to lean against him again.

Her hair was still damp, but the roaring fire and their nest of blankets kept them warm. He didn't care how late he'd have to work tonight to make up for the time spent here. The extra hours were worth it for the small window into Madison's world.

"Sometimes, back then, I wanted to be an only child," he said. "Even prayed to be alone for a day or two, but I've never been alone. I was certainly never alone like you were. That wasn't fair to you."

She turned the topic right back on him. "Wasn't exactly fair on you to have to raise three kids at the ripe old age of prepubescence."

"Eh. I survived. Anyone else would've done the same."

She shifted her weight against him, pinning him with a flash of her green eyes. "No. Not anyone."

"Yeah, but—"

"No. You didn't have to take care of them, pretty much raise them, when you're only a few years their senior, but you did. It's such a . . . *you* thing to do. Taking responsibility, getting stuff done, looking out for the people you care about. Trust me—that is not something just anyone does. It's what *you* do."

Madison wasn't going to come right out and say she respected or admired him, or anything that telling and bordering on the emotional. But she didn't have to. It was there in her unwavering stare, the vehemence in her voice.

Roark wanted to kiss her for it.

So that's exactly what he did.

Chapter 19

Warmly and softly, he kissed her. He brushed his lips over hers, less demanding than last night, coaxing her open until he deepened the kiss. A flick of his tongue, and Madison let him in, pulling him down on top of her.

"I make a very good blanket," he teased.

She laughed, covering her mouth.

"Don't cover up your laugh," he said, moving down to kiss her neck, her collarbone. "I love your laugh."

She urged him into another kiss, afraid of what she might say. He "loved" her laugh; he "loved" her hair when it was a mess. He tossed that word around so comfortably. A word she never heard, and *never* used.

She kissed him deeper, needing the urgency instead of sweetness. If he kept kissing her softly, touching her as though she were precious—if he kept being the person that he was—then she would truly break.

Roark had flaws, the same as anyone else, but his flaws helped him understand her. Perfectly. And it was too much.

"I need you," she said, wanting to move things along.

"I need you too." He went back to kissing her neck until he got to that tender spot that she liked so much, right at her collarbone. He laved over it with his tongue.

"No. I mean . . . right now."

"Okay." He breathed the words against her skin. "But what's the rush? You cold?"

She was far from cold. She was a growing fire, and it was because of him. Like the embers beside them, she was dancing flame, with the same risk of burning everything in sight.

He slid his hands up and down her sides, warming her with his touch. Her nipples tightened hard and he cupped her breasts, thumbing one while flicking his tongue over the other. She jerked against him, clutching his arms with both hands.

"Roark." She sighed.

"Okay . . . okay." He moved away and one of the blankets fell away from him, so he wrapped it tighter around her upper half and sat up.

"Where are you going? You're going to get cold."

He glanced at the fire. "Doubtful. I run hot anyway."

She noticed.

"Besides, I'm not going anywhere." He put hands under the backs of her knees and tugged until her legs were on either side of him.

She formed a small, silent, "Oh," with her mouth.

"I don't think I'll be cold," he said, settling between her thighs.

He concentrated his attention on her with the same focus and enthusiasm as last night. Touching and licking, teasing and coaxing at the bundle of nerves until she went from being a woman in control to a babbling, quivering woman in need.

Roark was relentless, even as her body tensed, her legs squeezing at his shoulders. All he did was hum happily—or smugly, who really cared?—and she pressed into his mouth, gripping at his hair. She rocked with each flick of his tongue, all thoughts of rushing forgotten.

"More."

He gave her more and more until she arched her back and . . .

"Oh. Holy . . . yes!" she cried out, pulling at his hair as the orgasm hit her. Writhing against him, she made a noise in her throat that shocked her. Roark wrapped his arms under her legs and held on, sucking gently at her cleft until she made it again.

"Damn. . . . it." Her legs went loose and numb as she slumped on the blanket, the shivers running through her again.

He kissed the inside of each thigh again, then her stomach, working his way back up and wriggling in to get under the edge of the blanket. He settled over her, but Madison kept her eyes closed, a smile on her face.

"I'm definitely not cold," she said after a moment.

"Me neither."

She hooked a leg over his, moving so that his erection nestled right into her hip. "You came prepared?"

"I'm always prepared." He reached out of the pile of blankets and made the quickest grab and tear of foil of anybody, ever.

"Let me put it on," she said, taking the condom from him as he settled back between her legs.

She reached down, stroking the length of him, running her fingers over his sac until he gave an involuntary jerk, his eyes rolling shut.

She rolled the condom on, watching his face the entire time. She stroked him again before lying back.

Roark followed her movement, leaning forward, the blanket falling away. He was built like the perfect outdoorsman.

He held Madison's hip, still touching her, still caressing her.

It had to be a little chilly for him, partially out of the blankets, but he didn't rush. Each time he'd gone about having sex like he was on a mission to make her one big trembling mess.

He succeeded each time.

And he wasn't turned off by a woman who liked to take the lead in bed sometimes, but today, right now, she wanted him to take her.

Roark pushed himself inside of her, and she felt every inch.

With both hands on her hips, he lifted her up, tilting her pelvis. "Wrap your legs around me," he told her, and she did. He rolled his hips, thrusting into her, a steady look of concentration on his face.

She studied that look, committing it to memory. Now, whenever she caught a glimpse of him studying his notes on his phone, she'd think of this.

"You're beautiful," he said, reaching out to hold her hand and kissing her temple.

With him, she felt beautiful. She tucked her forehead into his shoulder, shivering despite the heat coursing through her body.

"Hey." Roark's breath tickled her ear. "You okay?"

She nodded, keeping her face hidden. She needed a second before she could look at him.

"You feel so good," he murmured.

He felt like everything she'd always wanted sex to be. Unhindered and hot and earthshaking. She didn't have to hold back, or worry about intimidating or scaring him away because she pounced on him in the forest or shoved him back onto a bed and took charge.

She had that with Roark, and having it was both wonderful—and terrifying.

Madison pushed the whisper of fear away, running her hands up Roark's forearms, the muscles taut from holding her. She didn't want to think about what this might mean. She only wanted to feel.

"Harder," she whispered to him. "I still want to feel you when I wake up tomorrow."

Her gaze locked with his, Roark's eyes dark and hungry. He thrust into her, steadily faster, working his jaw. They kept going, moving against one another until they were slick with the sheen of sweat.

He grabbed her left leg, hoisting it higher, changing the angle so that it shot sparks into her core. "I want to feel you too," he said. "So tomorrow . . . we can look at each other . . . and know."

With his words, her orgasm rushed toward her. Arching her back, she welcomed it. Know what? She wasn't sure, but her climax hit as though the campfire beside them had exploded and all around her were sparks and fire.

She eased down with Roark holding her. He tried to shift off of her, but she held on. Shivering, embracing him, not wanting to lose him just yet.

Eventually, she let him roll to the side to dispose of the condom before settling down with her, the blankets draped over his chest. He ran his hand over her hair, threading his fingers through the strands until he worked all of the tangles loose.

They lay that way for what might have been a few minutes or it could've been an hour. She didn't care, because she didn't want to leave. Finally, the fire began to dwindle.

"We didn't get to the s'mores," Roark said.

"You brought s'mores?"

"Can't have a campfire without them." His words were warm against her hair. "But we should probably head back."

"I know." But she didn't want to. Working with the Bradleys might be one of her easiest and most enjoyable jobs so far, but still . . . it was work. Real life. Escaping all of that with Roark satisfied a gaping need she didn't know she had.

"I'm glad we did this today," he said, his low voice and drawl vibrating his chest, making her want to curl up and purr. "Not just the sex either. I mean . . . hanging out, and talking."

Talking. Like when she'd opened up to him despite herself, despite her better judgment.

He eased up and reached for her underwear and pants, handing them to her. Then he grabbed his boxers and jeans and managed to wiggle into them while under the blanket. "Hang on."

He hurried from under the blankets to grab her shoes, top, and bra, which she'd strewn farther up the bank.

Madison dressed in silence, studying the man beside her.

"Thank you," she said, drawing his attention and then finding herself at a loss. Thank you for what? Not hating her? Not running away when she tried a burnout with his truck? For seeing who she really was, and still finding her beautiful? "For . . . you know . . . going to get my stuff."

Roark shrugged it off but gave her a smile like he knew what she really meant.

And anyway, what kind of guy was nice enough to dart out, half dressed, to get the clothes she'd flung everywhere while in a huff?

The same kind of guy who could run a family business while taking care of his family, and still have wild notions about going skinny-dipping in September.

Roark kept her guessing, yet he made perfect sense. She understood his need for order and control, for hard work and responsibility. She couldn't wrap her mind around how someone so disciplined could also be free and fun loving, but she was learning how good it felt to let go.

With Roark she wasn't just living, she was alive. For the first time in her life, she wanted something outside of work and her own drive to survive. She wanted more.

She wanted Roark.

The realization hit her like jumping into a cold lake. If she had on her running shoes right now, she'd be tempted to take off without him.

"You ready?" she rushed to ask, slipping on her shoes and standing up.

He stood up too, shaking out the blanket and packing stuff away. "Yeah."

She almost told Roark to go ahead and drive back, she'd run home.

No. Not home.

Honeywilde was not home, it was an inn, like every other inn or bed and breakfast or hotel she'd used before. The man who ran it was wonderful, but that was in the here and now. It meant nothing long-term. She was only projecting because she finally had someone's attention. Someone who was decent and kind, not some ass trying to take advantage.

In a week, the wedding would be over. She'd leave and start planning another event, the same as always.

This was not home.

Madison slipped on her shoes and led the way back toward the truck. She had to force herself not to run or rush, but act normally. Pretend like everything that just happened had no effect.

She'd told Roark about her past. Some of it anyway. About her childhood, about her parents. A story she hadn't shared with anyone since she was twenty, because she'd learned it hurt less to simply bury the hurt deep and pretend like life had always been fine.

She was fine. She was always fine.

Her lungs burned as though she'd run too far, too fast. She quickened her pace across the clearing, leaving Roark behind. If he noticed her sudden kick into high gear, he didn't say anything. She reached the truck and rushed to the passenger side, holding on to the handle, gripping it hard enough to turn her knuckles white.

Don't freak out, don't freak out. Do not freak out.

She'd only said a few words about her past. Sharing some of herself and knowing more about him should be okay. He still wasn't in any position to hurt her. She would leave Honeywilde when this wedding was over, and it wouldn't matter that he knew her or that she'd let him in momentarily.

In the end, she'd be the same as always.

"Hey," Roark called over the bed of the truck, throwing the bag of damp towels in. "You okay?"

Madison took a deep breath, brushing her hair off her face before she leaned over and met his gaze, with a painfully big smile. "Of course. I'm fine."

Chapter 20

The next morning, Roark sat at breakfast with his morning paper, his brother and sister eating entirely too fast for proper digestion, and Madison, across from him, pushing scrambled eggs around her plate like she was putting together a puzzle. She hadn't said more than a dozen words to him all morning, and those had been reserved.

Being around her, like this, was stepping back in time to when they first met, and he bet he knew why.

Their time together was running out. They had just under a week until the first guests arrived, then all of this would wrap up and it'd be back to their regularly scheduled lives. And yesterday they'd shared something. They'd had a moment of intimacy that went beyond sex, and it was amazing. Perfect.

He felt wonderful about it, but now Madison was shutting down on him. He couldn't ask her about specifics here, in front of everyone, but maybe yesterday had been too much for her.

Sophie slurped at her coffee so fast she started to cough.

"Okay. What's the matter with all of you?" He folded his paper and laid it aside. "All of our remaining guests are checking out today and we have four days to focus on nothing but the coming weekend. This is one morning we can actually sit and have breakfast and breathe, and you-all are acting like the train's about to pull out of the station *or* like it's run over your toe."

Sophie swallowed her bite of toast. "I'm having housekeeping and grounds help clear out some of the furniture and roll up rugs near the back of the great room, to open it up and make room for the dance floor. We'll leave the seating nearest the fireplace though."

"I have some thoughts about what could go where," he told her.

She patted his arm. "Of course you do."

"You have opinions on everything," Dev added. "Don't worry though, I'll incorporate the 'Great Room According to Roark' in my decisions."

"Don't be a smart-ass," he told his brother.

Madison cleared her throat. "Brenda is coming by today as well, to talk layout and where to put which flower arrangements." She kept her gaze on her eggs, studying them like they were one of life's great mysteries.

"And I'm going to help by giving them my two cents." Dev sipped his coffee.

Sophie perked up. "You're using Brenda for flowers? I didn't know that. That's awesome."

"Roark said she was the best." Madison quickly glanced up at him.

"Oh, she is, and she loves the Bradley boys."

"I'm pretty sure you're her favorite though." Devlin stole the last triangle of toast.

"Wait until you see this list of arrangements," Roark told them. "Madison may make it on her favorites list ahead of all of us. There are at least ten of those big . . ." He glanced at Madison for help, but she'd moved on to fiddling with the handle of her coffee cup. "What are those things called?"

"Centerpieces?" She quirked a brow at him.

"No, the large arrangements, that 'anchor the room,' as you call it."

"Features."

"Yes, features, plus a list of centerpieces and bouquets that's longer than Brenda is tall."

Devlin leaned back in his seat and looked at Madison. "We need to meet to discuss the trips I lined up to visit the winery and the shopping downtown. I was thinking too, maybe have Steve set up a little champagne bar for the day of arrival. Mimosas for the early people, straight up for the latecomers, sort of set the tone for the weekend."

A champagne bar was exactly the sort of frivolousness that normally sent Roark into a budgeting-induced tirade. He had to remind himself this was all being paid for, by the couple, and he was not in charge right now.

"I think that's a cool idea," Sophie answered first, immediately sneaking a look at Roark, waiting for his reaction. He glanced across the table to find Madison staring and waiting as well.

Her words came back to him. *You're pretty tough on your siblings.*

He knew he was. He'd always known. From the time Dev was learning to dress himself, through the disaster that were his high school and college years, yes, he was hard on his brother, because someone had to be.

Dev sipped his coffee, an edge sharpening in his gaze, as though he knew Roark was about to squash his fledgling idea to a pulp.

"Yeah, I think that'd be a nice welcoming gesture. Nothing too formal, but a little bubbly always brightens up the atmosphere and makes it festive."

Madison didn't exactly smile at his response; more of a flash in her eyes. Whether the flash was good or bad, he couldn't quite tell.

Roark picked up his coffee mug, the weight of three people staring at him making it hard to swallow. "What?"

Sophie was the first to speak. Naturally. "Are you feeling okay?"

"I'm great. Why?"

"I bet I know why." Beside him, Dev half mumbled, half coughed into his napkin so only Roark could hear.

Roark gave him a warning glare and Sophie leaned over to say, "Okay, that's more like it. For a minute I thought maybe I'd woken up in an alternate universe. Don't get me wrong, you two getting along is stellar, but you can't just spring it on me. I need time to adjust."

That got a mild smirk out of Madison. The most life she'd shown all morning.

"I'm going to go so I can meet my crew in a few minutes." Sophie slid her chair out, taking one last sip of coffee as she stood.

"I'll go up with you. Brush my teeth and stuff before Brenda gets here. See you in a few." Dev nodded to Madison before they left the restaurant.

Roark watched them go, both siblings still as aggravating as ever, but he was a little more thankful that he had them around. That he'd always had them around.

"The eggs no good?" he asked Madison, her plate still full of food. Even the biscuits and honey remained untouched.

"Not hungry."

"If you do get hungry later, let Wright know and he'll hook you up with something. Since everyone is checking out today, I think he's mostly cleaning and doing prep work for Thursday. Don't want you to get peckish."

"I'm fine." The words came out clipped, edgier.

"Okay. Just trying to look out for you."

"I need you to worry about making sure the rest of the inn is top-notch. I know Sophie has the great room and guest rooms covered and Dev is going to help me and Brenda with the layout of the floral arrangements. I want to make sure the inn has never run smoother."

He felt compelled to remind her he was as invested in this as she was. "I'm anxious about this event too, but it's going to be great. I'll check in with everyone today to make sure."

"I'm not anxious."

Sure she wasn't. "All right, then you're fine, but I admit I have some nervous energy, which always makes me the picture of diligence. Everything will be shipshape. I promise."

Madison put her silverware on her plate. "Great. That's all I ask. I'm going to go meet with our—I mean, the florist."

She couldn't have left the restaurant faster if her ass was on fire. Hightailing it into fifth gear, Madison was out the door and out of sight in seconds.

"Any more coffee?" the waitress asked him.

What he wanted to do was chase down Madison and ask her what the hell was the matter with her. He wasn't an amateur when it came to people giving him the cold shoulder. Something was up, and they might as well talk about it to get it out of the way.

He also knew if he pushed and prodded her, she'd shut down completely. Better to let some of the day go by, casually talk with her again later, and gauge her disposition.

But he'd find out what was going on, chilliness be damned.

After making his rounds to practically every single employee of Honeywilde, making sure they were all bolstered and buffered for the coming weekend, along with resolving a few issues and gripes, the day was half over.

After lunch, he found Madison, still talking with Brenda, and Dev standing a few steps away from them, arms flung wide in a gesture toward the stone fireplace.

"Are we discussing flowers or playing charades?"

"Hey, honey!" Brenda hugged him right away as Madison hung back.

"I'm trying to convince Madison and Brenda that something for the mantel might look nice. Evergreens or whatever would last the weekend. Liven it up a bit." Dev lowered his arms and looked at him, an expression on his face like he was just waiting for Roark to shoot him down.

"I think you're right. Something up there besides the clock and candlesticks would look nice."

A little crease appeared between Devlin's eyebrows as he blinked at him. "Seriously?"

"Yeah. Seriously. It draws attention to the fireplace too." He intentionally looked at Madison. "With our recently fixed and resealed hearth."

Her gaze barely brushed his.

His brother shook his head, looking a little shell-shocked. "Okay."

Brenda swatted at his arm. "We are going to have this place looking like a one-of-a-kind wonder. I can't wait to see it myself. I've got some flowers coming in that I have never used before. I'm so excited."

No one got a thrill out of flowers like Brenda. He tried to catch Madison's gaze again, to smile about her enthusiasm, or make some kind of basic eye contact.

He got nothing. Madison kept her focus on the mantel, tapping her pen against her lips in thought. Her aloofness could be written off as her just being in work mode, but Roark knew that wasn't the whole reason.

"Evergreens, and let's use some chrysanthemums of the same colors as in the features, to tie it all together," Madison said.

Brenda made a note in a little spiral notebook. "I have plenty. Not a problem."

"Then I think we're all set." Madison at least made eye contact with her, and got a hug in return.

"I will be here Thursday with some flowers for the arrivals, and then I will see y'all early Saturday with a van of flowers fit to marry off a princess." Brenda hugged Roark goodbye and did the same to Devlin with an added, "Behave" tacked onto the end.

They stood and watched her as she walked away.

Dev was the first to break the silence. "Well, I'm glad you liked the mantel idea and . . ." He looked back and forth between them. "I'm going to go find Wright and Sophie. Catch you guys later."

He all but ran away from them and the tense silence that hung in the air. Roark stared at Madison's profile. After a long moment, he cracked.

"That's it." Roark was suddenly in front of her, like he'd popped up from the floor. "What is going on with you? You've been acting weird ever since we got back from . . ." He looked around to make sure the great room was still empty. "Skinny-dipping."

She crossed her arms in front of her, but finally met his gaze. The tension showed in his eyes, and in the tight way he held himself. "How do you know I'm acting weird? You haven't known me long enough to know what weird looks like on me."

"*This* is what weird looks like on you." He moved one hand up and down as though presenting her to herself. "Normally you say exactly what's on your mind and today you've been sullen and quiet. There's obviously something wrong and I know it's not the sex."

She stared back at him, and all of his confidence and fortitude visibly crumbled.

"Oh shit. It's not the sex, is it?" He stepped closer. "Because I'm pretty sure both of us—"

Madison shook her head. "No, it's not the sex." She wasn't okay, but for him to think that the sex was anything less than phenomenal was just wrong. "The sex is great. Better than great."

"Then what is it?"

She looked away, out the window, wishing the long, rolling silhouette of the Smoky Mountains could give her the right words. Even better if the mountains would help her understand what was wrong with her.

Approaching the fireplace, she let out the breath she'd been holding and sank down to sit on the newly refurbished hearth. "I don't know."

Roark shook his head and sat down next her, looking determined yet so confused. "I'm trying to understand here, but you've got to give me something beyond *I don't know*."

She did know that she never let anyone get close to her, and yesterday she'd done exactly that. Not only was she getting too attached to Roark's company, she enjoyed his family, this place, all of it.

Devlin was a wandering soul, wrapped in a wild package. Anyone from the outside looking in could see he did half of what he did just to get under Roark's skin, the other half he did to gain his approval. Sophie's personality matched her spitfire appearance. The redhead stereotype was tired, yet couldn't be any truer in her case.

Never a moment of boredom with the Bradley clan, but she was still able to work and find solitude without ever feeling solitary. The problem wasn't that she didn't understand why she was freaking out. The problem was she shouldn't be freaking out at all.

Normal people didn't have sleepless nights and mounting anxiety just because they'd found someone they liked, and happened to enjoy their family too.

"Maybe you're more nervous about the wedding than you can admit?" Roark suggested. "Even to yourself?"

She wished it were that simple. A few nerves flitted around her brain, but that was the rush of her job. She thrived on the excitement level. "Sure. That's probably it."

He studied her before smoothing his hands down his thighs to settle on his knees. "Y'know, you lie about as well as you play a dumb blonde, but if you don't want to tell me what's wrong with you, just say that you don't want to talk to me. Don't be scared. I'm a big boy, I can take it."

Madison straightened at the challenge. "It's not that I don't want to talk to you. I do want to talk to you, but I don't like that I told you all that stuff yesterday. The stuff about me."

Roark's expression remained neutral. He was giving her silence in case she didn't want to say any more, but he was also waiting, his pupils wide with the hope she'd open up a little bit more.

"Dammit. And I hate that you can get to me."

"I'm not trying to get to . . ." He tilted his head to the side. "Okay, maybe I am."

She hit him with a loaded look. "I know! You sit there looking so patient and accepting and I just *blah*." She opened her mouth in imitation of spewing out all her feelings.

He leaned an elbow on his thigh, and angled forward so he could face her. So she'd have to look at him. "I'd say I'm sorry, but I'm not. Anything is better than you stonewalling me with 'I'm fine.' I'm sure you're aware, but you're kind of hard to get through to sometimes. I'm glad I can."

But why did he want to get through? What was the point? She didn't have anything to get through to.

"Do you want to tell me *why* you don't like that you told me about your folks?" he asked, his expression suddenly full of concern.

His attempt at pushing through didn't concern her as much as how well it worked. "It—It's that I . . . I don't talk about my mother, or my father, to anyone. The fact that I did, to you, freaks me out. A lot." She couldn't believe she was telling him that either.

"Okay."

"And . . . I know I've been sullen, but now you know why. Personal chitchat and sharing my past, that isn't my thing. It makes me uncomfortable." She took a deep breath and smoothed her hair over her chignon. "But we need to move on. We have a lot to do today and tomorrow. So let's go get it done."

She pushed herself off the stone hearth, but Roark still sat, his pale gaze piercing her with a look that went straight through. He didn't say anything; he didn't have to. That look said plenty. He didn't buy her moving-on speech, and he didn't look thrilled that opening up about personal details screwed with her head enough to make her shut down and then act like a manic workaholic.

Maybe now he'd understand that the effort of trying to get through to her wasn't worth it. She wasn't that great to be around and her head was a big mess. She was a freak; a highly functioning, successful freak. He might as well learn that now.

Roark stood, his gaze icy. "As long as you're *fine*, then I guess I worried for nothing." He turned and walked away from the fireplace, leaving her behind.

It stung, but she deserved it. Roark was better off walking away from her.

Everybody did, and she didn't know how to deal with anything else.

Chapter 21

He waited one more day before showing up at Madison's room. She'd spoken to him yesterday, a little, some of the casual camaraderie back between them, but she'd been *fine* all day yesterday too. She kept insisting she was so okay that he wanted to bang his head against the stone fireplace.

Things were not fine. They had less than three days until the wedding party arrived; that meant only five more days together. Madison would go back to the city, and Roark would get back to running a resort. Their time together would come to an end and there'd be no reason for them to see each other again unless they chose to. Nothing about that was okay, and Madison knew it, but hell would freeze over before she'd ever say as much.

If one of his siblings acted this bullheaded, he would've called them on it immediately. Problem was, he had called Madison out. She'd told him why she was acting odd, but he didn't like her logic. Or lack of it. Maybe she'd spoken the truth. Maybe opening up to him was all that bothered her and she really was *fine* that she'd be leaving in a few days. Possibly, Roark was the only one becoming invested in what they had—

Regardless, the fact remained that Madison was freezing him out. Withdrawing and shutting herself off. And he wasn't having it.

Pressuring someone like Madison or holding on too tight would only guarantee her hightailing it in the opposite direction. A heavy-handed approach wouldn't work, and if her inevitable exit from Honeywilde really didn't bother her, then all they had were a few days.

Days. The thought of it knotted his stomach. No way could she be satisfied with wrapping up this thing between them, within days. He damn sure wouldn't be. Their remaining time together had to count; he'd see to it. Then he'd see to somehow dragging it out a little longer.

If she didn't want to overshare or open up emotionally in the meantime, fine.

Damn, he hated that word.

A new plan was necessary. He wouldn't ask too many questions, prod too hard, or ask too much of her. He was capable of being smooth, somewhat, of hanging back and being the opposite of proactive. There were plenty of other things to talk about. They could chat about work or the weather . . . or work.

He knocked on her door, and the realization struck him that he'd never been in her room, or her in his. She'd been here for almost two weeks, but never once had they been in each other's room.

On the other hand, they weren't *a thing*, as she called it, and when you weren't a thing, you didn't stay over at each other's place. This wasn't even Madison's place. She had a room at Honeywilde. A temporary location while she planned an event that quickly approached and would be over faster than that.

Temporary.

The word ran through his mind again, and he let it. He mouthed the word because he needed the reminder. She would leave in a few days, without hesitation, and he'd have to let her. In the meantime, he needed to get his shit together and accept what she offered at face value.

Madison opened the door, already in her running gear and shoes. "Hi." She scanned him from the skull cap on his head to the Mizunos on his feet. "Great minds think alike?"

Keep it light and keep it simple, he reminded himself. Unimportant chitchat. Like trying not to scare off a damn deer.

"Figured the rest of the week will be hectic as hell. I need to get out before it starts, wondered if you might as well."

She smiled, her green eyes bright, but something else reflected in their shine.

"There's another trail, with a steeper incline, if you're willing to go up the mountain a little ways." And little chance of talking while running. The trail was a killer. "Hell of a view too."

Madison closed her door, sliding the room key into the tiny pocket of her running pants. "I could do some uphill. Is the view even better than the one from the veranda? Don't say yes, because I don't have time to move this ceremony."

"It's not that good and it is no place for a wedding. You'll see."

She followed him down the quiet hall of empty rooms. Downstairs, the smell of coffee drifted through the great room, the sound of laughter from the restaurant. It had to be Sophie and Wright because Dev was nowhere near up at this hour.

"You want coffee or anything?" Roark asked Madison.

"No, I had some in my room. Made it with the teeny tiny coffeepot."

"We're lucky we even have those. The red tape it took to get four-cup coffeepots in a room was unbelievable."

They walked outside, the crisp fall morning making him come alive more than any caffeine ever could. Roark took a deep breath in, the faint scent of wood smoke overlaid by the smell of dry leaves and grass filling his senses.

"That is such a great smell," Madison said beside him.

"Addictive."

They walked and stretched on their way down the path and driveway, starting out barely jogging as they headed up the mountain. After a couple of bends, it steepened, the burn already starting in the backs of his legs. The trail cut off to the right and he pointed to it, up ahead.

"You lead the way," Madison panted out.

"You sure? You're not going to race me this time?"

She shook her head. "Might be some spiderwebs. You get to go first. Take them all down with your face."

He managed to breathe out a laugh and turned onto the path. "Should've known there was a catch."

"Just getting you back for the spider crack last time we ran."

"That was over a week ago," he joked, but inside he fist pumped that she'd lightened up enough to tease him.

As they made their way to the path, she commented on the oncoming fall color, her tone lighter than yesterday, her face less stony and tight. If he could get her to relax again and joke with him, he'd take her running every day, and use his face to take down every spiderweb he could find.

Madison jogged up beside him. "How many did you hit?"

"Two or three webs, no spiders. That I know of. But thanks for asking."

This time she didn't push to run past him, so he didn't ramp up his speed. Instead they matched their pace, both of them falling into a rhythm, not saying a word for miles.

Once they neared the vista, Roark pointed up ahead. "We got about another quarter mile, if you want to slow down."

Madison slowed her pace and he did the same, until they were down to a swift walk, panting for air.

"Hey," she called for his attention. "Thanks for . . ." She gestured toward the path.

"For what?"

"Inviting me to run with you."

"Why wouldn't I?" His words came out in short puffs.

She flung her hands up. "Because I was a moody pain in the ass the last couple of days?"

"You were?" He turned to her, his eyes wide.

"I was." She bumped her arm against him.

"You were our pita guest yesterday."

She rolled her eyes but didn't argue.

Regardless, she ought to know he enjoyed spending time with her, whether they were planning a wedding or jogging or sleeping together, or even dealing with her poor mood. What was he going to do, *not* run with her? Not spend time with her? Ignore the issue so they couldn't enjoy what little time was left?

Not an option.

They followed the path around a few bends, jumping the occasional hole or thick root.

Madison took a quick breath in, but then stopped. A moment later she flung her hand out as though tossing away a thought. "It's just that . . . a lot of people find me . . . difficult. This isn't news to me. I'm not the sort of person who relaxes well. Doesn't make me much fun to hang out with."

Roark looked over at her, watching until she glanced back at him. "You call this relaxing?"

"You know what I mean. I'm not great at hanging out or whatever. I work, I talk about work, and I make plans, for work. That's what I'm good at. It gets beyond that and I . . . I don't know."

But she was talking to him again, and about more than work. Whether she realized it or not, she was sharing.

"You're also great at sex. Don't sell yourself short there."

She laughed, shoving at his shoulder, making him step out wide. "True. Sex I'm pretty great at too. But this is . . . This is okay."

Which meant they should stick with this type of activity. Running and small talk, sex and work. That was all on the table. Intimate reveals about her past while cuddled naked together under some quilts: too much for her to handle.

Too bad the time with her by the campfire was also one of the best moments of his life. A moment when he'd shared a part of himself he never spoke about. Roark didn't off-load on people, but he'd opened up to Madison. She'd opened up to him about her past. Something he couldn't heal, but a similarity they shared. Neither of them was used to relying on someone else, laying their weaknesses and hurts bare, but they had.

They'd been honest and vulnerable, and the moment connected them like the threads of those quilts. He was stronger as a result, but it'd scared the shit out of her.

He slowed down, seeing the curve in the trail ahead, the way it swung wide, rock meeting dirt and opening up so hikers could see the valley below. "Up there. That's us."

Madison peered over at him. "We don't have to climb out on some rock or something, do we?"

"No. Come on. Have a little faith." Roark found the trail, overgrown by some evergreen branches. He held them back so Madison could follow.

"Why does it seem like you're always leading me out into perilous territory? Dead-end paths, secluded lakesides. It'd be like a horror movie if this place wasn't so freaking charming."

Roark stopped and Madison collided with his back.

"It's not a horror movie." He turned to her. "You'll see, and then you're going to feel very bad for saying that. All we have to do is pick our way through some trees and walk out on this rock, which is about a half mile wide, and you can see the valley below. It isn't dangerous, it's gorgeous."

He began walking again, with Madison jerking on the back of his shirt. "I specifically asked if I had to climb out on some rock and you said no."

"We're not climbing. We're walking."

They ducked under and around a few more tree branches until several feet in front of them, the rock widened up to a long, slightly sloping surface, perfect for sitting or lying down on at night and stargazing. During the day though, it provided a spot to enjoy the beautiful view of the valley and town below.

"Come see." Roark held on to her arm, helping her forward. "I want you to be in awe, so I can say I told you so."

Madison elbowed him with the arm he held, but her smile was worth it.

"You can see the steeple of the Lutheran church." He pointed to the left. "And a few of the buildings right outside of town. That's Stewart Farms. The post office."

Madison rocked up onto her toes, quietly taking in the panorama. Roark didn't let go of her arm. He slowly, and slyly, tucked it under, until she was holding his arm.

The longest minute went by and she didn't pull away, or speak.

"This is an incredible view," she finally said, looking up at him. "It's adorable. Have you ever come up here when it snows?"

He took a second to answer, first soaking up this small victory. "Yes, but not since I was a kid. The grown-up in me isn't interested in hiking uphill, over four miles, in a foot of snow."

"I bet it looks like a Christmas postcard though. A real Currier and Ives come to life."

Roark turned to her. He wasn't really shocked, but he knew an opening when he saw one. "What do you know about Currier and Ives?"

"Come on. I know picturesque romanticism. It's my job to know. One of these days, someone is going to want a winter-wonderland wedding, and *I* will have to be the queen of snow."

"I think I'd rather deal with horses than snow." He grimaced. "No, I *know* I'd rather deal with horses."

Madison walked farther out on the rock and he went with her. Their breath was barely visible in the early morning chill. She looked like a snow bunny, pale pink hat pulled down over her ears, blond braid trailing down to brush her shoulder, gray and pink running gear and shoes.

She was a snow bunny liable to bite him, but he liked that about her.

"It's so quiet up here," she said. "We aren't far from the inn and I can see the town, but it feels so secluded. Serene and . . ."

"Insulated."

"Yes." She glanced up at him. "Insulated."

"That's why they call it being nestled in the mountains. You might be thousands of feet above sea level, but you're surrounded by some of the oldest mountains on the planet. It's a pretty secure feeling, whether it's physical or psychological."

Her expression was incomprehensible, to the point he had to say something else or risk her shutting down on him again. "The leaves are starting to change too, but in a few weeks? Now *that* is a sight. Like a patchwork of golds and reds and orange, laid over the mountains."

"You love it here, don't you?" she asked, her gaze never wavering.

"Yeah. Of course."

"And you've never lived anywhere else? Never wanted to?"

He shrugged. "Why would I? Even when I went to college and grad school, I was right down the road at App State. The resort is here, my family. This." He spread his free arm out at the view before them. "Don't get me wrong, I love to travel and get away when I can, but nowhere else can compare to this."

She scuffed her running shoe along the rock, finally dropping her gaze. "And it's not all too much? With running Honeywilde and your family right there, all the time?"

He studied the top of her pink hat, wondering what his life must look like to her. He had a never ending list of responsibilities; so did she. But his was anchored to a single place.

"It's too much all the damn time. The resort is a huge responsibility. There are days I want to run higher into the mountains and hide, try my hand at being the reclusive mountain man Brenda teases me about, but . . ." He shrugged again. "I love it. Running Honeywilde takes effort, and can stress me out, but that doesn't mean I don't want it. When my grandfather was alive, I remember how he thrived on it. He was proud of the inn, but he worked hard. You've seen how I am; that's probably why I love it. I wouldn't know what to do if something was easy."

Madison glanced up again, no judgment, her gaze open as she took him in. "You're a lucky man, Roark Bradley."

He turned to her, moving his hands so he held her arms. "Believe me, I know."

"I'm not talking about m—"

Roark pressed his lips to hers, silencing what she was about to say. He pulled away after a second, making sure this wasn't something she'd object to.

Madison stepped closer, lifting her chin ever so slightly.

He kissed her again, her hands on his waist, then caressing his back. "I've missed you. Even though it's only been a couple of days."

She buried her face into his shoulder. "I'm sorry."

He cupped the side of her face, making her look at him. "I don't want to waste the next few days."

"Me either." Madison rubbed her cheek against his palm, then tilted her head so his hand slid down her neck.

He brushed his thumb over her pulse, a strong, thumping reminder that she was here with him now, and that's what mattered.

He kissed her again, dragging his tongue over her bottom lip until she leaned into him.

"We have to go back and do actual work today," she warned. "A lot of it."

"I know, but I have an idea."

"Uh-oh."

"Shhh. You love my ideas." Rather than stop kissing her, he moved over to her cheek, brushing his lips over the edge of her jaw and slender column of her neck, speaking against her skin. "When we clock out tonight. Meet me in the suite downstairs again. We can make up for lost time."

"That *is* a good idea."

He leaned away. "Told you."

Her eyes sparked with a challenge and a mischievous grin curled her lips again.

Damn, he'd missed that look on her. It'd only been two days, but he'd mourned the loss of it like it was water.

"I have an idea too," she said.

"Do tell."

"We're going to race back down the mountain and whoever wins gets to call the shots tonight."

"You're on," Roark said, as they both took off. But regardless of who came in first, he'd already won.

Chapter 22

She woke in her own bed the next morning, too sore for another run. That's what she got for racing Roark all the way back to the inn—she'd won, but only by a hair and she was pretty sure he threw the race—and spending the night with him downstairs, before sneaking back up in the wee hours.

Madison smiled, remembering the way he'd touched her, his hands on her waist, tilting her, lifting her, until the friction was just right and she felt like a starburst exploding across the night.

A shiver ran through her as she sat up, the sensations of the night before still fresh in her body. Just as well there'd be no running this day. She wouldn't make it a mile, *and* the wedding party arrived this afternoon.

They'd rushed to plan, preparing for days, and today they'd begin to execute. She and Roark needed their heads in the game.

Downstairs, a fire already crackled in the stone fireplace, but she couldn't find anyone. At this hour, Roark and Sophie were normally up, bustling around.

That's when Madison heard them: the buzz of many voices, all talking at once, and then total silence. She followed the odd rhythm of conversation to Roark's office. The door was pushed to, but not closed all the way. She eased it open in time for the clamor of conversation to stop once again, as everyone turned to stare at her.

Inside his office, Roark glowered from behind the desk, Sophie lurked near the window, and on the other side of the desk stood Devlin and a man she hadn't met. He was a few years younger, but with the same distinctive dark hair and piercing blue eyes of the other two Bradley boys.

It had to be Trevor.

Beau yipped in excitement, running over to her for a quick lick before circling the guy's legs, all but bouncing up and down.

Definitely Trevor.

Madison eased her hand up in greeting. She should back out of the room quickly and let everyone pretend her sudden appearance was only their imagination. If this was truly the prodigal son, returned from his adventures abroad, she shouldn't have any part of it.

Roark wasn't secretive about his feelings on the situation with Trevor. Add to that the events scheduled to kick off today and the sour looks currently marring everyone's faces, this was clearly not a cheerful reunion.

"Might as well come on in and join the party." The sarcasm dripped from Devlin's words as he waved her in. "I'm sure we can squeeze two or three more in here. No reason to miss out on all the fun—"

"Don't do that," Roark said, interrupting his brother. "Don't make light of this and don't try to drag her into it. It's got nothing to do with her." His voice was level, but the tone steely and strong.

"The hell it doesn't."

"It doesn't. Madison is at Honeywilde for business. She's not a part of our personal issues," Roark argued, shooting her an apologetic look. He knew how uncomfortable this would be for her.

"Oh, okay. Right," Devlin said, but his petulant tone meant Roark was the furthest thing from right.

"She doesn't need to be involved in our family drama." Roark tried another point of argument, this time with a little more volume behind it.

And he was right. Really, she didn't need to be in the middle of this. She wasn't big on drama and family wasn't her forte, but for some reason, Roark insisting she wanted nothing to do with them or their personal lives, made her skin prickle in defense.

As twisted as it was—and she knew it was really freaking twisted—she didn't want to be left out of whatever the Bradleys had going on. She knew who Trevor was, and because she knew how Roark felt about things with his brother, a part of her wanted to be here.

Hell if she could explain it, but rather than wanting to hide, she wanted to know what was going on.

Devlin jabbed his thumb over his shoulder toward her. "Her big wedding is the reason you're trying to kick our brother out."

"What?" Madison stepped fully into the office. "You don't have to—"

Roark shook his head. "Devlin is being overdramatic." He turned toward his middle brother, placing the tip of his finger on his desk blotter. "I am not kicking Trevor out. I'm saying, of all the times he could show back up, now isn't ideal. He took off without any consideration for us, he shows up here without a word of notice, and his return has thrown you all into an uproar. He can't treat this place like a hotel."

"It *is* a hotel." Devlin raised his voice. "We live in a hotel."

"Hey!" Sophie pointed at him. " No yelling. You know the rules."

"Thanks," Roark muttered off to the side.

"Don't thank me. I agree with Dev. I'm as ticked as anyone that Trev left and we haven't heard a peep from him, but this is our home. He's here, his room is unoccupied—hell, the whole floor he lives on is unoccupied. He stays."

Roark's gaze caught with Madison's. That floor had been a *little* occupied.

Trevor finally spoke up. "I'm right here. You guys keep talking about me like I'm not here, but I am. It's not a big deal. Seriously. I can crash with a friend till Monday. Keep the peace and all that."

"No. That's bullshit." Devlin turned around, looking at Madison.

What was she supposed to say? She knew what Trevor meant to Roark. What they all meant, but here was the lost baby brother, for the love of god. Roark bellyached about him, but the deep groove in his brow and the clench of his jaw meant he was doing this because, for some reason, he thought he had to.

If he thought it was best for his family and Honeywilde that Trevor not be here right now, he was wrong.

"Dev, it's okay. Not worth arguing over." Trevor shrugged, as casually as if he was deciding on what to order for dinner. "I have people I can visit for a few days. Whatever." He shrugged again, his gestures so much like Roark's.

More so than Devlin, Trevor looked like a younger Roark. A very tan, relaxed version of Roark, and even though he said *whatever*, the guy looked like someone had just kicked Beau. Madison had to speak up.

"It's not going to bother me or disrupt the wedding if he's here." She attempted a casual tone, even though it suddenly mattered very much that he stay and that Roark stop looking so miserable. "As long as it's not a distraction for all of you, I'm certainly not opposed to him coming home." At least Trevor had a home, so, by god, he ought to be back in it.

Every Bradley in the room turned to look at her. Madison arched an eyebrow, waiting.

"See?" Sophie opened her hand toward Madison. "Reasonable. Trevor could even be another set of hands for the weekend. We could use his help setting up chairs, and definitely in the kitchen."

Roark studied his sister. She looked at each of her brothers in turn. "And I'm sure we can all be grown-ups and deal with our drama later. Right?" The cutting edge in her gaze meant they all had better agree with her, and quickly.

"Of course we can." Roark crossed his arms. "It's not that. I don't want there to be *any* issues this weekend. Everything is set to go. Nothing, and no one, is allowed to screw it up."

Dev nodded, running a hand through his hair. Way too long on top to be considered professional, it flopped over as soon as he was done touching it, a strand falling in his face. "We get it, Roark. No trouble, no commotion."

"Good." Grabbing his phone, Roark stood and came from behind his desk, arms out in the international sign for *everyone get the hell out of my office*.

As everyone began to vacate the premises, Sophie moved close to Madison.

"Thank you," she said.

"For what?"

Sophie looked back and forth between Roark and Trevor, as Trevor stepped right into Roark's outstretched arms and hugged him.

Sophie nudged her. "I think you know why. It's nice not being the only peacekeeper around here."

But she wasn't a peacekeeper. She stared back at Sophie, unsure of how to take the compliment.

As Sophie walked away, Trevor squeezed Roark, and Madison couldn't look away from the expression on Roark's face.

Roark gripped his brother's shoulder. "You could've died in some damn jungle and how would we know?"

Trevor laughed, patting him on the back as he let go. "I wasn't going to die in a jungle."

He walked past Madison and gave her a grin, the width and shape of which was disarmingly similar to Roark's. "Sorry I didn't get to introduce myself, but I heard all about the famous event specialist extraordinaire."

"Go." Roark turned his brother toward the door with both hands on his shoulders. "Unpack and settle in before I change my mind."

But she'd noticed Roark had never actually said Trevor couldn't stay. He'd merely argued for reasons why the situation wouldn't be ideal, and then accepted that his staying was going to happen anyway. The Bradley family had had an entire debate and argument over what seemed to be a foregone conclusion, that of course Trevor was going to stay in his home.

Madison shook her head. Maybe someday she'd understand the way this family worked.

The thought froze the smile on her face.

There would be no someday. She hadn't freaking moved in with the Bradleys to live, she was here for a job. In a matter of days, she'd be gone. She couldn't keep trying to understand how the Bradleys operated, why Devlin was often so quietly unsettled, or how Sophie had mastered the art of saying about half a dozen things with a single look. No biscuits and honey every day, and no more Roark.

After Sunday there'd be no more of his steady presence and humor, his straightforward take on life that she completely understood. She would no longer get to stretch out beneath him or rise above him as they wrung climaxes from each other with the kind of dogged determination only they could appreciate.

She'd always known their arrangement was temporary, but the time frame suddenly felt too short. What if they could keep it temporary, but make it . . . temporarily longer?

"You okay?" Roark turned to her as his brother left the office.

"Yeah." She blinked. "Yeah, I'm okay. Just going over this afternoon in my head." All she could do was hope she was a marginally better liar than the other day, because she wasn't even in the same zip code as okay. She needed some time to come up with a different plan. If she suggested she come up some weekend, would that be too much like a commitment? Like long-distance dating?

She didn't do long distance. Hell, she didn't usually *do* anything.

He tapped at his phone, looking over his list. "Big day today. It's finally here."

Finally here. That meant no time for her to think, no days left for her to come up with a brilliant plan. Today she had to kick into full-time event supervision mode.

"Want to grab some coffee really quick?" Roark asked.

A nod was all she managed. No more sipping black coffee with Roark either, stealing his because it tasted better, and knowing he'd let her, because that's how he was.

She dragged her feet on the way to the coffee trolley. The wedding of her career was finally here, and all she wanted to do was put it off.

Chapter 23

The next day, a menagerie of people unlike any Roark had ever seen, strolled into the lobby of Honeywilde. He did his best not to so much as twitch an eyebrow.

The bride and groom, their band, and the wedding party totaled twelve all together, sporting everything from denim and leather, rivets and studs, and what looked like crushed red velvet, to a jacket of pink shag carpet. They had a lot more than their ears pierced, and hair that covered the spectrum from platinum to deep purple. One girl had streaks of what could only be described as cheetah print. It actually looked really good on her.

His mother would be having a fit if she still ran the place.

Roark smiled, delighted.

The bride and groom's band, Red Left Hand, enjoyed the contradiction of having fresh-faced, sweet-looking Whitney as lead vocalist, backed by a bunch of guys who looked like they'd done several stints in county.

Madison made all of the introductions and maintained such casual calm that any outsider would swear all of this was no big deal.

But Roark noticed the tightness around her eyes, the smile that he knew as her business smile. Her hair was smoothed back in the perfect low ponytail. Not a thing out of place.

"Roark, you've met Whitney Blake, the bride to be, and Jack Winter, the groom." Madison stepped aside so they could shake.

"Welcome to Honeywilde," he said, Sophie beside him, vibrating with excitement.

Jack tilted his chin and shook first. The black tattooed letters were more striking in person, curling over his knuckles, the sleeve of tattoos more intricate, traveling up his arm and disappearing beneath his rolled-up shirt sleeve.

Whitney shook Roark's hand next.

"Hey." Her accent came out Southern sweet and smooth, looking and sounding like someone's favorite granddaughter. She was the antithesis of Jack, yet when she looked at him and said, "We're thrilled we get to be here," she looked absolutely elated.

"We're glad to have you." He smiled, not only thinking about what this wedding meant for the couple, but how much it meant to Honeywilde and his family.

Sophie caught his gaze, giving him a threat-laden stare. She'd pop up from her spot like one of those suction-cup toys if he didn't introduce her soon.

Roark held his arm out toward his sister. "Allow me to introduce you to the people who run Honeywilde. We're all here to help you in any way."

Sophie's arm shot straight out to shake Whitney's hand.

Madison went on to introduce the staff to the band members, and Roark stepped aside. This was her event, after all.

Staff gathered the luggage from cars and took it to the appropriate rooms while the guests mingled and enjoyed champagne at the side bar Devlin had arranged. Madison stepped close to Roark's side, remaining quiet and watchful.

"Everyone looks pleased, all smiles so far," he said.

"You think?" She nibbled at the inside of her cheek.

"Absolutely. Look at them." The whole group looked like they were on vacation. Not a stress line among them.

"You did well. And Dev was right with his side bar suggestion." He kept his hand low, but opened it, palm facing out. She gave in and joined him in a surreptitious high five.

Eventually, the wedding party was shown to their rooms, where they'd find the lavish welcome baskets that Madison and Sophie had put together. Roark had seen the contents as Sophie topped them with apricot-colored bows. He'd asked her if he could have one too.

As soon as the great room was free of guests, Madison spun toward him and the rest of the staff gathered there. "We have exactly an hour and a half to have this area ready for a casual dinner of mixed grill, and the requisite relaxing evening."

Beside him, Trevor chuckled. "As long as it's requisite chilling out."

Roark nudged him with his elbow on his way to help everyone set up. Madison was in the zone, so everything was requisite. He dug that about her.

The list on his phone had four check marks as they covered everything discussed: tables, food, drinks, background guitar music. Check, check, check *and* check.

Madison fussed with a strand of her ponytail as they waited for the guests to reappear.

"Nervous?" Roark asked, moving to stand by her side.

She released the strand of hair. "No."

Their small party of early arrivals began to trickle down, sitting at the oversized round table set up in the great room.

Once the bride and groom were downstairs, everyone seated and stuffing their faces with barbecue and all the fixings, Roark stepped around the corner toward the lobby. He leaned against the wall by the stairs, out of the room where he could still keep an eye on everything but not *look* like he was keeping an eye on everything.

"How do you think it's going so far?" Madison appeared behind him.

He had to clench his teeth to keep from cursing in surprise. "You scared the hell out of me. Where'd you come from?"

She peeked around him to check on the guests. "I was back here spying before you thought of it, but I went to check with your head of housekeeping to make sure they were doing turn-down service and all that."

Roark pinched his lips. "They know what they're doing. We've had guests stay here before."

Madison returned his pinched-lip look. "You asked Devlin about icing the beers three times today. I'm allowed to check with housekeeping."

He put his hands up. "Okay, you're right. You warned me you'd be all up in my business and micromanaging my people. You manage away, because it's going great so far."

"I think it is, anyway."

Roark glanced at the table of people, all laughing and talking a lot louder than necessary, then turned to Madison.

She was twirling her hair again, sucking on the inside of her cheek. She was legitimately worried. Of course she'd never admit as much, but he'd been around her long enough to know this wasn't her normal look. Madison was somewhere between fretting and quietly freaking the hell out.

"Hey," he said, trying to get her attention.

She kept studying the table of guests.

"Hey." He moved to block her view so that she had to look at him. "It's going great. Fantastic, if you ask me. This weekend is going to be epic. Don't worry."

Madison studied him before standing a little taller. "I'm not worried."

He considered arguing the point. He'd never seen her this way. She was obviously worried, but it wouldn't help her if he pointed it out. He wanted to remind her that to be nervous was normal, as was needing reassurance. And he was there for her.

It was exactly the kind of statement and offer that would freak her out even more.

"I know you're not worried," he said instead. "You've got nothing to be worried about. The inn has never looked better. I'm merely making an observation."

The tightness around her eyes softened as she released her hair, her shoulders relaxing. She didn't thank him with words, but she closed the short gap between him and reached for his hand. Tangling their fingers together, she held his hand. Only seconds passed, but in the short span of time, her eyes said thank you a thousand times.

She gave his hand a gentle squeeze before letting go. "I need to go check with Wright on dessert."

Madison was a blur of motion, gone in an instant, and it didn't matter. Because that was the first time she'd reached for him that had nothing to do with sex and everything to do with intimacy.

Once dinner and dessert were over, the plates picked up and the table clean, the wedding party sipped on their drinks and shared stories about being on tour—a few of which had to be made up. No way that stuff happened in real life.

The drum player started debating the merits of a song they were working on. "It's brilliant, and commercial radio will hate it," he said.

"No one is going to hate it," Whitney insisted.

"Why don't you let us hear some of it and we can tell you if it's crap?" one of the three bridesmaids asked.

The bass player groaned, slumping in his chair. "I thought we were taking a break from the tour so these two could bend to social standards and participate in an institution known for its failures." He gestured toward Whitney and Jack.

Jack flipped him off. "If you guys are in such a fucking twist about this song, what's it hurt to play it for someone?"

"You just like to hear you're right." The bass player returned his middle finger with a smile.

Madison nudged Roark in the arm. "I know someone like that."

He reached over, skating his fingers across her ribs enough to make her squirm before she shushed him.

The band bickered a little more, but it ended in Jack going to get his guitar and Whitney shaking her head about singing. It took a little coaxing, but she eventually buckled to the encouragement of their friends.

Whitney's voice was low, a little raspy, sounding nothing like she looked. The song was beautiful, but that wasn't what captured his attention.

What stood out, even more than Whitney's voice and the chords Jack played, was the depth of affection in their eyes as they looked at each other.

Jack stared at Whitney, eyes wide, like he was watching for falling stars, afraid he'd miss the best of them. When he'd glance toward his guitar, Whitney would study him, smiling like she was in on a secret that only the two of them shared.

The two of them didn't just love each other; they were amazed by one another.

Roark glanced around to see if he was the only one noticing this. Finally, he braved looking over at Madison. Her face was a mask of porcelain calm, but she fiddled at the ends of her hair, staring at the two of them without blinking.

Surely she saw it too. These two people loved each other, and in less than two days, he and Madison were going to give them the kind of wedding that suited who they were. Not a wedding for anyone else, only for them.

The mood was—dare he say—romantic. A thrill of pride tickled him, and even as he relished taking part in the event, it meant the inevitable drew closer.

"Hey," he whispered, waiting until she looked at him. He mouthed the rest, his fingers crossed beneath his crossed arms. "Come by my room when we're done here? Late dinner?"

The corner of her mouth curled up as she nodded.

Time might not be on his side, but he was damn well going to make it count.

Chapter 24

"I have everything we need, with congratulations from the kitchen and a request that we finish up some leftovers." Roark wheeled a trolley toward her, with two platters, presumably of grilled meat and veggies, and a bucket with four beers on ice.

She helped him carry the plates over to the coffee table in his den area, then the platter and bucket of beer.

So. This was Roark's room, and it was exactly what she expected. Clean, orderly, nice quality, and comfortable. Neutrals ruled the color wheel, with the odd splash of color in picture frames and paintings. She guaranteed those were Sophie's doing.

And his room was *covered* in pictures. His brothers and sister, Beau, Roark hiking with his family, pictures of the inn, several of him as a boy with a distinguished-looking gentleman who had to be his grandfather, and two pictures that she assumed were of his parents when the Bradley kids were all very young.

"Is that your grandfather and that's your family?" She nodded to the pictures on the table below his television. Against her better judgment, she was opening that door, but she had to know. The Bradleys as kids were all too freaking cute.

"That's us." Roark already had a bite of kabob in his mouth.

"Heathen."

"I'm hungry," he said around it.

She looked away, taking a plate and placing a Portobello kabob on it before sitting.

"But yes." He finished chewing as he got up to grab two pictures and bring them over. "This is me and Granddad, back in the day, and that's all of us with Mom and Dad."

She took the pictures, even though the last thing she needed was to see adorable prepubescent Roark, already being the little man of the family for his younger siblings. A quick look down, and yep. He was all that and more. A head taller than the rest of them, he wore a smile but held a seriousness in his eyes. He even had his arms thrown around his family, rather than looking like a disgruntled preteen. "Look at how adorable you all are."

Roark sat down, a solid weight beside her. "I was already hitting that awkward preteen stage. And look at Devlin. He'd rather be anywhere than posing for a family photo."

"Where . . ." She was treading on dangerous ground again. "Where are your parents now?"

Roark grabbed a beer and twisted it open, taking a long swig before he spoke. "Mom moved to Asheville, so she's not far away. Dad is in Greenville. They rarely come up, never together. It's awkward for everyone if they're here at the same time. But they're happier now, so . . ."

"You were close to your grandfather though, huh?"

He sat up, tilting the picture still in her hands. Rhododendrons in full bloom all around them in the photo, and a misty view of the mountains behind them that'd make an artist weep.

"He was my idol growing up. One of those people who knew a little about everything and could do anything from fix a car to grow the perfect tomatoes. I loved him."

The sincerity in his voice, the loss that still remained, cracked something open inside of her, a fracture with light shining out.

She shifted on the couch beside him, the mood suddenly too deep. "And look at your little shaggy haircut."

"It was the style. And it's horrible, I know."

"No, it's cute."

"Well, I try." He winked at her.

"Actually, I have a confession to make."

"Nice." Roark took the pictures from her and set them on the coffee table. He opened another beer and handed it over. "Confessions. Do tell."

Instead of debating how honest she should be, she spat it out. "Before I even visited Honeywilde, that first time, I did some research on you guys."

"It's normal to check a place out before you visit."

"Yeah," she said, dragging the word out. "But I researched you. All of you, but mostly you. Online."

"Really?" He sounded impressed instead of creeped out.

"I saw that you went to App State, that you studied business and played baseball there, then got your MBA."

"Did you look up a picture of me in my baseball uniform? I was pretty cute in that too."

"Very cute."

"You *did* look me up in my uniform."

"Of course. Baseball uniforms are hot." He was hotter now.

He rubbed his hand on the napkin over his thigh. "Not gonna lie, the fact that you looked me up is pretty hot too."

"You are so weird." She took a long drink of her beer. "I didn't go to college." The bitter truth was out of her mouth before she could stop it. A close, personal fact that she had no reason to share with him, but after seeing him with Trevor, seeing with her own eyes what really made Roark tick, her truth wanted out.

The thing was, she'd wanted to go. She remembered kids taking the tests and talking about going away to school. They were getting out, getting on with their lives in this bright, positive way. She hadn't had the means or the grades. Her long swig of beer was cold enough to make her eyes water, but that's not why she blinked and looked away.

"Didn't slow you down though. You learned all about business and stuff the old-fashioned way."

"You mean the only way I could."

He nodded, eating his food, and into the quiet of the room she told him the rest. "I had no money for college, obviously, but I didn't have the grades either."

"How is that possible? You're one of the most intelligent people I've ever met."

That compliment was not going to get to her, even though it did. "Self-taught and clever. Not the same thing."

"Cleverness got you to where you are now, and you seem to be doing all right."

Except, she wasn't all right. Yes, she did fine now, but she'd had to scrape and scavenge to get here. She'd always worked her ass off for everything she had, and it left her with nothing else but work.

Her teen years weren't spent studying and her early twenties weren't full of stories about carefree weekends and playing baseball. They were full of scrounging to get by, then thinking she'd finally found love, only for it to fall apart.

"I was more concerned about having a meal at night than history and math. School was something I had to do until I was eighteen, but I was also waiting tables so at least I knew I would eat."

His expression might look placid to someone else, but the set of Roark's jaw showed how hard he was working not to rage against her past. "Damn, I want to drop-kick your parents, in spite of the fact that you're doing better now."

She hadn't meant to say all of that, but . . . it wasn't fair. People might think she was okay now, or even that she was cold and stuck-up, but that was only because they knew nothing about where she came from or how she got here. Madison stuck a potato wedge in her mouth to keep from telling Roark more. She could barely taste it, but chewing gave her time to get it together. "I don't mean to vent. Life is good now. That's what matters. It's—"

"Fine." Roark said the word for her, setting his plate down. "You're going to say it's fine and I swear to god I cannot hear that word one more time, okay? It is *not* fine." The vehemence in his voice brought Madison up short. In the time she'd been at Honey-wilde, she'd never heard him like this. His tone brokered no argument.

He turned to face her, taking her plate away to set it on the coffee table as well.

Everything inside her screamed to run and hide from whatever he saw or thought he saw.

"You keep saying you're fine or it's fine that you got the shit end of the deal as a kid, and it is not fine. You deserved to be a kid and have fun and not worry about having a hot meal. Working to eat and survive at fifteen or sixteen is not okay. There's nothing fine about it, so stop pretending otherwise."

"I'm not pretending, I—" She snapped at him, then clamped her mouth shut.

"Don't you dare hermit up on me right now."

Madison stared at him, clutching her beer until her hand hurt from the cold.

"You're the most outspoken person I know. Say it."

"I'm not pretending my childhood was okay," she ground out. "This is just how I deal with it. I've moved on because I have to. What's my option? Stay in bed for days, or pay for years of therapy? Cry all over you? Not going to happen."

Roark straightened, his lips pinched, then he nodded to himself as if he'd decided. "All right. You want to know what I do? To deal with it all?"

She was lost on how to answer. Roark always seemed so together.

"I make lists. All the time, lists. You've seen them. My brother gives me shit about it, but what you don't know—what no one knows—is I make a list for almost everything. I make one at night and sometimes in the morning, and I check each item off to keep me on track. If I don't, I'd wake up completely lost inside my head. I couldn't sleep for the jumble of thoughts about to swallow me whole. If I can't look at something that tells me what I need to do, what needs to be done, my mind starts to wander and I start to think. That is not a good thing, and you want to know why?"

Madison blinked.

"Because I start thinking about my brothers and my sister, and when I think about them, I worry about them. I worry and then I get angry for them because of what we should've had and didn't. I worry about what we went through, I worry because I've worried for so long, I can't turn it off. I was responsible for them in some way from the time I started kindergarten. Then, when I'm done stressing over them and their lives, I start to think about how much they resent the hell out of me for it."

"They don't," she tried to argue.

He shook his head, unconvinced. "And I don't blame them. I hover over them and get too bossy sometimes. Dad gave me a larger share of the inn than them, and even though they know it makes good business sense, it still bothers them. They see me with a degree of separation. Dev and Sophie? They can have an hour-long conversation without opening their mouths. Trevor and Soph were two of a kind when we were kids. Me? I'm the manager. Was then and I am now."

"You're more than a manager to them. You have to know that."

"Maybe, but the fact that I had to basically take over to save Honeywilde, that my folks were too wrapped up in themselves and their misery to keep this place in good shape—it pisses me off. It pisses me off that I was never given any option *but* to play the responsible-leader role, my whole life, yet somehow *I'm* the asshole. I'm the asshole because they wouldn't do their jobs as parents or as owners of this place, and it is *not* fine. It's shitty and it's okay for *you* to tell me it's shitty. You don't have to insist everything is fine. Not with me."

"I hate my mother," she blurted. The one thing she never said aloud came pouring out, making her throat burn. But this time, she wasn't going to shut herself up. "I mean, *hate* her. She was the reason Dad left and she . . . she was *horrible*."

Madison could still hear the spite in her mother's voice when she told a sixteen-year-old Madison that if she didn't like this new boyfriend's place, she was more than welcome to try her luck on the streets.

"If she'd tried, if she'd even given half a damn, I would've felt like the luckiest girl alive. She resented me for existing. I could see it in her eyes. I wish I would've had an older brother or sister who gave a damn about me. Believe me. Your family loves you for what you did."

At first, she wasn't going to say the rest. It wasn't her place or any of her business, but she saw something in Roark's family. A bond that, though strained at times, went deeper and held stronger than anything she'd ever experienced. What they had mattered, and if she could help Roark, she would.

"Just . . . maybe. Maybe your brothers and sister don't want you to do so much for them *now*?" She eased into her suggestion. "Maybe they want you to trust them a little more. Give Devlin more responsibility or, I don't know, let them do things all on their own, without your help. Even if it means they mess up sometimes."

Roark leaned back on the couch, his gaze steady on the photographs in front of them. He didn't say anything for a moment and doubt flooded her senses. She couldn't feel the beer in her hand anymore. The low throb of numbness spread to every limb.

Finally, he sighed. "I know. You're right, and I want to let go a little. The thing is, I don't know if I can. I trust them; it's me I'm not so sure about." He lifted his shoulders and let them drop.

Madison reached for him. Without hesitation or uncertainty, she put her hand over the top of his, and held on tight.

She'd done her best not to know Roark, not to fall for him and like him more and more. She didn't want to understand him or for him to understand her, but she did. She knew how hard he tried and how much those around him meant. And no matter how walled up she tried to be, he got her.

More importantly, he accepted her.

She met his gaze.

"C'mere." Roark tilted his chin and tugged at her elbow.

"What?"

"You're sitting too far away." But he was the one who made the move to sit even closer, taking the beer bottle from her hand and setting it on the coffee table. "I can't kiss you over there and I need to kiss you right now."

She pressed into him and their lips met, his kiss slow and soft, his fingers in her hair, skimming her face and neck. He brushed his hand over her hair, cupping the back of her head, savoring the kiss like he was savoring her. Cherishing. He slipped his tongue past her lips, coaxing her open, giving her everything that she wanted in that moment. An acceptance, without words, of who she was, all that she was, on the outside and the complicated inside.

In that moment, she knew what she needed.

This.

Not explosive sex or undeniable chemistry, but something even more potent.

He leaned back, still holding her close. "Will you spend the night with me? Here. I don't care if we stay right here on this couch and fall asleep with our clothes on, but I want you to stay with me tonight."

She couldn't let herself overthink what it'd mean. "I want that too."

He brushed her hair back, his expression so open that the wall inside her cracked further; something long forgotten tried to fight every withering effect in her life to bloom, big and beautiful.

Murmuring words she could barely make out but didn't need to hear to understand, he touched her, stroked her hair, raining the smallest kisses over her cheek.

Affection, in its truest and deepest form, not because he wanted sex or because the sex was great, but because he wanted her.

Madison turned her face and he kissed her temple, but she did it so he wouldn't see. Tears pricked her eyes and she squeezed them shut, not because she was scared but because here, in this calm quiet, she was allowed to feel, and it was exactly where she wanted to be.

Maybe, if she sat very still and promised not to want it too much, she could feel this way forever.

Chapter 25

A few weeks ago, all he'd wanted was for this wedding to happen, Honeywilde to get the publicity from it so that he, his family, and the resort would be in a secure spot. Now, he'd give anything to put this weekend off another week or two. A month. Three months. As long as it was further into the future and he got a little more time with Madison.

But that wasn't reality. Reality was a great room full of pretentious wedding guests, with so much fake hugging and cheek kissing, he wanted to hurl himself off the veranda.

A distinct line differentiated the wedding folks who were family and old friends from those who were industry people.

Whitney and Jack's friends and family looked like anyone you might run into at the local Target *or* someone from juvie. The industry folks were deceptively casual, wearing five-hundred-dollar distressed jeans, and shirts you'd only see in a magazine ad. They greeted each other with loud exclamations of joy and lots of hand gestures, none of it with an ounce of sincerity.

Madison worked the room though, skirting the edges, watching the guests for any needs, working with the inn staff to have those needs met. Her efforts were making the party a success, but her presence was never obvious.

Except to Roark. He couldn't take his eyes off her. Soaking up all he could, while he could, that was his excuse.

What else was he supposed to do? Ask her to stay? She'd already been very clear about what she wanted and expected. Even though they'd grown closer, that didn't mean she'd stay, and in fairness, she'd been nothing but honest from the start. They never said anything about after the wedding.

Maybe he should bring up her coming to see him some weekend, or he could visit her in the city. But to what end? An extra weekend or two would only make it worse. Putting off the inevitable so it'd hurt all the more when they finally said goodbye.

He swallowed the bitter thought as Madison approached him.

"It's like a show but without the stage," she whispered.

"It is. Normally I'm into people-watching, but this is . . ." He pulled a face.

"Yeah. Talk about schmoozing. There's more here than I can stand."

"Where are Whitney and Jack?"

"Around. Probably avoiding"—Madison moved her palm in a circle—"this."

She lowered her hand to her blouse, fiddling with the top button.

"Stop worrying. Everything is going well, I've seen what Wright has ready for dinner and I'm still drooling, and these people look happy in their hobnobbing." He tried to reassure her, but she kept fidgeting.

"I have a bad feeling."

"Probably just nerves. It's a big weekend." He wouldn't share his nerves about the two of them. About it ending. The anxiety radiating off her would be work related, same as always, and he needed to accept things as they were.

Tomorrow they were done. He wasn't going to ask her for some kind of long-distance nonsense, so this would be it. She'd hate the idea of dragging out their "not a thing," and if he pressed her for any kind of promises, she'd likely panic. Or worse, agree when it wasn't what she really wanted.

The last thing he needed was another person growing to resent him.

Damn. Why was he even thinking this way?

"It's not my nerves." She shook her head. "There are some signs. Namely the bride and groom aren't here right now, and this is their party. Troutman is flouncing around like this is his weekend."

As soon as she said that, ol' fish face lumbered toward them.

"Mr. Troutman." Madison nodded politely. "I hope you're enjoying yourself."

"I'm here. That's all I can say for it."

Roark clenched his teeth. Troutman had already drank himself beet-red, eaten enough canapés to leave no room for dinner, and schmoozed with 80 percent of the room.

Roark prompted him for some kind of compliment. "Still, it's a great party and tomorrow will be even better."

Any kind of compliment.

Trout tilted his head, noncommittal. "I guess it's okay for a back-woods feel. Oh!" He flagged down some other blowhard and turned his back on them.

Madison remained stock-still as he left, but she clung to the button on her blouse.

"Ignore him. Everyone else is having the time of their lives."

"I wish I could ignore him. Unfortunately, my wish is that he brag about me to his inner circle, and I don't see that happening in this lifetime."

"The bride and groom will more than make up for it."

"If they turn up." She glanced around, fiddling with her button again. "I need to find them before rehearsal. See if there's anything else they need. Oh, and don't forget, keep everyone else in here, sipping champagne and chattering while the wedding party runs through what they need to do. I don't want interference on the veranda. But don't be too heavy-handed about it."

"Madison."

She jerked her chin toward him, worrying the inside of her lip.

"It's all under control. We'll keep everyone in here happy so you can run through the ceremony."

He wanted so badly to touch her, do whatever necessary to strengthen the confidence that Troutman had chipped away. He also wanted to hold her close as they stood there, but this was work. They couldn't be cuddled up in a corner and have anyone take them seriously.

Settling for a quick yet pointed gesture, Roark turned to stand in front of her, his back to the crowd of people as he blocked her view of the room. He grinned as her gaze flashed up, and he brushed the tips of his fingers along the line of her neck.

"You're going to have them eating out of your hand." He knew from personal experience.

Madison's pulse thrummed beneath his touch and, after a slow sweep of her lashes, he peeled her fingers off the button and moved her hand down to her side.

He wished he could say he'd gotten through, that he'd convinced her, but he knew better.

"I should go find the couple."

"Okay. But remember, you've got this." Roark let go of her hand and stepped aside.

Her gaze stayed locked with his as she walked toward the outer edge of the wedding party and only at the very last minute did she look away.

At the rehearsal dinner, Madison's tension spiraled so high that it rolled off of her and onto him, a full room-length away. Several times he'd tried to make eye contact, but she'd scurried off to take care of something else. He studied the bride and groom, remembering what Madison had said about her bad feeling.

To him, Whitney and Jack looked fine. Smiling and talking with their guests.

Then, he looked again.

They were both all smiles for others, and several times Jack would glance over for Whitney's attention, only to be left hanging. She wouldn't look at him, and damn if Roark didn't know how that felt.

He eased his way around the outside of the great room and its collection of round tables and raucous conversation. The kitchen was even louder, but that's where he found Madison, supervising the timing between appetizers and main course.

"Hey." He nudged her elbow.

At first she didn't hear him or was too caught up to notice.

"Hey." He nudged again.

"What?" She turned.

"Did you talk to Whitney before this dinner?"

Madison shook her head, waving some of the waitstaff past. "Yes, but I didn't get a solid answer. She said they didn't need anything, but . . ."

"I see what you mean about them being off, or just different than last night."

"And how they've been every time we talk or when we met weeks ago. Is it my imagination?"

"No." Roark shrugged, because what could they do about it? More than likely this was typical bride and groom nerves. Pre-wedding jitters. Surely even rock stars got them.

"I'll check on them again after the dinner." Madison was tugged away by a harried-looking Wright in full king-of-the-kitchen mode.

Roark looked around the kitchen. The waitstaff moved in and out of the swinging doors, through the restaurant and into the great room, waiting on some of the most high-maintenance clients that Honeywilde had ever known, the rest of the wedding party easy to please. A crowd of total opposites.

It wasn't as though he didn't know how Madison managed it all. He knew, because his job was the same. But it was because he knew, that he respected her all the more.

"Roark," Sophie hissed, suddenly at his side. "We need you in the great room, pronto."

By the time he was done in the great room, the evening was gone. All of the partygoers retired to their rooms, the bride and groom to their suite. Roark checked in the kitchen and billiard room but couldn't find Madison. He finally found her out front, pacing up and down the portico, arms wrapped around herself in the chilly night air.

"Where's your coat?" He strode over, whipping off his suit jacket and holding it open for her to wear.

She made a vague gesture, but the dark blotches under her eyes said what she couldn't.

"Why don't you go get some rest? You had a successful night and tomorrow's the big day."

She kept pacing, with him right beside her, her boots clicking over the bricks. "I know. But I'm worried about the bride and groom."

"Why?"

"You know why. Tonight was fine, but they didn't seem . . . I expected them to be happier. And what if they aren't happy because this isn't the weekend they wanted? What if I've screwed up but they won't tell me? What if I've ruined everything?"

"You haven't ruined anything. Tonight was wonderful. If they weren't happy, it's got nothing to do with what you've done for their weekend."

"Maybe." Her shoulders drooped. "But I've been thinking—"

"It's late and you're exhausted." Roark steered Madison toward one of the woven-wood benches along the front patio. "Tomorrow is a big deal, for everyone. I think you all just have nerves, but it's all going to be—"

"Fine?" She sat down hard at the end of a bench. "That's my line."

"This time it's true." He sat as well, leaning back and wrapping his arm around her shoulders.

They sat that way until he felt like he might zone right off to sleep.

Then she spoke. "Three weeks can fly by."

"Yep." His answer was a pop of pale breath in the night air. "The day you booked the inn seems like a long time ago. But it's gone by too fast."

Madison nodded, and leaned her head over to rest against his shoulder. It was nothing. A small gesture, but three weeks ago she would never have allowed the support or taken the comfort.

He nodded. "And on Sunday, you head back to Charlotte."

She was quiet, picking at some invisible lint on her pants. He knew enough about her by now to know she didn't want to answer. Didn't want to discuss it. But he wasn't made that way. He had to say something.

"You know that night, at your door? The first time we kissed?"

She hummed her yes.

"Then, you said when this was all over, when we were done with business . . ." Roark shrugged with barely a lift of his shoulders, but it was enough to make her glance up.

"I remember what I said. I thought I could resist you until our work was done, but—"

"Then you didn't have to."

She shook her head.

"But before all that, back when you suggested we wait and hang out after the wedding, were you planning on sticking around for a little while after the wedding? Coming back for a long weekend trip to the mountains?"

Madison sat back again, leaning into him so she was no longer looking at him. "I have no idea what I was planning to do. I don't think I'd planned at all. I knew I wanted you, but I was smart enough to know we should hold off until the job was done. Turns out, I'm not that smart after all."

"Or I was too irresistible."

"That too."

"But now you're going to take off?"

That made her sit up. "I am not *taking off.* You make it sound like I'm Trevor. I'm not running away."

"No one said you were. I meant, after Sunday, are you going to leave or . . .?"

She opened her mouth and then clamped it shut on whatever she was about to say. After a moment, she looked over his shoulder as if talking to the stone wall of the inn. "I-I have to go eventually. Everything I have is in Charlotte."

"I know."

Her gaze shot to his, irritation flashing in the brilliant green. "And you knew that when we began this."

"I know I knew. I'm just saying . . ."

"Saying *what?*"

"That I'm going to miss you, dammit!"

Chapter 26

Those were not the words she wanted to hear.

Of course he'd miss her; she would miss him. That much was so painfully clear now, she wanted to scream. What she needed him to say was . . . something more than that. She wanted the impossible.

"Maybe you could visit? Or I could visit you?" He tried to catch her gaze, his offer strained, either because he was reluctant to say it or expected her to shoot him down.

Visiting meant prolonging the inevitable. The occasional visits were scraps, and they deserved more. He did anyway.

"You work all the time," she said.

"I can take time off. It's what, two hours to Charlotte?"

"Three."

"Three hours. I can come to the city for a day or two."

"So . . . visit when you have the time?" Something neither of them had. Ever. This was a ruse, a lie they were telling themselves to make it all okay. For the first time in her life, she knew a situation wasn't going to be fine and she didn't want to pretend otherwise.

"Yeah, that'd work."

The pinched look in his eyes and the stiffness of his body told her it wouldn't.

"Or . . . what if you extended your time here? Leave on Monday. Or Tuesday. When do you absolutely have to be back?"

She could extend her stay, but then she'd still have to leave. Their time together would still have an expiration date. If they arranged to keep seeing each other, that meant commitment. And what if he asked her to stay indefinitely? She had no idea how to handle an offer for more, so for her to want him to ask was selfish and crazy.

She was a cement-mixer of emotions she didn't understand. If she couldn't understand them, how could she expect Roark to? She didn't know what she wanted, but she knew she needed him to take the first step. He couldn't count on her to navigate through territory that was completely foreign.

She'd never be capable. It had to be Roark.

And that's how she knew she was losing her mind. Complete lunacy to want him to offer himself up, when she could promise nothing in return. Even if she kept seeing him, he'd be getting a raw deal. Short term, maybe she wouldn't ruin everything. Maybe she wouldn't run him off. Long term?

She'd never had anything last very long.

Roark should never put himself out there like that, not for a wreck like her.

The only explanation for her wish was that she was worse than her mother, no better than her father, wanting everything to be all about her. The same as saying to hell with what Roark might want or deserve, *she* needed this. Him.

But she had to look beyond it. See past her own selfish need and look out for him.

A cough and a string of curses made both of them jump.

Jack stomped through the portico, toward the drive, like he was looking for someone to fight.

"Jack?" Roark got to his feet.

Jack spun around, his eyes like onyx in the moonlight. "Shit, you scared me."

"Kind of scared us too. Everything okay?" Roark moved closer and she followed right behind him.

"Far from fucking okay. You don't happen to have a smoke and a light on you, do you?"

Roark shot Madison a confused look. She shrugged back at him, no clue what was going on. "We don't smoke."

Jack scuffed his black boot along the cobbled part of the drive, looking a lot like he was considering kicking over a potted plant. "I used to, but Whitney wanted me to quit, so of course I did." He forced out a laugh of pure bitterness.

"I can get you some cigarettes if it will help," Madison offered, anything to bring back the contented guy from last night and get rid of the angry man who was here tonight.

"Nah." Jack huffed out a breath, a white puff in the night air. "Won't fix it."

"Fix what?"

Jack finally turned to them, stuffing his hands in his worn leather jacket. "Might as well let you know so you can be off the hook, huh?"

The signs all surged toward her, like a wave bearing down, but she pushed it back. No. That couldn't happen. Not this wedding or this couple, not to her and Roark.

"The wedding is off." Jack cursed, dragging a hand through his hair. "Utter fucking bullshit, but it's off."

"What?" Roark asked, as silently the truth of what she already knew broke over her.

"I want you to know I appreciate everything you've both done. Last night was . . . it's all been great."

Screw being appreciated.

"What happened?" she asked, her voice calm while inside she stormed.

"Good damn question." Jack flung his hands out of his jacket. "Whitney and I, we got into a stupid argument after dinner tonight. You ever get in one of those fights that you don't even know what it's about? She was pissed, but I was fine. Then, all of a sudden, she's yelling and I'm defensive, and I don't know how it got to that point. She said that was it, and there's no way we can get married."

"Are you sure she meant it? Maybe she's just nervous," Roark tried.

"Whitney doesn't get nervous."

Madison would bet anything Whitney wasn't nervous, she was scared. She stepped closer. "Where is Whitney now?"

"Hell if I know. She took off. Look, it's no good going after her. This shit has happened before. We worked it out, but fuck me if it hasn't happened again."

Madison looked back at Roark, then to Jack. "But we've seen the two of you together. It's obvious she loves you."

"I thought so too. I knew so. But maybe Phil was right. Working together and trying to be a couple, it's too much. Maybe the new has worn off and she's sick of me. You've seen us. We don't exactly match."

"That's bullshit." Roark stopped him. "You might be opposites, but everything was fine until today. You have to fix this."

She and Jack jerked around to look at him.

Jack stared hard. "You don't think I've tried? I'd still try, but you don't get it, man. She's gone. The wedding is over."

Roark held up a hand, a clear sign he was getting ready to take over on a matter, and Madison bristled. This was her wedding and Whitney wasn't her first running bride.

"Then I'll go find her." Roark pulled out his phone, firing off a text to god knew who. "I'm sure this can be fixed."

Jack scrubbed at his face and cursed again. "You're not going to find her. I've tried before and failed." He turned and stormed back into the inn.

As soon as Jack was gone, Madison turned to glare at Roark. "You can't go storming after Whitney or barking at Jack. You're not helping matters."

"What are you talking about? I'm being proactive."

"But you're doing it wrong." This was her area of expertise. She understood wedding jitters and she knew the fear of forever better than anyone.

"At least I'm doing something."

"Excuse me?" Madison raised her voice. Maybe it wasn't fair of her to be angry, but she didn't care. She had a wedding and a no-strings attached affair that were both falling apart, and right now Roark cared more about the wedding.

She pushed past him. "I don't need you swooping in to save the day on this. Just let me handle it."

Roark stepped right back in her way. "We have a skittish bride who's running away from her relationship."

"I know."

"And you think you're the best person to talk to her? To convince her not to go?"

She stood a little taller to look him square in the eyes. "What the hell is that supposed to mean?"

"Whoa! I didn't mean—"

"Yes, you did. You don't think I'm good enough to talk to her, to fix this." She wasn't blinking and she stared at him so hard her face hurt. But who the hell did he think he was? This was her wedding and her bride. She wasn't going to let him step over her.

"Madison . . ." He ran a rough hand over his hair. "You struggle to talk about your past, never mind the present. You hate commitments, so how is that going to help a reluctant bride?"

His words blew a hole through her.

"I've helped *plenty* of reluctant brides. Believe it or not, I know how to do my damn job. And I've told you more about me than I've ever told anyone. Now you throw it in my face?"

"No. That's not . . . I know you've opened up to me, and you've got no idea what it means to me. But this has to be fixed and I'm better suited to handle it."

"You don't think I'm capable." And it hurt more than she should've ever allowed.

"It's not that."

"You don't think I can fix my own wedding. This is *my* wedding. My bride."

He leaned toward her. "This is my wedding too. And it's too damn important for me to stand aside."

"Because of some publicity?"

"It's a lot more important than some promo shots."

"What aren't you telling me?"

"This wedding doesn't go off, and the publicity with it, Honeywilde might not make it through the winter. *I* have to fix this."

Madison took a step back, that bit of information stunning her numb. "How could you not tell me this wedding was that important to you? That important to the resort?"

Roark stiffened. "Because it's my family and my problem. Not yours. You're leaving Sunday, remember?"

Her blood froze in her veins, the truth a cold reminder she'd so easily forgotten. This was not her family, not her family business, and these were not her people.

She was all alone.

Madison jerked her gaze away. Roark hadn't forgotten the truth, but to hell with him for keeping something that important from her after all she'd told him, then trying to step over her to take charge.

She pinched her eyes closed and counted to ten.

Thinking what they had was different, thinking that she'd found something and someone that might last . . . she'd been kidding herself. This was why she was alone; because that's all she understood and it was easier. Letting him in meant he knew what made her tick, meant he was capable of hurting her. And that's exactly what he was doing. Just like everyone else, he didn't believe in her, didn't trust her. How could he ever want her? His words were a mirror, showing her who she really was.

But she didn't have to be hurt by him, or anyone else. It wasn't so hard, not caring what he thought. Turning off her feelings was something she'd learned to do long ago. People couldn't hurt you if you didn't let them in.

She could shove Roark out of her heart before he ever got the chance to break it, and every crack in her walls, the ones he'd created with his trust and sincerity, would seal shut.

When she opened her eyes, Roark took a step back.

"Whitney won't want your help," she told him, her tone emotionless.

"No, *you* don't want my help. You're the one who doesn't want me involved, but this isn't about you."

"No, this is about you having to fix everything and always be in charge. Even things you have no business sticking your nose in."

"Are you always this damn difficult?"

"Yes." She stepped closer. "Yes, as a matter of fact, I am. Surprised it took you this long to notice. But then, it doesn't really matter how much of a pain in the ass I am when all we're doing is having sex for a couple of weeks and I leave on Sunday. Actually trying to deal with me or have me around longer is a whole other matter."

"That is not—What are you talking about? You're the one who said—"

"But I guess it's a good thing you're realizing that now because this"—she pointed to the center of her chest—"is me. I'm difficult, demanding, and I will drive you crazy. Maybe I haven't yet, but eventually I would. Give me the time and I'll make you hate me. I always have."

"Madison." He stepped toward her, but she moved away.

"No." She shook her head, refusing to give in to the waver threatening to shake her voice. "It's good that we got this out of the way. Now we can focus on saving this wedding."

As soon as she got the words out, she walked away. She waited until she was out of his sight to start running. She let her legs carry her, fast as she could go, taking stairs and turning corners, eyes blurry, until she got so lost inside Honeywilde, even she didn't know where she was.

Chapter 27

Jerking his tie off, Roark cursed his inability to find the runaway bride.

He rolled the tie up into a neat bundle and stuffed it in his pants pocket. He'd searched every nook and cranny—even the nooks of crannies—for Whitney, and Jack was right: She was gone.

He couldn't find Madison either.

He had no clue what he'd say to her or how to right whatever he'd done wrong, but if she was still at Honeywilde, she was well hidden.

Dying embers in the fireplace called to him. If he couldn't fix things with Whitney, and he damn sure couldn't fix things with Madison, the least he could do was build a fire. A fire and some coffee might help him figure out how to solve this.

After slipping off his jacket, he grabbed the poker and some choice splits of wood, and coaxed and babied the flame until it blazed anew. He left the screen off and sat in his favorite spot on the sofa.

The seat lost something without Madison beside him.

He stared into the fire, the embers glowing and tumbling together, hypnotizing him. Since he was a kid, he'd loved late-night fires, always welcoming and warm, comfort for the soul. Tonight the fire wasn't making so much as a dent in his mood.

"You mind?" Jack appeared from the far dark corner of the great room, pointing at the chair nearest the hearth.

Roark tilted his head in welcome. If he was going to give in to a moment of wallowing, he might as well not wallow alone.

Jack slumped down in the chair, laying his phone on the arm, face up so if any communication came in, he couldn't miss it. He kept his emotionless gaze on the flames and, for a guy with a tough-as-nails appearance, he looked beaten.

Roark didn't blame him. He was pretty damn broken himself.

Madison had torn off like he'd been the one to call her a demanding pain in the ass. He'd done no such thing. He'd been trying to help, only ever tried to help for the last three weeks. She'd fought him at first, but they'd gotten past that. Or so he'd thought.

He knew he had a tendency to take over, but he had no choice. If he didn't find the bride and fix this whole situation, then there'd be no wedding. If there was no wedding, there was no special press for Honeywilde. Without it, the resort's finances wouldn't survive the slower winter season.

What was he without Honeywilde? He could not lose his family's legacy. They'd have nothing. He was the leader of his family and owner of the resort. When you're in charge, you have to take charge. Madison ought to know that better than anyone.

Of course, she hadn't known just how important this wedding was to Honeywilde or why he needed to step over her to get this event back on the tracks. She hadn't known because he hadn't told her.

Roark huffed and shifted his ankle off his leg, only to cross them the other way and hold his head up with an elbow propped on the sofa arm.

He needed to think. There had to be a way to fix this without dragging everyone down with him. Screwing up and failing was something reserved for his shaky relationships with his brothers and sister. In business, he knew how to deal, how to succeed. With the people closest to him . . . it was a crapshoot.

Madison knew that too. She knew how much he regretted the way things were with his siblings. He'd mucked things up with them, and now he'd mucked things up with her. And they weren't even in a relationship.

Had to be a new record for him, ruining a good thing he didn't have.

"Glad to see I'm not the only one up at this lovely hour." Devlin strolled in, eating a plate of leftover hors d'oeuvres.

"Why are you up?" Roark shifted again as his brother sat down.

"I'm hungry. You want?" Dev held out the plate.

Roark shook his head, but a hand suddenly appeared from over his shoulder, snatching up one of the dates.

"Don't tell me you've started having middle-of-the-night meetings too." Trevor chomped on the date as he flopped down between the two of them. "Not that I'd mind. Can't sleep anyway; my bed's too soft after weeks of a sleeping bag."

Devlin stopped chewing. "I should lead the night meetings, seeing how I have the most experience with insomnia."

Roark's brothers laughed, until they looked over at him and Jack.

"Uh-oh," Dev muttered. "What happened?"

Roark looked over, battling with the decision of what to say and how much. He didn't need them all in a panic because the bride took off. If he couldn't fix this disaster, how could they? He also didn't want to spill Jack's business out in the open.

"Roark." Devlin said his name in the exact same tone Roark often used on him. "Don't sit there not saying shit and looking like the world has ended. Tell us."

Madison's words came back to him. What if his family didn't want him to fix everything anymore? Maybe they did want him to trust them more. Let them help.

Maybe they wanted him to let them in, the same way he wanted Madison to let him in.

"Whitney, the bride, she's gone." He spat out the truth before he could convince himself he had to carry this burden alone.

"What?" his brothers said in unison.

Jack groaned, rubbing at the side of his head. "She called the wedding off and ran."

"I did look for her," Roark told him.

"Yeah?" Jack studied the fire. "How'd that work out for you?"

He held out his empty hands and shrugged.

"Told you. Thanks for trying and all, but I did warn you."

Damn. The man sounded like him. *Told you so.*

He told people stuff all the time. Told his family what to do growing up; still tried to tell them how to function, daily.

"Does Madison know?" Devlin asked. "This is her wedding. We need to—"

"She knows," Roark said.

"Then where is she?"

"I don't know." He hoped he didn't look and sound as defeated as he felt.

"Oh god. What'd you do?" Dev's question was laced with weariness.

Roark could keep everything to himself, try to handle this all alone, or he could tell them the truth.

"I think I screwed things up with Madison and I don't know how to fix any of this."

Dev set a half-eaten shrimp on his plate. "We have to find Madison. She's got to be around here somewhere, and hell, we're up. We can help you look."

Trevor leaned forward to catch Roark's gaze. "We find Madison and I bet she could find the missing bride. Madison could convince her to at least come back and talk to sad sack over there."

"Trevor." Devlin buried his face in his hands.

"I'm kidding. Rock star knows I'm kidding, don't you?"

Jack looked a little stunned, but then a ghost of a smile crossed his lips. "Yeah, somehow I do."

Trevor stared down his nose at Roark. "I mean, Madison did talk *you* into doing this wedding and letting me stay. I bet she could talk a bride into coming back around."

"Exactly." Dev nodded. "But first you've got fix whatever you screwed up with your woman."

Roark blinked, unsure of how to respond.

Dev rolled his eyes. "Oh come on. Like we don't all know you're head over heels for Madison? It's obvious. We've known you your whole life and you've never been as happy as these past few weeks. Maybe you just need to find Madison and make sure *she* knows that."

Roark kept staring at his brothers.

They were right.

In her time at the hotel, Madison's tough nature and strong will had been the perfect balance to Roark's. He enjoyed having someone who pushed him and pushed back.

And he'd told her as much, but had he told her how happy she made him? How every day was brighter, more invigorating, simply because she was there.

He'd told her plenty of other stuff. Told her the view at Honeywilde was great, that she had to use Brenda because no one was better, told her that she ought to go skinny-dipping, and that she shouldn't beat herself up for the past, that she was capable of anything.

He'd told her everything but how he really felt about her.

How strongly it gripped him when he watched her from across the room. When he'd been knocked flat with the urge to run up and grab her, and shout about how amazing she was to a world that couldn't see it. To Madison, who couldn't see it either.

He cut his gaze back to Jack, who'd gone back to staring into the fire.

Both of them were mourning the loss of the women they wanted, and sitting here doing nothing about it. Pathetic. The two of them. A rock star and a resort owner. On their asses like they'd given up.

Giving up was pointless, and he didn't do pointless.

He might not be able to fix Jack's issue, but he'd be damned if he was going to sit here and let Madison hate him without knowing the truth. All of it. The truth about Honeywilde, and how he felt about her.

He looked at his brothers, both awake, both there to support him when he didn't expect to need them so much.

Roark rose from the sofa and put his jacket back on. "Dev, Trevor. I need your help. I have to find Madison."

There was a high probability that she didn't want him or his truths, but he had to do everything he could to make sure she knew and understood that Roark Bradley didn't give up. Not when his parents checked out, not when his siblings needed him, not on Honeywilde, and not on her.

Chapter 28

She could've hidden in the warm safety of her own guest room, but no. Madison rocked on the basement patio swing, her knees pulled up under the quilt she'd stolen from the common room nearby.

This was a bad idea because it was freaking cold in the mountains in the middle of the night; a good idea because no one would look for her here. Then again, who said Roark was even looking? If he was half as smart as he thought he was, he'd take tonight as a blessing.

She buried her face in the quilt. That wasn't fair. He was twice as smart as he thought, and his confidence was a problem for her, not him. She was the one who wished she had what came to him so naturally. She was the one who faked it, so when it came time to really woman up, she ran.

All because she was scared; more frightened than she'd ever been, even more than when she'd gotten thrown out of her poor excuse of a home at eighteen, with an entire fifty bucks to her name.

That was nothing. Hell, when it came to being alone and surviving, she was the champ. But when she felt the pull of needing someone, wanting to be with someone, that's what sent her into a panic.

She wanted Roark to care about her, and that was the problem. She'd spent her life protecting herself so that she'd never want or need anyone's love again. But she did.

She'd been so worried about letting Roark in, scared to get close . . . but it was already too late for that. He was in. She cared about him, his family, his inn—all of it—more than she'd ever thought possible.

Roark hadn't asked her for more, because she'd been so adamant about them not being "a thing." Because she was an idiot. Now she wanted him to ask her for more, and it scared the shit out of her.

Why would he want her? No one else did. Then he'd stepped right over her when something important was on the line. She was a fool for ever believing it'd be any other way.

And she still had a wedding to save.

Whitney was gone, but even if she did find her, then what? She didn't want Roark to be right about her not being able to convince Whitney to stay.

But he was.

She sighed, lifting her head to rest her chin on her knees.

Who the hell was she to give anyone a pep talk about relationships? *She* needed the pep talk. The thought of her trying to sing the praises of love and commitment, encourage settling down and trusting another person with your heart? What a load.

"Hey." Whitney stuck her head around one of the giant stone pillars that supported the back of the inn.

Madison came up off the swing, clutching her chest. "You're here."

Whitney grimaced, but came closer, her strawberry blond hair catching the moonlight, face so pale she could be a ghost.

"Yeah. "

Madison's heart thumped in her chest like a bass.

Whitney eased toward her. The coat she wore was overlarge and the sleeves hung down over her hands. Madison could still tell that beneath all that fabric, where she held her hands together, she was wringing them.

"Do you . . . do you want to sit down?"

Whitney smiled, but it was weak. A sad impression of her smiles from the night before. "You don't mind?"

"No." Normally, she'd mind very much. But she needed to do this, not only to save this wedding and save her own ass, but to be there for Whitney. She sure as hell needed to be there for someone.

They sat on the swing. Whitney pulled the blanket up to her chin, sitting the same way Madison sat earlier. Instead of bombarding her with questions, Madison asked her only one. "Mind if we swing back and forth a little?"

Whitney shook her head, so Madison pushed off with both feet, the swing swaying back and forth, back and forth. With each swing, the chain's links whined a little.

"When I was little, I thought the noise from squeaky swings was strangely musical."

Madison didn't say a word but turned to look at her. Her chin was wrinkled as she fought to keep it from trembling.

"Strangely *bad* music, but there's still a rhythm if you listen. I would swing faster and slower, changing the tempo." Whitney swiped at the corner of her eye with the edge of the quilt, her chin finally succumbing to the trembles as the tears fell. "I've always been such a weirdo."

Madison shook her head, the claim *No, you're not* on the tip of her tongue, but how would she know? She hardly knew Whitney; plus, whenever people cooed *no* at her, she shut out whatever else they had to say.

She bit at the inside of her cheek. Think. *Think.* "I used to swing as high as I could and stay that way, just to see how long I could. I'd make myself motion sick, but I wasn't about to stop. Guess I'm a weirdo too."

Whitney nodded, pinching her lips together, her face shiny with tear tracks.

"So . . . have you been—*where* have you been? Hiding in the woods?"

Whitney's laugh surprised them both, and Whitney snorted with another laugh. "Sort of? There's an empty round, tent-looking thing near here and the door was open."

Madison thought of Roark, and the smile on her lips twisted her heart. "It's called a yurt."

"I've been sitting in there for . . . I don't know how long."

"Three hours. At least, that's when I found out you'd left."

"That long?"

Madison nodded, pulling the quilt closer. "You went there alone, in the dark?"

Whitney pushed her feet against the concrete floor, making them swing a little faster. "Too numb to care about the dark."

Madison didn't know what else to say, and she wasn't about to open her mouth and say something stupid. Instead, she helped Whitney keep up the swinging.

Time went by—it could've been a few minutes or thirty—but Madison had to say something or Whitney would stay hidden all night.

Hiding wasn't helping matters. If Madison couldn't open up and talk about her feelings—all the squishy stuff that let people in—to help herself, then the least she could do was help the bride.

She shifted on the swing, turning to face Whitney. "Jack told us what happened."

Whitney stared straight ahead.

She reminded Madison so much of herself, trying to put on the strong front. A strong front that wouldn't fool everyone, and could very well ruin this wonderful thing in her life.

Madison could've cried right along with her.

"I'm sorry," Whitney whispered. "All of the work you guys did, the trouble you went through for us."

"You weren't trouble. I enjoyed planning your wedding." She meant it too. Every moment of arranging their event had been an experience unlike the dozens of events before. From talking about bolted-down furniture, to cake tasting, to debating with Devlin over how much dance-floor space they needed, to Sophie and her looks that said a million words, to Roark and his . . . everything.

She didn't want the wedding to be off because it'd damage her business. That was unavoidable, but she'd bounce back from it. She always did. The universe had dealt her worse hands than this, and she'd always made it through. But what about Roark? Would he bounce back? Now that she knew how shaky things were here at Honeywilde, she wasn't sure.

And would she bounce back from having Roark in her life?

In Whitney and Jack, she saw two people who cared for one another, one sitting here in tears, and they were letting some kind of bullshit keep them apart. And, for once, she wanted love—real love—to prevail.

"I don't care about the wedding, Whitney. I'm just sorry you guys aren't getting married." As she spoke the words, she realized it was true. Her regrets weren't about the notoriety or what it'd do to her business. She was upset that these two people, who seemed perfect for each other, who were clearly in love, were apart.

She regretted that she'd had something so special right within her reach and was too scared to grab on and refuse to let go.

"I'm sorry too," Whitney said between sniffles. "I really wanted to marry Jack tomorrow, and dance and eat chocolate bourbon cake."

"Then . . ." Madison shook her head, struggling to keep up. "I don't understand. If you want to marry Jack, then why don't you? You called it off, you can call it back on."

Whitney squeezed her eyes closed and shook her head. "I can't. I left him. He hates me."

Madison stared at Whitney, who was trying to keep a stiff upper lip about it but the agony was oozing off her.

"He doesn't hate you. If you want to be with him, why'd you call it off?" Her tone bordered on harsh, she heard it. She was demanding an answer, but to hell with sitting silent. Whitney needed to answer to herself on this one, and this might be the only way.

She shook her head, strawberry blond waves bouncing.

"*Why?*" Madison repeated.

"What if getting married ruins everything? Being together all the time, working and living together. We'll end up killing each other."

"That's what Jack said." Madison tilted her head, remembering. "Actually, that's what Jack said Troutman said."

"Yeah."

"Whitney . . . I'm just going to say it. I think your manager is trying to sabotage your relationship."

She wiped at her nose. "That isn't new. He hates us being together, but it's not him. He couldn't sow doubt if it wasn't already there. For me anyway. Did Jack talk to you?"

"A little."

"A little is a lot for Jack. What did he say? Was he upset?"

"Of course, he's upset. The man loves you. You have to know that."

"I do, but . . ." She turned toward Madison, her fingers curled into the quilt. "Can I tell you something?"

"I think you'd better."

Whitney looked away, as if she was bolstering herself for something. "Everyone thinks Jack is this bad boy, troubled lead guitarist. And he is, to an extent. But he's also driven and professional and focused. Like, he *really* has his stuff together. I don't have anything together. Nothing. I'm the biggest mess you'll ever meet, but I hide it well. Scary well."

Madison rubbed at her temple. The girl had a point here somewhere.

"Don't you see? I'm the trouble in this relationship, not him. People think I'm the Goody Two-shoes and that he'll somehow bring me down." She tossed her head back. "Jack is the one who's got it together, I'm the wreckage. Just . . . no one knows. I will drag him down."

Madison studied her; the pained expression proved the truth of her words. Whitney thought she was too damaged for the man she loved. It was a sentiment Madison understood all too well. She pulled the quilt up higher; she was colder than before, a shiver running through her arms.

"Does Jack know?" she dared to ask.

"Know what?"

"That you're a mess and you're scared of hurting him?"

Whitney started, then turned and gave her a sad smile. "He knew before I did."

Madison's eyes burned at the sight of that smile. She knew what lay behind it, and exactly how Whitney felt. She tightened her grip, trying to hang on as the broken parts of her shook loose and flew around her. She'd held herself together so tightly, for so long, but she was wreckage, just like Whitney.

Jack knew the real Whitney, the good and the bad, and he didn't care. It was obvious to anyone paying attention.

And Roark knew Madison. More than anyone, he got her. He saw who she really was and had never once turned away. He'd tried to take over earlier tonight, sure, but he wasn't the one who ran. And he wasn't the one leaving.

What if he knew she needed him? He was there for the people who needed him—sometimes a little too there—but even so, it showed he was the last person who'd ever turn his back on her.

"Jack—" She cleared her throat, trying to steady her shaking voice. "Jack must be okay with you, just as you are, because I've seen how he looks at you."

Whitney's laugh was wet as she pressed her face into the blanket. "But I'm scared," she said, giving words to how they both felt. "I'm scared out of my mind and I feel awful because I shouldn't be. I'm supposed to be this . . . this . . ."

"Strong woman." Madison filled in the blank.

"Yes. This strong woman who has it together, and I don't have shit together. On stage, sure, but in my life? No. Nowhere close. What if I screw this up? What if he gets sick of me? What if he—"

"Realizes what he got himself into."

"Yes." Whitney rubbed at the corners of her eyes.

Madison knew how she felt. Oh god, did she know. These were her own fears, laid bare in the words of someone else. If Whitney could tell her, a relative stranger, then maybe Madison could tell Roark.

"Do you want to be with Jack?"

Whitney nodded, her face blotchy and wet, but conviction sharp in her eyes.

"Do you love him?"

"Of course."

"Then be scared about it, be freaked out, but marry him anyway."

Whitney's eyes went wide, her face expressing precisely how Madison felt.

"W-what?" Whitney stammered.

Madison couldn't believe that was her advice either, but when it came down to the very root of things, these were two people who loved each other. They loved each other enough that they could work through everything else, including Whitney's insecurities. After all, wasn't that what love did? Stuck with you, supported you, and believed in you? Wasn't that what made it love?

"Jack loves you too and it's okay to be scared, but you go find him right now and you marry him anyway. Don't let your fear and insecurity cause you to lose him."

Do as I say, not as I do.

Whitney took a deep breath. "But . . . what if—"

"No. No what-if, you go talk to him now." She sounded more like herself when she was trying to close a deal, except this time she had real conviction behind it, not just a front.

"Then you have to go with me. To find him."

"This should be a private—"

Whitney grabbed Madison's forearm, squeezing. "Please. You have to come with me, at least until I find him. I'll talk to him, but I can't approach him alone. I'll back out."

"Okay." Madison patted her hand. "Let's go find him." Then she could find Roark, and hope he wouldn't let her back out either.

Chapter 29

He almost plowed into them as he barreled through the portico in search of Madison.

Whitney stood there, bedraggled in an oversized coat, Madison by her side, staring at him, one of the inn's quilts clutched in her hands.

"Have you seen Jack?" Whitney asked first.

"Yeah, he's . . . come on, he's inside." He led them over to Jack, Madison eerily still when they reached the great room.

Jack looked up and the four of them stayed frozen that way, until finally Madison cleared her throat, encouraging Whitney with a hand on her arm.

"Go on." Madison pointed to the chair closest to Jack.

Whitney hesitated. "Is . . . is it okay if I talk to you for a second?" she asked Jack.

He nodded, watching her sit down.

They stared at each other in a painful silence, until Madison spoke up. "Whitney has something she'd like to say."

Jack studied Whitney, not a trace of resentment or anger on his face, but it still took him reaching over and touching her hand for her to speak.

"I'm sorry that I said us sharing a life would be the biggest mistake anyone could make."

Jack flinched, pain in the fine lines around his eyes.

"It's . . . that's not at all true. Not in the way I said it." Whitney slid toward the edge of her seat, closer to Jack. "I meant it's a huge mistake for *you* to get stuck with me. I ran off because I didn't want you to be stuck with me. Because I know how I am and . . ." She looked to Madison, and Madison nodded.

"And I'm scared," she said.

Jack sat forward too, holding her hand in both of his. "I know. I know how you are too, remember?"

"But what if I'm not enough, what if you only think you love me, but end up hating me later? You deserve someone who isn't so messed up."

Roark's gaze clashed with Madison's, and he refused to look away.

"I deserve you. I want *you*," Jack said.

Madison stared back. "Can we . . . ?" She tilted her head toward the veranda.

Roark nodded and strode toward her.

"We need to talk," she said.

The wash of relief that came over Roark came with anxiety right on its heels. She might only want to remind him that things were over. That she was right after all. That she'd fixed things with the bride and groom and he had no business in Whitney and Jack's business. That she'd never needed him for any of this and he was tromping on toes, as usual.

They stepped out onto the veranda, the early morning air a cold slap in the face. She wandered to the banister, and Roark followed.

Her shoulders curled in as she folded her arms around the quilt, trembling.

"Here." Roark eased the quilt from her hands and put it around her shoulders. "You mind?" He held an edge up to join her because she wasn't the only one shivering.

They pulled it tight around them, holding it closed in the front.

"I'm . . . I'm sorry I didn't tell you about how much Honeywilde needed this wedding." It was the first among many things he needed to tell her.

"I know." She shook her head. "But it's okay. I understand why you didn't."

"No, it's really not okay. After all we've shared . . . I could've confided in you. I know that."

Little white lights hung on the topiary trees, ready for a party, casting a glow across the veranda. The first time he'd come out here with her, he was already captivated. In a way, he knew it then. He couldn't figure her out, and that intrigued him. The tough outer shell and the vulnerability underneath that no one got to see—except then he did.

"You wanted to talk?" He had none of his usual certainty. In fact, he wasn't sure of anything, other than Madison wasn't leaving here without knowing how he felt about her. She needed to know he was an idiot for not doing everything in his power to convince her to stay. He'd persuaded her not to wait for them to be together until after the wedding. Convinced her to be with him for as long as she was here; surely he could talk her into being with him indefinitely.

Madison turned, clinging to her end of the quilt. Staring at the center of his chest, she worried her cheek. "When we first started out, I told you that the last thing I wanted was for us to be any kind of thing."

"I know." But it'd happened for him anyway.

"Because I was leaving and this was going to be short and sweet. And fun. Right?"

"Right."

She finally lifted her gaze to look at him, and what Roark saw in her eyes knocked the air from his lungs. Madison open and vulnerable, and scared out of her mind.

"It's not fun anymore." Her voice shook, as she blinked back the tears threatening to spill over. "You were supposed to be like anyone else. We'd enjoy each other and it'd be over, and it'd be fine. Same as always. But I'm leaving and I'm not fine, and that scares me because . . ." She glanced away before carrying on. "Because I don't know how to handle feeling this way. This wasn't supposed to be hard. Leaving here, leaving *you*, it wasn't supposed to hurt. But it does!"

Roark reached for her, offering her comfort with a hand on her arm, and she kept going.

"I was so worried—so scared of letting you in, but you're already in here." She pointed to the center of her chest again. "I know I never said I wanted anything more from you than the here and now, but I was wrong. The thought of leaving you—"

"Stay." He couldn't get the word out fast enough. "Don't leave. Stay here, with me." He shifted his hold on her arm to grip her hand. "I don't want you to leave. Since you walked in that front door, I've wanted you here. I want you in my life. By my side. Always."

She opened her mouth to say something, but he stopped her. Because knowing her, knowing what she'd been through, this mattered. "And I want you to know, even if you say no, even if you're too scared to stay, and you reject me completely, I still want you to know, *I* want *you*. You are worth me taking this chance. And you don't have to say anything else if you don't want to. But I need you to know, I love you."

The tears that'd pricked her eyes, threatening to fall, spilled over. The dam she built decades ago, broke. All she could do was bury her face in his chest and let it flow. In her life, she'd never heard those words. Not from anyone. And she never expected to.

"I don't want to go," she mumbled into his shirt.

Roark stroked her tangled hair. "Then don't. You don't have to go anywhere."

"But. Why?" she asked moments later, watery eyed and rubbing her face on the quilt. *Why would anyone love me?*

"Why what? Why do I love you?"

She managed a sniffling nod.

"Because of you." Roark shrugged, like it was all so simple. "Have you met you? You're pretty damn special."

"But you'd put yourself out there like that, for me? Knowing how I am. Knowing I'm messed up. I might run off like Whitney."

Another shrug. "She came back. That's what love does. It hurts and then it heals. I want to be with you and if you say no or yes, that doesn't change how I feel about you. You need to know that. I can't let you walk out of my life without knowing exactly how much I want you in it, and if I can convince you to stay then you definitely need to know I love you. And if you break my heart, then I give it to you to break. You're worth that risk to me."

She'd thought she was done crying. But she was wrong.

Roark pulled her close, his strong arms around her as she wept and shook. She cried because she didn't deserve him, and she cried because somehow she'd gotten him anyway.

She kept her face pressed to his shirt. "But I'm such a mess."

"You've met my family. You'll fit right in."

Her laugh was watery as she mopped at her face with the quilt.

"I don't want you to go," he said. "I know you have a life that isn't here. I get that and I don't know how we'll work this out, but I don't want to lose you."

Madison shook her head. "This is the most life I've ever had. I can do my job anywhere."

He nodded, studying her face, which could not be a pretty sight right now.

The thought of saying the next few words, of putting the truth out there, made her want to throw up in the topiaries. But she had to say it. She needed to step past the fear of him walking away, for her.

She looked in his pale eyes and prayed for the best. "I *love* being with you. I like your big old inn and family. I like Beau the dog. I don't . . . I don't want to leave you. I want you in my life. You and Honeywilde and all of it. I would be okay . . . being here. In this place. With you."

He reached for her hands, and with him holding on to her, she grew stronger. Braver. "I want all of this, and that scares me. I can't pretend like it doesn't anymore. Wanting you scares the hell out of me, but the thought of leaving here on Sunday, of driving off and never seeing you again, never feeling the way I've felt the last few weeks, scares me more."

"You don't have to be scared," he said. "I should've said it last night or the night before or a week ago when I first felt it. I want to be with you, always, and somehow, we'll figure it out. The rest, all of the hows and whens, we'll figure out together. All that matters is that you'll be with me."

Madison nodded, her throat knotted up so that all she could get out was, "I will."

Roark kissed her. Kissed her with all of the affection and desperation she felt. He held her, murmuring the most beautiful words into her ear. The sky began to brighten and, at some point, the quilt fell from her shoulders. But she wasn't cold. She had him and the promise of tomorrow to keep her warm.

"Told you she'd fix everything if you could find her!"

They turned, and Devlin waved at them from the veranda doors. Beyond him, huddled close together on the couch by the fire, were Jack and Whitney.

Roark's chuckle was a warm vibration at her back.

"Should I make coffee?" Dev yelled.

Madison moaned, resting her head against his shoulder. "Oh god, yes."

"Please!" Roark called back.

He kissed her once more on her temple before brushing her hair back as she wiped her eyes, enough that she looked halfway presentable.

"Think our wedding is back on?"

"God, I hope so." Roark threw his eyes to heaven. "Let's go make sure and get them hitched before anything else can happen."

"Agreed."

"But first." He pulled her into him and kissed her, as fully as always, but what swept over her was something different altogether. Still the same mix of excitement and lust, but along with it, complete acceptance. Of whatever she wanted to give him, of all that she was, unconditionally.

And for the first time in her lifetime, Madison was home.

Chapter 30

Whitney gave them both a thumbs-up right before Madison shooed her down the aisle to the sound of a guitarist playing Pachelbel's Canon in a version unlike any other.

She hurried to Roark's side, tucking her arm into his and observing the whole beautiful event from the premier seating of the back row.

"She looks amazing." Pride dripped from her voice. As it should. His Madison had made the impossible happen.

Whitney did look amazing. She practically skipped down the aisle with happiness for her wedding day, and for being strong enough to follow her heart. Jack, biker gang-looking fellow that he was, radiated joy. He glowed with it, and in a million years, Roark figured he'd never see a more contradictory sight.

He brushed his fingers over Madison's where she held his arm, feeling pretty damn glowy himself.

This morning, he'd thought his knees were going to buckle as she spoke. Certain she was going to walk out of his life forever, he'd had to force himself to stand there and listen. Take whatever she had to dish out, because he was sure he deserved it. Then she said she was scared, and his knees really had gone out a bit.

Roark intertwined their fingers and glanced at her. She'd worn her hair *mostly* loose today. Blond waves fell to her shoulders, inviting and touchable, the same way she was—with him. One side was pulled back, a burnt-orange flower pinned there, courtesy of Whitney's insisting that if she had to wear shoes to get married, then all the women had to have flowers in their hair.

Sensing his gaze, Madison looked over.

They'd figure out this relationship stuff. She was here, and that's what mattered. She'd go back to Charlotte in a few days, work on settling things up there so she could home base out of Honeywilde, and then they'd be together.

Home.

He wasn't sure how the logistics would work, and he wasn't the least bit worried. Between the two of them? If they both put their minds to it, and their lists, they'd make it work.

Now that they both knew they wanted the same thing, everything else they'd conquer in time, and together. When they ran upon hard times, they'd solve that together too.

He mouthed the words to her, silently. "I love you."

"I love you too," she mouthed back.

She told him again later, after dinner was served and the cake was cut. The cake was, of course, a huge success.

"Thank goodness you convinced me to go with some random cake no one has ever heard of." Madison rolled her eyes over another bite.

Roark used his fork to pick up the crumbs left on his plate. "My pleasure."

Sophie found them, holding up the corner of the great room. She pointed at Roark. "*You* are in big trouble."

"What'd I do?"

"I have heard two people ask to speak to the chef and ask if he's available for freelance work. You're probably going to have to give Wright a raise after this because he's not allowed to leave. None of these music hoity-toits are allowed to take him away."

"He's not going to leave."

"He better not." Sophie looked both of them over. "Why are you two over here anyway?"

"We're eating cake." Roark held up his empty plate. "What's it look like?"

Devlin half walked, half glided up to all of them. "Quit holding up the walls. There's dancing to be done."

Roark barked with a laugh. "You do not want me to dance. You know this."

Sophie grinned. "Why do you think *I* want you out there? You make me look like I have skills."

"Get Madison out there. I'm going to get one more itty-bitty slice of cake." He nudged Madison in Sophie's direction.

"Oh no. No, sir." She dug her heels in. "If I have to dance, you have to dance."

He started laughing as his sister and his girlfriend—he really liked thinking of her in those terms—dragged him toward the dancing. "This is not going to be pretty."

Madison shook her head. "We're both going to lower the quality of the dance floor just by getting near it."

The *large* dance floor, to be exact. Devlin had been right, the reception party overflowed even the large expanse of parquet flooring.

He and Madison lucked out though. As they closed in on the crowd, the DJ slowed things down with a ballad.

Dev spun Sophie in some fancy turn Roark would never dare try, and he raised an eyebrow at Madison.

"Don't go getting any ideas. I might be able to manage a little side-to-side for a slow song. That's it." He took her hand and pulled her into him.

"I've experienced your side-to-side." She cocked an eyebrow. "*And* your front-to-back. You've got nothing to be ashamed of. Believe me."

They shared a private smile until Madison began to giggle.

"You know . . . it's that charming little grin of yours that started things in the first place."

"Oh really?"

"Really. The sheepish little smile on the boss-man? It's irresistible."

"That is good to know." He tried his best at a dance turn, making them both laugh.

"You're going to use that little smile on me every day of my life now, aren't you?"

He pulled Madison closer into his arms, holding her tight, promising he'd never let go.

A lifetime sounded like a great plan to him.

Epilogue

One month later...

S he sauntered into the great room, knowing she wore a smug grin, not caring one bit. "Are you ready for this? Because I don't think you're ready."

Roark tried to grab a magazine out of her hands and she dodged to the side.

"Oh, come on. We're dying over here." Sophie clapped her hands, looking the furthest thing from dying.

"Okay, but you have to share. No hogging the publicity." Madison set copies of five different magazines down on the coffee table, and the Bradleys dove in like a pack of wild dogs.

"Holy shit, we're in *Southern Living*." Dev reached across the table.

"And *People*. We made *People*!" Sophie screeched, flapping one of the magazines around in the air like it was a pom-pom.

Trevor grabbed the biggest magazine from the pile. "Why is there a *Rolling Stone* issue in here?"

"Because . . ." Madison drew out the word, walking around to sit on the arm of the sofa, next to Roark. "Honeywilde may or may not be mentioned by name, in a little article about Red Left Hand's front man and -woman, and their high-speed romance and nuptials."

"No way." Trevor started flipping through the pages.

Roark's dark head was buried in the middle of a ten-page spread in *Carolina Style*. It was the smallest name among the magazines, but the largest article. Each of the pieces gushed over the pictures from the wedding, how picturesque the resort was, how romantic and ideal.

There was no way bookings at Honeywilde wouldn't skyrocket this fall, indefinitely, because she'd gotten the name out everywhere she could. She'd called in some connections, favors, even some of her former coworkers who still owed her.

"This is..." Roark looked up, shaking his head. "This is amazing. I can't believe you did this. I mean, I can... but... *damn*."

"I can totally believe it." Sophie clutched the magazine to her chest. "And Whitney and Jack said they'd autograph one for me if I mail it to their new manager."

Madison winked at Roark. As soon as Jack and Whitney were married, their next order of business had been to fire Phil Troutman.

"This is epic." Devlin put down his magazine, pulling at Roark's arm. "Bookings are going to start coming in. We're going to be slammed all fall. We have to start planning."

Roark tossed his head back, a grin to rival Madison's. "*You* want to plan?"

"Yes. We have to live up to the hype. Whip out that phone. I have ideas."

As Devlin and Sophie got into an animated discussion about other events and possible celebrity bookings, Roark turned to her.

"Enjoy basking in this glow. You've earned it." She kissed the top of his head.

"*We've* earned it." Roark pulled her down into his lap and kissed her fully on the mouth.

"I'll enjoy more of the glow when I get back," she told him.

"Damn. That's right. You have to head to Charlotte today."

"Just for three days. I have an event there, and then I'm going to pack up the rest of my apartment. You're about to be stuck with me."

"I can't wait." He squeezed her.

"You'll have a lot to do around here once these magazines spread the word."

"I hope so. You know how much I love a lot of to-dos."

She kissed him again. "I better get my bags. The sooner I get to the city, the sooner I'll be back."

Roark stood with her. "I'll help you with your stuff, see you off, and then get back to basking." He nodded to the magazines, spread all over the coffee table. "Thank you for this. For everything."

She shook her head. "No. Thank *you*." Madison reached for his hand, and Roark held on tight.

The Bradleys had given her more than she could ever give them. With Roark, she'd found love, happiness, and acceptance.

She'd found home.

ABOUT THE AUTHOR

Heather McGovern writes contemporary romance in swoony, Southern settings. While her love of travel and adventure takes her far, there is no place quite like home. She lives in South Carolina with her husband and son, and a collection of Legos that's threatening to take over the house. When she isn't writing, she's working out, or binging on books and Netflix.

She is a member of Romance Writers of America, as well as Carolina Romance Writers, and she's represented by Nicole Resciniti of The Seymour Agency.

Connect with Heather on her website, Facebook, Twitter, or her group blog. She'd love to hear to from you!

https://heathermcgovernnovels.com
https://www.facebook.com/Heather.McGovern.Novels
https://twitter.com/heathermcgovern
https://badgirlzwrite.com

Please turn the page for an exciting sneak peek of

Heather McGovern's next

Honeywilde Romance

A DATE WITH DESIRE

coming in December 2016!

Chapter 1

L ooking at the Bradley brothers was like staring into the sun.
A beautiful, blue-eyed sun, so big and bright the sight hurt a little, but Anna still studied them with a sharp eye as they buzzed around the check-in area.

They were all tall, with hair the color of rich coffee, and in the kind of rugged shape that came from working in the mountains. The family photo on the resort's website didn't do them justice, especially not the rakish-looking one in the corner.

He was more like a sun god.

A sun god sent to whisk a weary traveler like her away from the ever-tightening grip of big city reality. Pamper her with luxury and cater to her every whim and wish.

Good Lord, she was word vomiting in ad copy.

Her brain whirred on high speed work mode when she was supposed to be checking into the Honeywilde Inn and Resort to relax and recover.

Her therapist was right. The time had come. She either took a break or had another break down. The choice was hers.

"You'll be in cabin number five," one of the other Bradley brothers said. His name badge announced him as Roark Bradley, General Manager. "Trevor will show you the way up. Cabin five sits at the highest point on the property." He turned to who she guessed was the youngest of the three. "Trev, take my truck and have Ms. Martel follow you. Five can be tricky to find until you know your way around."

While he murmured to Trevor about offering to help with her luggage and watching the steep bend in the last turn, the third brother stepped out of his corner.

Devlin Bradley, Hospitality Manager, his name badge read.

Devil Bradley might be more fitting.

The slow, sly drag of his gaze up her body, from the tips of her toes to the sunglasses on top of her head, would be lewd if he didn't look so adorable trying to hide it.

Arms crossed over his body, he leaned against the reception desk and scratched along his temple, checking her out around the side of his hand and in between his fingers.

Smooth.

All of this she noticed from the corner of her eyes because she was *not* checking him out too. But if she were checking him out, she'd say he was easily the handsomest of the three.

No, handsome wasn't right. His brother, the manager, was handsome.

Devlin was sexy.

Tall and filled out, he was still a little leaner than his brothers. His dark hair was too long on top to be considered professional, eyes hooded like he'd recently woken from a post-sex nap, and his jaw line would make any model jealous. Broody in a classic James Dean way, but with a hint of boyish charm.

He was the type they hired to advertise trendy clothing lines, and she was half tempted to call her office and let them know.

But she was not working right now. She was supposed to be on vacation.

Just a woman on vacation, admiring a good looking guy as he proceeded to fake cough so she'd look in his direction.

Anna pinched her lips together to keep from smiling.

Devlin was tempting, no doubt a handful, and she couldn't deal with any of that at the moment.

Taking a break from her burgeoning career, leaving her job in the lurch, that was enough to handle. Following her therapist's advice of rest, recovery and "participating in the process of grief" would likely prove too much.

She had no room in her vacation for blue-eyed devils, she sucked at relaxing, and the process of grief could take a flying leap off this mountain.

"Are you all set, ma'am?" Trevor Bradley straight up ma'am-ed her as he walked by.

Fantastic.

With a smile that weighed more than her luggage, she nodded. "I'm ready if you are."

Trevor bounded toward the front door and she turned to follow. But her gaze snagged with Devlin's.

She meant to look away. Follow the harmless younger Bradley who would lead the way to her cabin.

If she had, she would've avoided the sensuous curl of Devlin's lips, the flicker of interest. She returned his smile unwittingly, and that got all of his attention.

His smile spread wider, revealing perfect white teeth and an all too knowing look in his eyes.

Heat rushed up the back of her neck, pin pricks dancing across her skin.

Encouraging him was a horrible idea, but her physical reaction was even worse. Whether she admitted it or not, her body knew what was up.

Devlin Bradley was all kinds of hot, and his being the last thing she needed to tangle with right now only made him hotter.

If his lingering looks were any indication, he didn't think she was too shabby either.

Anna turned on the heels of her wedge sandals and got the heck out of there.

By the time she left the lobby of Honeywilde's Inn, the back of her neck was on fire. Hopefully her hair hid everything, because once it flared up, her skin would be cherry red back there.

Trevor led the way to cabin five in a big black pickup truck, the wheels of her Lexus spinning a couple of times as she tried to keep up on the curvy incline.

Her car wasn't made for off-road mountain driving. *She* wasn't made for off-road mountain driving, but she'd been told to choose a vacation at a legitimate resort *or* one of those "retreats." The kind where she'd be in therapy and meditation all day because she couldn't cope with what life had dealt her.

No thanks.

She'd opted for the first appealing vacation spot that popped up on her Google search for upscale North Carolina mountain getaways.

If she was going to take time away from work, it had to be the mountains. Maybe then she would stop putting off her responsibility.

But upscale meant she wouldn't wind up in a pup tent or a cabin with no running water.

Honeywilde boasted peace and quiet, lovely strolls around the lake, hiking, delicious dining, legendary sunsets, and a warm, luxurious atmosphere.

Sold, she'd booked in to one of their private cabins immediately, for two and a half weeks.

Take my money, she'd thought. *Just please don't let me fall apart.*

The black pickup stopped in front of a sturdy log cabin, a covered porch stretched across the front with two Adirondack chairs and two rockers.

A little sign post at the bottom of the stairs read: *Cabin Five: Highpoint Escape.*

Escape. "Perfect." She popped the trunk of her car.

Before she could get out, Trevor was at the back, unloading both of her suitcases.

"I've got it." He pulled out the shoulder bag as well, but Anna took the bag from his hands. That one was precious. "I'll get this"— she played it off—"I know my two suitcases aren't light."

Had she over packed? Probably. But did she have any idea what a person needed to bring for a vacation in the mountains? Absolutely not.

The weather could be hot or cold, dry or damp. Was dinner at Honeywilde dressy or casual? Did she need hiking boots *and* sneakers? Until yesterday, she hadn't owned hiking boots.

Now she did.

Along with something called a rope bag and a pair of god-awful shoes one was supposed to wear in the river. As if she had plans to walk in the river.

The salesman at the outdoor store swore she'd need all of it. He'd known a sucker as soon as he saw her.

All that remained in the trunk was her train case, full of cosmetics, toiletries, and a bottle of Xanax she'd refused to crack open—so far. Anna grabbed the case and her purse and hurried after Trevor.

Once he'd off loaded her things, he wished her an awesome stay and took off, leaving her all alone in her Highpoint Escape.

"Well. Here we are," she said, doing a slow three-sixty in the middle of the cabin's den, her announcement met with silence.

A two-foot-tall bear, carved out of wood, stared back from beside the fireplace.

He was cute, but fat chance of him responding.

When she was six or seven, her father brought her to North Carolina to see the bears. She'd been terrified, but he'd assured her everything was safe. The bear cubs were cute, the momma bear not so much.

Anna grabbed her phone to take a picture. Her dad would get such a kick out of the bear statue.

The phone suddenly turned to a block of cement in her hand, the picture on the lock screen shaking before she tossed it back in her purse.

Her father was gone. She could no longer send him anything. No funny pictures, no one-line comments that only he would appreciate.

She sank to the arm of the sofa, the wave of sadness like gravity.

She'd asked her therapist, Susan, about inviting a friend or boyfriend to join her on her break, phrasing the question like she had a boyfriend or knew anyone who'd be willing to put their lives on hold to go away to the mountains with her.

In her mind, she'd figured a traveling companion might make the time more enjoyable. Distract her from loss and the ripple effect that was ruining her life.

Susan's answer was a hard and fast no.

The point of her time off was to focus on herself, not others; no distractions so she could overcome her denial of grief, reflection and yadda, yadda something about actualization. Anna was supposed to be taking the time to think about what she wanted out of life and how she'd function in this "new normal."

God, if she never heard that term again it'd be wonderful.

She carefully set her shoulder bag on the coffee table and made herself get up and look around. Missing her father was not going to dissolve into wallowing again.

She'd already tried that, and it didn't help.

The one bedroom, one bath cabin turned out to be as lovely as the pictures on the website. Everything was on one level except the loft-style bedroom. The floors were rich hardwoods, with big windows, and no over-the-top moose or bear themed décor. Just the one cute bear guarding the fireplace.

The place was tastefully decorated in neutrals with warm apricot accents, exactly how she would've set up a log cabin if she happened to own one.

Except—

If cabin five were her place, she probably would've remembered one *very* important detail.

Nice Jacuzzi tub, porcelain pedestal sink, and the toilet looked shiny and clean.

And completely without a seat.

"That is not going to work," she announced to the cabin.

How the heck did you forget a toilet seat?

Then again, if three brothers ran the place, toilet seats probably didn't top their priorities.

Normally she'd unpack first and worry about it later, but later might be too late and she was here to visit the mountains in style, not cop a squat in the woods.

Flipping through the handy binder by the phone, she found the number for guest services. It only rang once before somebody answered.

"Thank you for calling Honeywilde. How may I be of service?"

Good Lord, the voice on him.

Deep and warm, raspy as if recently over-used, with a southern accent slightly thicker than the ones she usually heard in Atlanta. The way the words dripped from his lips made the question sound pornographic.

She'd bet anything, with nothing more to go on than a voice, she was talking to Devlin.

"Hello. May I help you?" His voice filled her ear, sending goose bumps down her arms.

"Yes. Hi. This is cabin five."

"Ms. Martel," he said, before she could get any further. "Are you settling in okay?"

"Uhm . . ." No. She wasn't settled at all, now that he'd purred in her ear, thank you very much. "Yes, everything is great, but there's one tiny problem. In the bathroom, there's no toilet seat."

Silence ruled for a few beats, then, "You're kidding." His voice remained phone sex material, but the dry note of wit made her smile.

"No. I wish was."

"I am so sorry." Embarrassment and urgency replaced the drawl. "We'll have someone over there immediately."

"Thank you." Hanging up, she realized she was still smiling. Smiling about a missing toilet seat.

When she opened the door to the cabin a few minutes later, the reason why was confirmed.

"Sorry again about the missing seat, but I'm here to take care of it." Devlin's eyes crinkled at the outer edges. In one hand, he held a still boxed and wrapped toilet seat, in the other dangled a tool belt. "At the start of the summer season we replace a lot of things and, unfortunately, your toilet seat was overlooked."

"I understand. Come on in." Lord help her, what if he put on that tool belt?

She stepped aside to let him in, and he headed straight through the den and past the kitchen.

As he reached the short hall, he jerked to a stop as if catching himself. "I'm Devlin, by the way. I didn't get to introduce myself earlier."

No, but he'd made quite the impression anyway.

"I'm Anna. Nice to meet you. Officially." For lack of knowing what else to do, and since his hands were full of tool belt, she gave him a slow, wide wave.

Because sometimes she was a giant goober.

"You too." The impish smile on his full lips made her breath catch.

Then he was gone, ducked into the bathroom.

Heat skittered up her neck again, and it wouldn't do. If she let her nervous reaction get out of control, she'd be all blotchy and itchy.

A super attractive look.

Once a stranger had asked if she was allergic to peanuts or shellfish or something. Nope. Just her body hated her.

She hung back, in the hall, furiously fanning her neck.

"My brother Trev was supposed to give the cabins a final inspection. We don't use them during the winter and in early spring they're rarely booked, so . . ." The clank of tools drifted down the hall. He was definitely putting on the tool belt.

She fanned faster.

"You might be our first guest up here this year."

Carefully, she moved closer to the bathroom door. On the one hand, she did not need to see him being handy and stuff, doing things with wrenches and whatever. But on the other hand she couldn't go the entire rest of her life having not checked out the tool belt situation.

"This shouldn't take but a minute. Is everything else okay with the cabin? Or have you even had a chance to check?" The rough edge in his voice soothed her senses, like someone gently scratching her back.

Before she bothered to look inside, she leaned against the wall outside the bathroom to listen to him talk. "Everything else is fine. The cabin is great, you know, besides the toilet. I can't wait to take a walk and have a look around. See what else is here." She rolled out the idea, hoping he'd offer suggestions, elaborate. Anything. As long as he kept talking.

"You checked in at a great time. Sunset is in just a little while, perfect for catching the colors during a stroll. You have a good view from your front porch, but the best view is at the main inn on the veranda, and you'd still have enough time to make it back here before dark."

Her toes curled in her wedges. A long walk near sunset sounded ideal, or maybe it was the way he said it.

Finally ready, she leaned in the doorway to find Devlin, tool belt on, squatted down and leaned over, jeans pulled tight around thick thighs, messing with something on the wall behind the toilet.

Wrong. She wasn't ready at all.

Who had legs like that? Long and solid looking, like he could hold a girl's weight if he had her up against the—oh good gosh, she was being a perv.

"The supply line is loose. Tightening it up while I'm down here."

"Uh huh."

"Oh. Hey." He jerked up, probably not expecting her to be all up in the doorway while he worked on a toilet.

She should say something. Quick. Before this got weird.

"So . . ." What to say, what to say?

Her line of sight, and therefore thought, was full of Devlin and blue jeans and *Wow*, and toilets. None of it made for appropriate small talk.

"Food." The word fell out of her mouth.

Of course she came up with food. "I have my own kitchen in the cabin, but I doubt I'll have time to make it to a grocery store today. Doesn't the main inn have a restaurant?" She knew the inn had a restaurant; she'd already picked out the first thing she wanted to order from the online menu. And possibly the second and third.

"We have an outstanding restaurant. Hold that thought." He leaned over again, doing something with a wrench that did delicious things to the muscles in his shoulders and back. Masking nothing, the thin gray T-shirt he wore clung to him, highlighting the dip of his spine, making her fingers itch to touch.

They were supposed to be talking about food. Her neck burned and she fanned it quickly, while he was distracted.

As bleak as her sex life already was, for over half a year now her desire for anything had gone ice cold. With no interest, she hadn't even looked twice at a guy. She hadn't read a book past page two, gone shopping except for this trip, or done anything other than work.

Nothing sent that zip of excitement through her body; nothing held her attention for longer than five minutes, so she'd buried herself in her job, more so than before.

Then that had fallen apart too. Her creativity, the flair that made her one of the top execs at the agency—gone.

But now, awareness danced across her skin. Her limbs tingled with anticipation, like when she was coming up with the perfect pitch for a sales campaign or seeing a gorgeous guy in well-fit blue jeans, bent over and doing some plumbing.

"There." Once he shoved the wrench in its spot on the belt, he stood with a groan.

Mercy, you shouldn't have.

The belt sat low on his hips, accentuating a narrow waist and flat stomach.

Maybe her desire wasn't as cold as she'd thought. Maybe she'd merely lacked the proper stimulus. Because right now, every part of her body was on high alert.

Normally, the first twinge of enjoying life was followed immediately by a pang of regret. A knot of guilt in the center of her chest. Her therapist said the reaction was normal when dealing with loss.

Normal didn't make it any more bearable.

Anna waited for the pang, but nothing came.

"Do you mind?" Devlin asked.

He'd caught her gawking. Of course he had. She was being so obvious, Pluto would notice. Her sophistication and manners had gone right out the window, and all it took was blue eyes and blue jeans.

Wasn't there a song about that? She'd have to look it up later. Except she didn't have her laptop and her phone was restrictive use only. Dear God, she was word vomiting in her head again.

His rumbling chuckle brought her back. "Is it okay?" he asked again.

When she looked up, he was indicating toward the sink. As in, did she mind if he washed his hands.

"*Oh*. No, no. Go ahead."

He washed up and she tried to look away, she really did. But she couldn't.

"I highly recommend you try the restaurant," he finally said, turning to her, thumbs hooked into the tool belt.

He had to be doing it on purpose. No way was anyone this attractive, this potent, without actually working his butt off to be so.

"Not only tonight though. You need to eat there for breakfast, without question, and lunch too. As a matter of fact, I can recommend a grocery store for quick food on hand, but you'll want to dine with us at Bradley's pretty much any opportunity you get. You won't regret it." Another smile, the corners of his mouth curling up like a promise.

Anna found herself leaning against the frame of the door for support. "You make a convincing case."

"I try." He moved to get past her, and he was inches away before she realized she blocked his path.

"Sorry." She backed into the hall until the heel of her shoes hit the baseboard.

"Don't be." He followed, stopping so he stood right in front of her.

Silence lingered, filling the cabin with a quiet tension. Electric.

Something was happening, though she was lost as to what exactly.

When she was ten years old, her father took her to Caesar's Head, and they'd gone way out on the big rock. They didn't go to the very edge, but Anna had still felt the pull of vertigo. The downdraft of the mountain winds. The call of the edge, luring her over.

The exact same sensation blew over her standing in the small hallway with Devlin.

He didn't hide his slow study of her. His gaze, like a lover's touch, brushed her face, down her neck, pausing in the vee of her shirt. Heat spread out from the point of his focus, slipping down, between her legs, making her squeeze them together.

She knew that look. It had to be identical to the one she'd given him while he was crouched in the bathroom floor. The difference was he hadn't been aware of her hungry stare, but good Lord, was she ever aware of his.

Too much time had gone by since a man had looked at her like that. The needle-toed dancers were back at her neck, twirling and tapping in tiny hot steps, her whole body lighting up.

If, with one look, Devlin had this effect on her, what would happen when he touched her?

Made in the USA
Las Vegas, NV
28 May 2024

90461701R00156